BOYFRIEND 101

(Fever Falls #6)

By Riley Hart

Copyright © 2019 by Riley Hart
Print Edition

All rights reserved.

No part of this book may be used, reproduced or transmitted in any form or by any means, electronic or mechanical, including photocopying, recording, or by any information storage and retrieval systems, without prior written permission of the author, except where permitted by law.

Published by:
Riley Hart

This book is a work of fiction. Names, characters, places and incidents are products of the author's imagination or are used fictitiously. Any similarity to actual persons, living or dead is coincidental and not intended by the author.

All products/brand names/Trademarks mentioned are registered trademarks of their respective holders/companies.

Cover Design by Black Jazz Designs
Cover Photo by Wander Aguiar
Edited by Keren Reed Editing
Proofread by Judy's Proofreading and Lyrical Lines

So, what is Fever Falls? It's a fictitious series with the city of Fever Falls serving as the backdrop to Riley Hart and Devon McCormack's newest collaboration. Unlike our previous collabs, where we wrote books together, we'll be sharing the Fever Falls sandbox and creating solo titles within it. The books are intended to be read as standalones; however, because there are overlapping characters between the books, it'll be a lot more fun to read them all!

Fever Falls has it all, including an inordinate amount of hot, curious, and eligible bachelors who learn the hard way that there's an unexpected consequence to living here: you just might fall in love.

Visit the Fever Falls website

www.feverfalls.com

Blurb

Camden

I'm a fun-loving guy who doesn't take life too seriously. If there's something I want, I go for it. Why not? Life's too short to slide into the grave with regrets. But what I don't do is go for men who aren't out and proud. Been there, done that. The only real way to get to me is to hurt my brother, but now that Sawyer's happy, he doesn't need me anymore. I'm stoked for him, I am! But seeing my friends and brother paired off is a constant reminder of the one thing I don't have but desperately want: Jude. There's something about this beautiful man who insists he's not into men. Even with my rules about guys who aren't out, I've craved him since the moment he stepped foot in Fever Falls. Now that he's one of my best friends, that desire has raged into an inferno I'm powerless to tame.

Jude

I've always considered myself straight. I wrote off the whole fascination with my longtime best friend Rush as something weird that happened. I've been over him for a while now, and the person who helped me was Camden Burke, the flirty man who calls me beautiful. I used to hate getting compliments about my looks, but when Cam does it... Well, let's say the way he makes me feel is my first clue that the thing with Rush wasn't a one-time deal. I'm bisexual. And Cam makes me laugh and always listens. Since I've been in Fever Falls, I've become closer to him than I've ever been with anyone, Rush included. So when I decide to explore my newfound sexuality, who better than Cam to show me all the pleasures of being with a man? Only, we get caught, and now it's not just Cam showing me what it's like to be with a guy—he's become my professor in what he calls Boyfriend 101, and apparently, I'm a *very* good student.

But unfortunately, I have some issues to work out and a few exam scores start slipping. Cam has already graded on a curve by breaking some of his rules to be with me. If I can't get my act together, I'll flunk out of Boyfriend 101, and I can't imagine retaking the course with anyone but him.

CHAPTER ONE

Jude

I think I might be a stalker. I'm obsessed with this guy—Jude, I think his name is—who lives in our building. ~ Theo

M Y SKIN FELT strangely too tight. Like if I moved wrong or stretched too much, it would crack open. I tried to ignore it. I mean, what the fuck? Why would I feel so weird just because Camden was at Fever with a woman? But I did feel all screwed up, off balance, and like my goddamned skin was splintering, and I didn't like it. I didn't like it one bit.

Fucking Camden Burke.

"Hey, gorgeous. Can I get a Long Island?" this bear asked me. That was a new term I'd learned—*bear*. If there was one thing I never thought I'd be doing, it would be working in a gay bar, using terms like *bear*, *twink*...oh, and *otter*.

My teeth automatically ground together when *gor-*

geous sank in. I was pretty good at ignoring it most of the time. I'd learned to block out shit like that over the years. It wasn't because he was a bear, or a dude, that it bothered me. I didn't like it when women said shit like that to me either. It made me feel…weird. I didn't know how else to explain it. I'd heard words like *pretty* and *gorgeous* enough in my life to figure it must be true, but I didn't see it. When I looked in the mirror, I didn't think I was ugly, but I didn't see anything special. It was just me.

The strangest part of the whole thing? It didn't bother me when Camden said it. What I was still working out the pieces to was *why*.

"Yeah, coming up," I replied to the guy. My jaw was still tight as I made his drink and took his payment. Every few minutes, my eyes would dart to the bar, where Cam sat with the blonde. All our friends were gone by now. Cam typically stayed later than everyone, hanging out and talking with me, but now he had a beautiful woman on his lap, and he was sucking on her neck instead of flirting with me.

The not-flirting-with-me thing was good.

Right? It was supposed to be good, but I felt any-fucking-thing other than that at the moment.

Since I'd moved to Fever Falls, Camden had become

one of my best friends. Rush had so much shit going on with his career and Lincoln that Cam was who I hung out with, who I spent my time with, who I talked to. I didn't want to lose his friendship, and I wasn't into men, so the not-flirting thing was supposed to be good.

Only, I'd been in love with Rush and he was a man. It was something I'd come to accept—with Cam's help. I'd been in love with my best friend who was a man, but we hadn't belonged together. He belonged with Linc, and I knew that, accepted it, was mostly over it… Cam's brown eyes caught mine, and he smiled, then winked, and yeah, I was staring.

Heat flooded my gut. Okay, so maybe I was attracted to Cam too…which meant Rush, Cam, and women? My head was a fucking confusing place to be. It had been for a long time.

Shoving Camden out of my thoughts, I buckled down and finished my shift. I wasn't closing the bar tonight, so as soon as midnight came around, I was getting the hell out of there. Typically, I would have a drink with Cam, or we would have at least walked out together, but my skin was still too tight and my head was still this twisting hurricane of confusion.

I grabbed my shit and went straight for the door. The second I stepped outside, I sucked in a lungful of fall air.

There, that was better. That helped. Since moving to Fever Falls, I'd learned little ways to deal with the stress in my life, stress I'd been feeling before my move, and it was amazing what a deep lungful of air could do sometimes.

It was only two steps later when I saw him…Cam and the sexy fucking blonde. He had his back against Fever and his hands on her waist. I saw his finger brushing back and forth between her skirt and her shirt, against her bare skin, and fuck if I didn't tremble.

She kissed his neck, he smiled, and then his eyes immediately snapped up, like somehow he'd known I was there. Our gazes held, and I couldn't move. Why the fuck couldn't I move? I had no business giving a shit who Camden was with. It wasn't something I had seen often, but I knew he hadn't been celibate since I moved there, and really, why the fuck should he be? We were friends. I'd told him I was straight except Rush. The end.

Cam cocked his head. He'd gotten a haircut recently, his light brown, almost dark blond, hair shorter on both the sides and on top than it typically was. He had some stubble along his jaw, which was perfectly sculpted and really fucking strong, no matter how many times I told myself I didn't notice.

Look away. Why the hell wasn't I looking away?

I saw his mouth move, noticed he was whispering something to Melissa? Melinda? I couldn't remember exactly what her name was, but I knew it started with an *M*.

Then he was walking over to me, and I rolled my eyes and took a few steps in the opposite direction, toward the corner of the building, where it was a little quieter.

"Hey...you okay?" Cam asked.

"Yeah, why wouldn't I be?" My voice had a sharp edge to it that I hadn't planned.

"Don't know. You seem a little off. You left without saying goodbye. You don't usually."

When I'd gone to the back room to clock out, he had still been at the bar. "So did you. You were already outside when I got here."

"Because I noticed you were gone. Wasn't sure when you left. We normally talk for a bit."

"You were busy."

Cam grinned, this mischievous half-grin he always did. "You jealous, Beautiful?"

I waited for the discomfort to slide down my spine, which often happened when someone gave me a compliment, but it didn't come. I knew if I ever asked

Cam not to call me that, he wouldn't, but I never did. I opened my mouth, and for a moment I thought that's what would fall out, but it didn't. "Did you ask her here to try and make me jealous?"

What. The. Fuck? Why had I asked that?

"Um…no? I asked her out because she's sexy as hell, sweet, and always a good time. This isn't a first with Mel, just the first time she's come to Fever. Are you really jealous?" Cam's forehead wrinkled as though the thought surprised him, which I guessed it should.

"What? No. That's ridiculous." But shit, I thought maybe a part of me was, and it was confusing and pissed me off.

"Come home with us," Cam said, serious as hell. He wasn't smiling, and there was nothing playful in his gaze.

"Are you fucking crazy?"

"No." He shook his head. "It'll be fun. I promise you, Melinda won't care. I'll ask her first, of course, but I know her. She'll fucking love it. You don't have to touch me, and I won't touch you. We'll just…share a beautiful woman."

Damned if my cock didn't begin to plump up. My skin wasn't too tight anymore, but started to tingle. "I can't do that."

"You can if you want to. It won't change anything.

We'll just have a little fun. You say no, and it stops. You say no right now, and I'll walk away."

Again, my mouth opened, but this time nothing came out. Have a threesome with Camden and a woman? My dick jerked, and fuck if it didn't obviously like the idea.

I'd done a lot of shit in my past, been with my fair share of women, but I'd never had a threesome with another man. Two women? Yes. But including a guy wasn't something I'd ever thought about, that I ever wanted. Rush I'd wanted all to myself, and there had never been another guy for me, but a part of me, one I wasn't sure how to deal with, wanted to say yes to Camden.

"I…" I started, just as Melinda wrapped her arms around Cam from behind.

"Our car is here. Is your friend going to come and play with us?" she asked, and Cam grinned at me, as if saying, *I told you she won't care.*

We stood there for what felt like a damn eternity. I wanted to say yes, fuck if I didn't want to say yes, but I couldn't make myself do it. He was right. It was just sex, but that felt different with him.

Cam seemed to know. He shrugged slightly, and I knew he meant, *I tried*, then he turned to Melinda. "Just going to be us tonight. Jude is straight."

My stomach twisted up, and my hands twitched. How many times had I said that very thing to him? Only it sounded wrong on his tongue.

"You want to watch? You can if you want," Melinda said.

Cam started, "That's nice of you, darlin', but—"

"Yes," I cut him off. I didn't know where that came from or what the fuck I was doing, but still, I said it again, "Yes."

"You sure?" Camden crossed his arms.

"Unless you're uninviting me." Now that I'd decided, I was going through with this. I wasn't backing down.

"You know that's not gonna happen. Let's go." There was a tightness to Camden's voice I was unfamiliar with. Still, the moment he began to walk, I followed.

We were quiet as the car took us to Cam's place. Quiet as we got out. Quiet as we went inside his house.

It wasn't the first time I'd been there, but it suddenly felt like it, felt different.

Camden grabbed Melinda's hand and went straight for the hallway. I followed, and then we were in his room, and it *was* the first time I'd been there.

A massive king-size bed was on the wall across from

the door. It had a dark-wood headboard that looked almost gothic, but no footboard. There was a TV and video-game consoles, which I knew he also had in his living room.

"You watching or participating?" Cam asked, jerking me out of my thoughts.

"Watching," just sort of fell out of my mouth.

"That get you off, Jude? You a dirty little voyeur?" His voice was deep, husky, and filled with sex, and damned if that didn't make me tremble. No one had ever spoken to me like that before, and I was pretty sure I liked it.

"We'll see." I shrugged, trying to play it off.

"Oh, this is gonna be fun," Melinda said.

"Sit down." Camden nodded toward the armchair in the far-right corner of the room.

Without a thought, I found myself doing what he said. I was on a diagonal from the bed, but on the same wall. Cam and Melinda walked over to the side I was on, and then they were kissing.

It was all sort of a blur from then on out, like I was there but wasn't. Participating, but not. Cam stripped her out of her clothes, then did the same for himself.

A shiver raced through me. My dick was hard, my whole body feeling jittery as I pushed against my shaft through my jeans.

Cam had a big cock, thicker than mine; long legs, hair on his chest, firm, sinewy muscles, and six-pack abs. The hair on my arms rose, my heart sped up, but I couldn't take my eyes off him, couldn't stop looking at Camden.

Melinda got on her knees and sucked his dick. His fingers tangled in her hair, and my eyes became riveted on his hands. He looked over at me and smiled the way he did, and damned if I didn't find myself unbuttoning…unzipping…pulling myself out and stroking.

"Fuck yessss," Cam hissed, and I knew he was talking about me just as much as he was talking about Melinda.

I had no idea what I was doing, what I had been thinking, but I couldn't stop. I didn't want to.

He picked her up and set her on the bed, his muscles twisting and constricting as he did so, and my dick ached. His tongue traced around her nipples, and he sucked her.

"Fuck…you have such a talented mouth," Melinda told him, and Cam chuckled against her. "Are you sure you don't want to play?" she asked me, but I couldn't find my voice.

I shook my head, ignoring the *No…I'm not sure…* floating around in my head.

"I hope you know what this is doing to me, Beautiful," Cam said. "How long I've wanted you in my bed, and now you're here, but you're really not." There was something so damn sincere, almost sad in his voice, and it stole my breath.

My voice was still gone. I was jerking myself with Cam's hot stare on me, and Melinda's. Part of me wanted to run, while another wanted to ask for his mouth on me too.

"Guess we'll have to show him what he's missing," Melinda said, and they did just that.

Camden suited up and pushed inside her. I watched his back muscles and the tightness in his legs as he fucked into her beautiful body…and he was too, beautiful, I mean, and I'd never thought that about a man before. Not even Rush, and I'd loved him. I knew Rush was good-looking, but things had been different with us. It was as if I'd woken one morning and realized the reason everything felt wrong in my life was because I didn't have him, but by then it had been too late.

Now it was a slower descent. Not that I was in love with Camden, because I wasn't, but I was attracted to him. I knew that as much as I knew my own name. I just didn't know if I planned to do anything about it. Or hell, how I even felt about it.

Cam pressed a kiss to Melinda's lips, then cocked his head to the side and looked at me. She did the same as little noises pulled from the back of her throat. She told me how good it felt, how good Cam was, and somehow I knew it. I *felt* it as if I was with Cam too.

The whole time he was watching me, staring at me, but not in a way that made it feel like he was using Melinda. She was watching me as well, talking to me, pulling me into this. It was as if they were both making me a part of their sex, but Cam's stare was hotter, deeper, like there was more behind it than Melinda's.

I didn't know what to think, so I tried not to. I just watched. Studied the way he moved, his muscles, groaned at the noises he made as they burrowed inside me. He was…fuck, he was sexy, and tonight was the first time I'd let myself really acknowledge that.

Then Melinda cried out that she was coming, and the muscles in Cam's neck tightened, his eyes blazing on me. When he dropped his head back, my orgasm slammed into me the second I could tell he was coming too.

We were quiet after that, and I couldn't look away. I wanted to run. To hide. To ask him to touch me.

Melinda said, "Good thing I don't have feelings for you outside of friendship and a good fuck, Cam.

Otherwise, I might have my feelings hurt because I'm positive it wasn't me you were fucking just now." She looked over at me. "Are you sure you don't wanna come over here with us? He can usually go again pretty quickly."

My head spun, and my face warmed with heat. My skin was too tight again, my whole body jittery.

"No…I gotta…I should go."

"Jude," Camden said simply, something in his voice I couldn't explain, but I shook my head. I wiped my come up with my shirt, tucked myself away, and walked out.

CHAPTER TWO

Camden

From the first time I saw you, it was hard to keep my eyes off you. ~ Letter from Henry

I WAS PRETTY sure I'd just made a big-ass mistake.

I hadn't planned on asking Jude to go home with us. Really, I'd just wanted to get laid, and Melinda had called, so I'd decided to go for it. Well, that, coupled with the fact that I was worried I was getting too wrapped up in Jude—in someone who was straight. I'd been down a similar road in the past, with my ex-boyfriend, Henry. But I'd be lying if I didn't admit I'd noticed Jude's eyes on me all night, that I'd seen the way he'd looked at me with Mel, and that I liked it.

It was no secret I was attracted to Jude. It had started as sort of a game. I mean, he *was* beautiful, with his sun-kissed skin, plump, kissable lips, bright-blue eyes that always looked so curious, and that hair…fuck that hair, with its soft waves. I liked it even better now that it was his natural brown. There was no denying he was gorgeous, but it had been mostly just for fun in the beginning. To see him blush. I was pretty sure, at least.

Jude wasn't the kind of guy I usually went for. If I were going to describe my perfect man, it would typically be someone like Lincoln. Twinks had always done it for me, and Jude wasn't that. He was six feet of long, lean muscles. But again, really fucking beautiful.

Then we'd become friends, and I realized I really did want to fuck him, but I also wasn't sure I ever would, because I valued his friendship. Not that I didn't think people could fuck and be friends. I did it all the time. My friends did it. Sex didn't have to make things awkward unless you let it, but I'd known Jude would. Plus, he'd always insisted he was straight, and I would never deny someone's sexuality. We were who we were, and if Jude said he was straight, he was straight, even if he had been in love with Rush Alexander.

But I also believed sexuality could be fluid, and when I'd been with Mel and he'd looked at me with fire in his eyes, I'd seen the shift in him. He'd wanted me tonight, which only made my desire for him skyrocket, and yep, that led to said big-ass mistake.

"So…that was awkward. Was it me?" Melinda asked.

"Nah, he's just going through some stuff. It'll be

fine."

"You want him."

"Yeah," I replied simply, because I did. "You did too."

"Who wouldn't? But you want him in a different way."

I shrugged because talking about it wasn't going to change anything. Yes, I wanted Jude. I'd wanted him for a long time, and that was that.

It had also killed me to tell him he didn't have to touch me if we all three hooked up. I'd never been insecure about my sexuality, but saying that to him made me feel strange.

"You know he wants you too, right?" she asked, and this weird-ass thing happened. I exhaled a breath, like I sort of relaxed, like I'd needed to hear that, and in no way was that normal for me.

"Obviously. Who doesn't?"

Melinda laughed and swatted my arm, then climbed out of bed and went for the bathroom. "I hate to leave so soon, but I have to be up early in the morning. I'll grab a car service."

I rolled my eyes. "You know I'm taking you home." What kind of asshole watched some dude while he fucked a beautiful woman and then sent her home in a random car?

We cleaned up, got dressed, and I drove Melinda to her apartment, which was only about fifteen minutes from my place.

When we got there, I let my truck idle out front. "I hope I didn't disrespect you in any way tonight," I said. It had been weighing on my mind. "Yes, I wanted him, but I wanted you too. You know I always love our time together." She was one of the few women I slept with. I was mostly with men, but I thought that was more because I spent most of my time with gay or bi men.

Melinda chuckled. "You're sweet, Camden Burke. I like having sex with you. That's all tonight was. I don't have my feelings hurt, and you didn't disrespect me. We're good."

She leaned over and kissed my cheek before hopping out of the truck. I watched her get inside safely, then pulled out my phone and shot a text to Jude. **Are we okay?**

Shit, I shouldn't have taken Mel to Fever, but again, why shouldn't I? I couldn't wait around for Jude forever.

I felt…needy. Like I was holding my breath while waiting for him to reply, which was weird as shit. His answer came back quickly: **Yes.**

And with that one-word reply, I knew we weren't

good. That I *had* fucked up, and things were going to be awkward between us. Jude always said more to me than that. I dropped my head back against the seat and sighed.

"Hi, Camden. Hi, Sawyer. Hi, Carter. Hi, Rush. Hi, Lincoln," Kenny continued saying each of our names and making me smile. He was Beau's brother and basically the best guy around. We all loved Kenny, but no one loved him more than Beau and Ashton.

"Hey, Kenny. How's it going, man?" As soon as I put my hand in the air, he gave me a high five.

"I'm great! I can't believe Beau and Ash are getting married in three weeks! Beau's a hero!"

"Yes, he is," I replied.

"Ashton is great too. He'll officially be my brother, but he already feels like my brother."

"He is your brother," Sawyer told him. He had his hand twined with Carter's. It felt so damn good seeing my brother happy. No one deserved it more than he did, and there was no one in the world more important to me than Sawyer, but it felt a little strange sometimes too. Like Sawyer was at this place I would never be, like there was a wall between us now, which I knew was a dumb thing to feel.

"Lincoln and I are Beau's best men. Ash says I'll walk with Wyatt," Kenny added.

We were all at Ash and Beau's, finalizing wedding plans. But I couldn't stop myself from wondering where Jude was…if he was coming. It had been a week since he'd gone home with me and Melinda, and we'd hardly talked and hadn't hung out once since then—not from my lack of trying either.

"Yep. We'll practice some today," Rush told Kenny. "I think that's what this is all about. But if you need help, you can come to me."

"Yeah, I don't wanna forget. Beau and Ash say I won't forget because I'm super smart, but if I do forget what I'm supposed to do, it's okay because everyone forgets."

"Yeah, just ask Rush. He forgets stuff *all* the time," Linc teased, and Rush playfully stuck his tongue out at him.

"Oh! Someone else just got here. I have to go say hi." Kenny ran off. He was so fucking great.

I turned to look at the door to see if it was Jude who had come in. It wasn't, so I let my gaze wander around the room, and nope, he wasn't there.

"Where's your BFF?" I asked Rush.

"He has some kind of stomach bug or something. He won't be here today."

Stomach bug, my ass. He was avoiding me. I glanced at Sawyer and saw his brows pull together. He was likely the only one who caught my expression, but it didn't surprise me that he did.

Dax and Jace approached us just as Lincoln and Rush made their way to Beau and Ash. Then Carter started discussing work stuff with Dax, and a second later, Sawyer was by my side.

"Trouble in paradise?" he joked.

"Don't know what you're talking about."

"Please don't tell me you had sex with Jude."

Falling in love with Carter had loosened my brother up in a lot of ways, but not all of them. "I didn't have sex with Jude, and if I did, it would be none of your business, and it would have been a decision we both made as adults."

Sawyer sighed. "Yeah, but you care about him. I don't want you to get hurt."

Well, shit. That was different. "Um…did we just trade places? I'm fine. Having sex with someone has never hurt me, and if I had sex with him, it wouldn't either. I've been told it's actually a life-changing experience."

"Oh God. I'd rather not talk about your prowess in bed."

"Eh, I'm sure he's not the beast you are," Carter said, and then it was my turn to freak out, because no, I didn't want to talk about that.

"Yeah, I'm done with this conversation. Not something I needed to know." Mostly, I just didn't want to talk about Jude, because Sawyer was right. I did care about him, and he was avoiding me, which wouldn't do at all.

We did a few rehearsals for the wedding. Kenny did great, as we knew he would. Beth, Beau's mom, had gotten ordained, and she was going to perform the ceremony, which I thought was cool.

The whole time, though, my thoughts were with Jude, and I got more and more restless. Once we finished our hundredth wedding meeting—which Ash was surprisingly anal about, determined it would go off without a hitch—I ducked out early and went straight to Jude's condo, which was actually Linc's condo. Short Stuff had moved in with Rush, and Jude was renting the place from him.

We were gonna figure this shit out, and we were gonna figure it out now.

My thumbs drummed on the steering wheel of my

truck as I made the drive into Fever Falls proper and to Jude's. I took the elevator, then walked down the steel-gray hallway to his apartment.

I knocked, and a few seconds later the door opened. "How did I know you would show up?" Jude asked. He wore a black tee and a pair of jeans.

"Because you know me, and you know you're being stupid."

Jude rolled his eyes and let me in. I went straight to the couch and plopped down on it. I'd been in this apartment a thousand times over the years, both when it belonged to Linc and now that Jude lived there. Jude and I spent a lot of time together, probably more than even our friends knew. "You're avoiding me."

"I watched you fuck someone while I jerked off."

"So? It was just sex. We had a little fun, and it was hot as hell, I might add. Are we really going to let that screw things up?" My pulse thumped against my skin, in fear of that happening. Jude's friendship meant a lot to me, and I'd never forgive myself if I lost it.

"No, we're not. I just…" Jude ran a hand through his hair, then sat on the chair across from me. His leg was bouncing up and down, and my fingers twitched with the urge to put a hand on his thigh to help settle him, but I wasn't sure if my touch would be a good thing or a bad thing at the moment. "I liked it…"

I released a heavy breath, but didn't want to make a big deal out of it, so I went for light. "I'd have my feelings hurt if you didn't. Everyone who sees me naked likes it."

Jude shook his head, but I could see a smile teasing those lips of his. Fuck if I didn't want to lick them, nibble them. They would be the death of me, I was pretty sure.

"I'm feeling weird about it all, trying to make sense of it. I mean, I spent my whole damn life thinking I was straight. Then one day I acknowledged I felt like shit. I was sad and lonely and missed my best friend. And every time he talked about this guy he was friends with, it felt like he was ripping my heart out."

My body tensed, but I tried to ignore it. I knew this story. Jude and I had talked about it before. I was the only one he'd ever really talked to about Rush, but lately, it'd felt like he was grinding up my insides. I figured I was jealous, and that didn't sit well with me.

"So I came here and still felt sort of fucked up, and oh, hey, I realized I was in love with my very male best friend. And oh, hey, again, he was in love with someone else. It fucked with my head. It was confusing as shit, but I worked it out. Talking to you and our friendship helped with that. Made me see I was in love with Rush and that was okay, but I thought it was just him, ya know? I'd never been attracted to another man before, and I thought the Rush thing was simply because I cared about him so much and we were so close. But I wanted to be in your bed that night, Cam. I wanted to be there without Melinda. Don't you get how that can be confusing for me? How I need some time to sort things out?"

Shit. I was an asshole. I should have given him space. "Yeah, I get it. And I'm sorry. But can I just say it makes me happy you're bi? Christ, Jude, you know I want you." It wasn't something I had any problem admitting. I wanted Jude. He was fucking beautiful. I wasn't in love with him, and I still felt like I'd been put through a meat grinder when he talked about loving Rush, but I was attracted to him and wanted to sleep with him, and I didn't think that was such a bad thing.

"But am I? When I'd never known it until I loved Rush and then didn't feel it for another man until I was attracted to you?"

He was attracted to me. Jude fucking Sandoval wanted me. There was no way to stop it—a smile stretched across my face.

"You're so fucking cocky. Focus, Cam."

"I can't help it!" It felt good as hell to hear him say he was attracted to me. "Okay…I'll behave." Sobering up a bit, I looked at him. "The thing is, sexuality is different for everyone. You can't expect it to play by the same rules for each person. Some people always know, others take longer to figure things out. But if you're searching for a label, there are options. You can be bisexual and mostly feel attraction toward women. It doesn't have to be this even split. I sleep mostly with men, but I love women too. You can be demisexual, but I'm not sure that's you. People who are demi don't typically feel sexual attraction unless there's a strong bond there. You feel attraction for people outside of me and Rush, right? Want to sleep with them?"

"Yeah," he replied. "That doesn't sound like me. I've had a lot of sex, and I really fucking wanted it." Jude chuckled.

"Well, maybe you're pan, which means you're attracted to anyone regardless of gender, but I think it's safe to say you're not straight, and that's what matters right now."

"Yeah…you're right. I just need to sort through my shit. And I don't know if I want to act on this. It's different with Rush now, and he doesn't even know the depth of how I felt."

Felt or *feel*, I couldn't help but wonder.

"I think you're saying I'm important to you and you don't want to lose me. If that's not the sweetest damn thing, I don't know what is." My hope was to lighten the mood. I didn't want him to think I wasn't taking this seriously, but I also wanted him to feel like this was all okay. It wasn't a big deal. We would be fine. When he grinned and flicked me off, I knew I'd answered the right way.

But then Jude turned serious, looked at me with those blue eyes of his all curious and penetrating. "Your friendship means a lot to me." He turned away.

Shit, this guy. He made me crazy in a way I was totally unfamiliar with. I wasn't sure there was anything I wouldn't do for him. "Hey," I said, and he looked up at me. "I'm not going anywhere—sex or not. Your friendship means a lot to me too."

Jude nodded. "Can we go back to how things were? Pretend it didn't happen?"

We could. I didn't want to, but I would. The most important thing was making him comfortable. Jude hadn't had an easy time of it. "Already done, Beautiful. Now, are we going to work on our puzzle or do something cool like play a video game?"

Jude had a secret puzzle addiction, and we'd been

working on one together for a while. And yeah, he liked video games, but he didn't enjoy playing them with me as much because I always kicked his ass.

He nodded, smiled, and I knew it was the damn puzzle. Still, I stood, walked over to the small table with him, and we got to work.

CHAPTER THREE

Jude

Well, not obsessed. That sounds like I'm a creeper. There's just…something about him. He sort of looks like he feels alone like me. ~ Theo

I COULDN'T STOP thinking about Cam and how things had gone down. It was fucking with my head. We'd still been hanging out over the past week since our chat, and I found myself watching him often—when he talked to Sawyer or when we went for a jog in the park; when he'd laugh and joke around with Rush or Ash, or how he always ruffled Linc's hair like he was a little brother to him. The way his throat moved when he took a drink.

I'd notice the veins in his arms and how strong his hands looked, and then I'd wonder what those calluses would feel like against my skin…

That was usually when I'd snap the hell out of it and quit obsessing about him, but the next time I saw him, it started over again.

It was making me fucking crazy.

Just like at the moment. I was walking to Fever Pitch to meet Rush for lunch, so why the fuck was I thinking about Camden goddamned Burke?

I shook those thoughts from my annoying brain as I walked into the restaurant. Fever Pitch has a sports bar/grill feel to it, tucked away on Fever Street, which I'd learned was the heart of the gayborhood. Mostly it was Lincoln who called it that, and I hadn't even known it was a thing until I moved to Fever Falls.

Rush had come out years ago, and it had never mattered to me. He'd always been my best friend, and that would never change, but I hadn't had any other friends in the LGBTQ community. Things were different where we grew up. There wasn't a Fever Street or gayborhood, and when I moved to Richmond, I assumed there was one there, but Rush had been in Fever Falls by then, and I hadn't known where it was.

And now…now I was pretty sure I was part of the LGBTQ community too. I mean, I knew I was. Having been in love with one dude and then wanting to bone another pretty much sealed the deal.

"Hey, man. What's up?" Rush asked. I'd been spacing off and almost passed by him. "You good?" He frowned.

"Yeah, just have a lot on my mind." *Oh, you know, like how I used to be in love with you and now I'm attracted to Camden. I guess that means I'm bi!*

None of those things came out of my mouth. Instead, I sat across from him and settled into the booth.

"Are you still seeing your therapist?" Rush asked.

"Yeah, but just once a month. The antidepressants help." When I'd first moved to Fever Falls, Rush made me acknowledge I was likely depressed. Despite growing up with a father who had been depressed my whole life, I hadn't seen it in myself. Hadn't thought I had a reason to be sad, other than wanting Rush, but now I understood that it didn't work that way. And I also knew there were a lot of things that bothered me, which I hadn't acknowledged before either, like my dad, but I didn't want to get into that. "It's nothing like that. I'm good. Stop babying me, or I'll throw something at you."

Rush laughed. "You're always throwing things at me."

"You always deserve it," I countered, and he chuckled again.

"Hey, guys, what's up?" Keeg, Jace's little brother, approached us. He waited tables part-time at Fever Pitch, and Jace worked at the fire station with Beau. I couldn't believe how large their group of friends was. It was still something I was adjusting to. I had never been close to a lot of people before. I just didn't work that way.

"Hey, how's it going?" Rush asked.

"Pretty good. Owen gets back from Parlaisa tomorrow. I can't wait." Keegan was dating a fucking prince, which was some crazy-ass shit if you asked me.

We talked to him for a moment, and then we both ordered bacon cheeseburgers and fries, and Keegan was on his way.

"I need to get my shit together and stop eating like this," Rush said. "January will be here before I know it." He was a motocross racer, and people didn't realize they were some of the most disciplined athletes there were.

"You'll do it. You always take care of your shit."

"That's because I'm fucking awesome."

I shrugged. "You're all right." My phone vibrated, and I pulled it out of my pocket.

Hey, Beautiful. Dinner tonight? Again, I waited for the discomfort to bubble up in me at Cam's compliment, but it didn't happen. I sneaked a quick reply to Camden, telling him sure.

"What are you smiling at?" Rush asked.

"Nothing." I shook my head. Sometimes I felt like I didn't know how to talk to Rush anymore, and I didn't know how to change that. "You wanna go riding sometime next week?"

"I would fucking love to go riding next week. I need it."

We started talking about Ashton and Beau's upcoming wedding.

We were halfway through our meal when Rush said softly, "I think I wanna ask Linc."

"Ask Linc what?"

"To marry me."

My eyes snapped to his just as my heart dropped to my stomach. I wasn't in love with Rush anymore. I wasn't, and I knew he belonged with Lincoln, but I'd never considered that Rush would want to get married. "Wow, that's…that's great." The words sort of stuck in my mouth, which pissed me off.

Rush glanced around, seeming uncertain, then shifted in his seat. I wasn't sure what that was about, but I didn't think it had to do with Lincoln. Or at least, not with how Rush felt about him. "I don't have a plan right now or anything. I don't even know if I'll do it soon. It's just something I've been thinking about. I'm scared it'll freak him out."

Somehow, I forced myself to shove my discomfort aside. In some ways, I could see where Rush was coming from. Linc had been skittish when it came to letting himself admit how he felt about Rush, but once he did, he was all in. "He loves you, man. He'll say yes. There's nothing Linc wants more than to spend his life with you."

"But married? He's never even talked about it. I'm probably out of my damn mind."

"No." I shook my head. "You're not. You're in love, and it makes us question ourselves...it can make us question everything, but that's because it matters so damn much." My eyes darted away. That was how it felt when I'd realized I was in love with him.

"Jude?" We'd had exactly one talk about my feelings, and at the time, I'd told him I was confused and thought I might have feelings for him. I'd never told him I was in love with him. What good could come from it? Plus, I was over it now. But Rush knew me, and regardless, he sensed something.

"Deflate that big-ass head of yours. I wasn't thinking about you. Being with Linc has made you an even bigger cocky motherfucker."

He laughed, but it was a bit forced. His eyes creased around the edges, the light that had just been there dimming. He looked...sad...like he was sad for me.

"Seriously, Rush. Cut that shit out. I, um...hell, I

moved on from that confusing stuff way back then. I actually might be kind of seeing someone, though it's not serious."

Why in the fuck had I said that? I sure as shit wasn't seeing any-damn-one, and I didn't want to.

"Really?" Rush asked, and I swear to God, I saw him let out a deep breath, maybe one he'd been holding since we had our one conversation about my possible feelings. It hit me then—and I didn't know why I hadn't seen it before—that Rush had worried about me. That maybe a part of him felt guilty that he loved Lincoln because he hadn't known how I felt about him. It was so typical Rush. He was the best man I knew.

And that was exactly why I said, "Yeah. We'll see what happens. I'm definitely not ready to propose…or to tell you who it is."

He held up his hands, chuckling. "I wasn't going to ask. I know you. Jude Sandoval never does anything before he's ready."

"Damn straight."

"I'm happy for you. I hope it turns into something, and if it does, don't run, okay? I can't handle the thought of you being alone."

Like my dad, he meant, who'd lost his wife when I was young, and never recovered.

"Stop getting all sappy on me," I said, but I knew he was right. I did always run when shit got too close…except I wouldn't have with him.

"So I really don't get her name or anything?" Rush asked.

Her. He automatically went to *her*, and I couldn't blame him. I mean, considering that the person I was seeing was made up as hell, they could be anyone. "Nope. Nothing."

We finished our lunch, and I pushed my lie aside. It wasn't that big a deal. I'd just tell him it didn't work out.

I went back home—well, to Linc's. Maybe I should look into getting a place I wasn't renting from Rush's boyfriend. I got out of the elevator, and the second I did, I saw the teenager who lived next door with his mom, sitting in front of the door.

"I don't know where I lost my keys. I'm sorry," he said into his cell as I walked toward him. "I know this is the third set I've lost." Pause. "Yes, Mom. I know I'm scatterbrained. You know how I get."

A frown tugged at my lips. He was about sixteen or seventeen, I thought. He wore a black beanie and had a skateboard beside him.

"Yeah, I know I'm almost eighteen. I get it. I screw up, and I need to grow up, okay? When will you be home so I can get in?"

I was stalling so I could hear the rest of the conversation, fumbling with my keys at the door.

"It's my art show tonight. You won't be able to go?" he asked, the melancholy radiating from his words to me. "Shit," he cursed when he got off the phone.

"No school?" I asked him.

"Some teacher-in-service day or something."

"Do you, um…need some help? I didn't mean to overhear. You're welcome to come inside and wait for your mom."

The kid's green eyes went wide, and I held up my hands.

"It was just an offer. You don't have to. My name is Jude. I rent this apartment from my friend Lincoln."

"I know Lincoln. Well, I don't know him, but I lived next door to him. I mean, obviously. No shit, I lived next door to him 'cuz I live here now. And I know you were just being nice. Did it look like I didn't know? Because I did. And I'm rambling. I ramble sometimes. It annoys people. I'm Theo, by the way."

I smiled. "Hi, Theo. It's nice to meet you."

"And sure. I'll come in. My mom is sending her assistant to bring me a key, but she said it'll take like an hour." Theo stood up, and I realized he had a sketchbook on his lap. He reached for his skateboard next.

"Maybe you should call your mom and tell her? Just to be safe."

"I'm seventeen. I don't need her permission. Plus, she never cares where I am. She's too busy for that."

Well, shit. I could hear the sadness in his voice, and I got it. My dad hadn't been too busy for me growing up, but I'd never felt like he was engaged with me. He was too damn sad and kept to himself. It was only because of Rush and his parents that I'd felt like I had family. "Maybe still just tell her to be safe."

Theo nodded. I unlocked the door, and he made a quick call to his mom, who really didn't seem to care that he was coming to my place.

I tossed the keys on the counter. "You thirsty or anything?"

"I'll have a beer," he replied. When I cocked my head at him, he laughed. "I'm kidding. It was a joke. Probably not a very good one, though. Maybe that's another bad habit? I always considered my sense of humor to be a good thing, but maybe it's not. So you've known me for five minutes, and you've seen I have a habit of losing things, I ramble, and I make inappropriate jokes."

I had to admit, it was a bit hard to keep up with him. Theo spoke rapid fire and went from subject to subject. I chuckled. "It's fine. You keep things interesting. And I'm sure you have a great sense of humor. Your choices are sweet tea, water, or orange juice."

"Sweet tea, please." I fixed Theo a glass of tea, and he walked around the kitchen, living room, and dining room, looking around. He studied the paintings on the walls and the books on the shelves. "This apartment doesn't seem like you. I mean, not that I know you. Obviously, I don't know anything about you other than the fact that your name is Jude and you rent this apartment from Lincoln and you have that construction guy over a lot."

That he'd noticed Cam surprised me. That he'd realized this place wasn't me surprised me more. "It's not. Most of this stuff is Linc's. My shit is in storage."

"Ooh! What about the puzzle?" Theo rushed over to the table in the corner. "Is that you or Linc?"

"Me." I walked over and gave him his tea, which he literally drank in five seconds flat. "Been a while since you had a drink?" I teased.

"No. One's mouth gets dry when they talk too much," he replied, and I laughed. He was a good kid. I liked him.

"You wanna do some of the puzzle with me?" I asked.

Theo nodded. His eyes were big, and he looked like an excited puppy. I couldn't help but wonder if his mom ever did shit like this with him and if his father was around.

So we sat down and started working on the puzzle of the Atlanta skyline. Theo did most of the talking. By the time he got a text that his mom's assistant was almost there, I'd discovered he was a senior at Fever Falls High, loved art and comics, his mom wasn't going to his show that night at seven, he had a few friends but no one close because he thought he was too much for people sometimes, and he liked riding his skateboard.

"Thank you for letting me come over. That was cool," Theo said as I walked him to the door.

"No problem. I'm always around if you ever get locked out again, or just want to visit." There was something about the kid. I felt for him. Now that I thought about it, I realized I hardly ever saw his mom. I'd seen him around a whole lot more, and I wasn't sure I'd ever seen them together.

"That's...thanks. I appreciate it."

We said our goodbyes, and the second we did, I found myself calling Cam.

"Hey, you. Miss me?" he teased.

"No," I replied. "Do you want to go to an art show

tonight?"

"Are you asking me on a date?" Cam said playfully.

"Nope."

"You're crushing me, Beautiful. And yeah, I don't know much about art, but I'm down."

The thing was, I didn't know much about art either, but I wanted to support Theo. I wanted him to have someone there. I thought maybe he might need it.

CHAPTER FOUR

Camden

Of course, you were the one who had the guts to talk to me first. I'm not sure there's anything you're afraid of. ~ Letter from Henry

"SO HOW IS it we ended up going to an art show at Fever Falls High tonight?" I asked Jude as I drove us to the school. His request had been a bit of a surprise, but I was glad he'd invited me. Things seemed to be going back to normal between us after the-hookup-that-shall-not-be-spoken-about. Well, except he watched me all the damn time, and I pretended not to notice, but ya know, just a normal day.

"This kid who lives in the condo next door to me."

"Beanie kid?" I'd seen him around.

"Yeah, him. I came home today and he was locked out. I heard him talking to his mom, who seemed not to have the time for him. He mentioned an art show. She can't go, and I just…I don't know. I wanted to support the kid. Is that weird?" Jude asked.

Fuck, this beautiful man was going to kill me. "No. It's not weird. It's sweet. Aww, you're so sweet. I'm gonna try and think of a new name I can call you—Joyful Jude? Your first name is hard, so we'll go with your last. We can be like Beau and Ash…hmm…Sweet Sandoval? Syrupy Sandoval?"

"You just might be the biggest dork I've ever met."

"Well, that wasn't very nice. Smelly Sandoval? Shut-up Sandoval. Stop-pretending-you-don't-like-me Sandoval, because when you do, you're so Satisfying Sandoval."

Jude let loose a deep, husky laugh that was contagious, so a second later I was doing the same.

"I really think there might be something wrong with you," he added, still snickering.

"Stop it, Sandoval."

"Make me, Crazy Camden."

"Ugh. My name is better and easier, Jilly Jude."

"Jilly?"

"Silly with a *J*."

"Or you could have paired it with Sandoval."

Glancing over, I winked at him. "I keep you interested by keeping you on your toes."

Jude shifted in the seat and looked away. I hoped I

hadn't overstepped. We said we were going back to normal, but the thing was, I always flirted with Jude, and he never cared. "Sorry. I—"

"Let it be, Charismatic Cam. Don't coddle me."

I liked that…him calling me charismatic, and I also understood his not wanting to be coddled. I would be the same. "So tell me more about this kid."

Jude told me what he knew about Theo as we finished our drive to the high school. The parking lot was nearly full, which was cool. Great turnout for an art show. We hadn't done that when I went to school there.

We were almost to the bright red and orange doors, when I stopped him. "Hey." I put a hand on Jude's shoulder. "This really is cool of you, supporting some kid you just met like this."

Jude shrugged it off, which I knew he would. "It's no problem…and wow, this school is bright."

"Fever Falls Fire, baby. You're talking to a previous homecoming king, most likely to accidentally set the school on fire, and district champion in high school football here. Are you impressed?" We'll forget that our team was so good because of Ash and Beau. Jude didn't need to know that.

He shook his head, but a smile played at his lips. "Most likely to accidentally set the school on fire? That doesn't sound good. So no, I'm not impressed, Cocky Cam."

"Eh, we can't use that one. Beau claimed it for Cocky Carmichael, though I'm sure my dick's bigger than Ash's, so it'd fit me better."

A woman gasped behind me, and Jude's eyes went wide. I mouthed a sorry, and then we hurried inside, trying to hold back our laughter. Christ, he was fun.

They asked for a small donation to get in, which Jude and I both did. Then we made our way to the gymnasium, where they had different sections for each high school artist.

"Wow…this is really cool," I told Jude, meaning it. We hadn't run across Theo's section yet, and had only made it to about three showcases, when I heard, "Camden? Isn't this a surprise." I froze up for a second, then shoved that feeling aside. There was no reason for me to get that way. Not after all this time.

I turned around and saw him holding his wife's hand.

"Jude, this is an old friend of mine, Henry, and his wife, Dee. They're both teachers at Fever Falls High. Henry, Dee, this is my friend Jude."

It was still awkward when Henry and I ran into each other. I guessed a shared secret past would do that to people. Especially when you'd thought you were in love at one point, only one of you said he would never come out, and despite saying he's gay, promptly proposed to a woman.

"Hey, Jude. It's so nice to meet you!" Dee said.

Henry's eyes darted from Jude to me, then back to Jude again. He seemed to notice everyone was looking at him. Henry shook his head, apologized, and said he had a bit of a headache, before shaking Jude's hand.

"Jude's neighbor's in the show, so we came to support him," I told them.

"Oh, that's so nice of you." Dee put a hand on her belly. Oh wow, she was pregnant again.

"How are the kids?" I asked.

"They're good," Dee replied. "They're both in elementary school. It feels like they're growing up too fast." Henry reached over and grabbed her hand, but he hadn't spoken, just sort of looked at me and Jude.

This was awkward as fuck, so I needed to get the hell out of there. "I'm glad things are going well. And congrats on the new baby coming. We need to be on our way, though."

The last thing I needed was for the conversation to drag on any longer. It was obviously uncomfortable for Henry…having his wife and the man he used to secretly love and sleep with speak to one another. I turned, and Jude was right behind me. It always shook me up a bit to see Henry. Not because I still had feelings for him, but because I was sad for him…and for Dee too. But then, maybe he'd realized he was bi and not gay? Maybe he loved Dee, but I also knew he had loved me, that it had been real, but that he hated that part of himself and wished it didn't exist.

When I felt Jude's hand at the small of my back, the tension melted out of me. "Are you okay? I sensed something there."

"That's, um…that's him. The guy I told you about." I'd told Jude about Henry when he'd talked to me about being in love with Rush, what felt like a lifetime ago. He was the only person I'd ever shared the story with, because it wasn't mine to share. Sawyer, Beau, and the others knew him, either from school or around town, but they hadn't known about us. No one was close with Henry, but they knew who he was, and so no, I couldn't share his business with them, even if there had been a time in my life when I'd needed to talk about it. I probably shouldn't have confirmed to Jude who that had been, but I trusted him.

"Shit…wow…I didn't put two and two together. Are you okay?"

"Yeah, I am. He made his decision, and I got over it a long time ago. We're here to see Theo, not to deal with old shit."

He nodded, but I wasn't sure he believed me.

"Jude? Holy crap! What are you doing here? And with Construction Guy. I can't believe you guys came. Like…did you come to see me, or were you already coming?"

My eyes caught on Theo, who was wearing slacks and a button-up shirt with a nice vest over it…with his beanie. The kid was cool as fuck. I could already tell.

"We came to check out your work," Jude told him.

The kid looked up at him like he hung the damn moon, and it hit me. It was something some people, straight or queer, didn't understand, but LGBTQ people had a way of finding each other, congregating together, whether we knew it or not, whether we were out or not. I'd seen it often throughout my life—people I'd been drawn to in school, coming out later in life. And somehow I knew Theo was queer. I could see it in the way he looked at Jude like he knew him. What I didn't know was if Jude knew or if Theo was out.

"Oh, wow, that's…" Theo's eyes darted down. "You really came to see me? Like only for me?"

Fuck. I really hoped this kid didn't have a crush on

Jude.

"Yeah, we did. We were curious about your work. This is Camden Burke, by the way—not Construction Guy."

Theo held out his hand. "Nice to meet you, Mr. Burke. I'm Theo."

We shook. "You can call me Cam, Camden, or Construction Guy, but please don't call me Mr. Burke. I'm too young for that shit." There was another gasp from a parent, and I was quickly discovering I wasn't good at being back in high school. That was the second time I'd been gasped at. "How about we go look at your art before I get kicked out?"

Theo smiled. "Yeah…I…of course. It's this way."

He was so excited, he looked like he was bursting at the seams. Damn, I was glad Theo had found Jude, and that Jude had invited me there with him. Having someone support you could make all the difference in someone's life. I'd always tried to be that person for Sawyer growing up, and I couldn't help but wonder if Theo had anyone.

He led us over to his cubicle, talking a thousand words a minute the whole time. I had no idea what he was saying most of the time, but he pointed to different pieces and told us a bit about them. One was a comic strip, and he said he wanted to make comics one day, but there were also some charcoal pieces, one of a clear box with someone inside looking out, and I thought maybe that was how he felt—trapped.

The kid was good. Really fucking good.

"Wow, Theo…this is incredible," Jude told him, and Theo nearly glowed.

"You really think so?"

"He's right," I added. "You're really fu—freaking talented. Oh my God. I don't think I've said freaking since I was fourteen."

Jude rolled his eyes playfully, and Theo laughed.

"This is what I want to do someday. Be an artist. Mom thinks it's silly, but…"

"It's not silly," Jude said. "It's your dream. You're lucky you know what it is. I had no clue at your age. Hell, I don't have a clue now." Jude's voice was low, sort of throaty.

"You're doin' all right if you ask me, Beautiful."

Theo's eyes went wide, and when I looked at Jude, I realized his were too. Shit, was I not supposed to call him that unless we were with our friends or around all queer people? The thought made my jaw go tight. I wasn't good at that—playing the game, denying who I was—but then, this wasn't about me, was it? It was about Jude.

Theo sucked in a breath that apparently seemed to choke him. He began to cough, his face turning red, and he reached for a water bottle and took a few long swallows.

"You okay?" Jude asked.

"Yes. I, um…yes. I just…choked…on air. I don't know why. But hey, did you see this one?" Theo asked, before telling us about a painting.

It was a distraction, and I stood back and let the two of them do their thing. Afterward, Jude asked Theo if he needed a ride home when it was over, but his mom's PA was picking him up.

We said our goodbyes and started to head out, when I told Jude, "Hold on a sec. I'll be right back."

I jogged over to Theo, and dropped my voice. "If you ever need someone to talk to, about anything, we can find someone, okay? I'm not saying there's something, but if there ever is, you can tell me or Jude. We have this friend named Trey. I think you guys might have a few things in common."

Theo's eyes darted away, but then he nodded. I walked away before it made things uncomfortable for him.

"What was that about?" Jude asked when I reached him again.

"Nothing. We okay, though? You looked a little shaken up when I called you…" I looked around playfully. "The *B* word."

Jude frowned, but I could see the spark in his eyes. "I hate you. Have I ever told you that?"

Laughing, I replied, "No you don't, B. You love me."

He flicked me off, which he loved to do, and we got our third gasp of the day. "We really might get ourselves kicked out of here," he said with a laugh.

"It happened to me a few times in high school too. Some of my favorite memories. Wanna make some new ones?" I waggled my eyebrows, then opened my mouth as though I was going to say something to get us in trouble.

Jude grabbed my wrist and tugged me out.

I laughed the whole way.

CHAPTER FIVE

Jude

Construction Guy called Jude beautiful. Like…just said it as though it was nothing. I wonder if they're boyfriends. If so, why does Jude seem so alone?
~ Theo

THE NEXT COUPLE of weeks went by in a blur. I was working like crazy at Fever, and we were all getting together often to help with final wedding plans for Ash and Beau. On top of that, Theo and I had hung out twice. I caught him lingering around in the hallway around our units, and I was pretty sure he was waiting for me, so we'd gone out and got coffee, and another time he brought over some of his art to show me.

I wasn't sure why he'd connected with me—maybe just because I was nice to him and spent time with him when it didn't seem like anyone in his life did. But whatever the reason, it was obvious Theo had decided he wanted to be friends with me, and I enjoyed hanging out with him too. He always seemed like he wanted to say something, like he was holding in a question, but he never asked it. I made sure to tell him I was there if he needed anything, but I didn't want to push.

Then there was Cam. I saw him probably every other day. He asked about Theo, and every time he did, I thought about our visit to the high school. It had meant a lot to me that Cam was so willing to go to an art show for a teenager he didn't know.

And Henry…that had been interesting. For as long as I'd known Camden, I'd never seen him uncomfortable. He was always steady and in control, but seeing Henry had been…different. I didn't know how to put it other than that. I knew he was the only man Cam had ever considered himself in love with, and I couldn't help but wonder if he still was.

But even more than that were thoughts of our night with Melinda, and the veins in his hands, and the curve of his lips, and what they would feel like against mine. I still couldn't get that night out of my head. It was twisting me up, the fierceness of the desire I suddenly had for him, so different than what I had felt for Rush.

Camden and I were friends. He was my best friend outside of Rush, but my feelings for Rush had stemmed from the love I always felt for him. I couldn't remember a time I hadn't loved Rush, whether it was friendship or later something more. With Cam...fuck, I wanted to *devour* him. I wanted to know what it would feel like to be devoured *by* him, and that was scary as hell.

Today wasn't the day to dwell on that, though. Well, it never should be the day to dwell on it, and I needed to cut that shit out. But especially today. It was Ash and Beau's wedding...which I was going to...which was still weird that I was friends with Ashton fucking Carmichael.

There was a knock at my door, and I frowned. Cam was picking me up, but he normally texted and I went downstairs. It wasn't like he was picking me up for a date and needed to come to my door. There was no reason the two of us had to ride together, but we were, and I wasn't surprised by that. It always felt good spending time with Cam. I wasn't sure I would have ended up staying in Fever Falls if it hadn't been for him.

I pulled open the door, and the second I did, my eyes snagged on Cam. He was wearing black slacks, a white dress shirt, the sleeves rolled to his elbows, with suspenders, and the first two buttons on his collar left open. "Holy fuck," rolled out of my mouth, my brain not having time to catch up. He hadn't shaved his stubble, but it was neat. His hair was somehow both messy and styled, and that goddamned jaw made me shiver. He looked…goddamn, he looked sexy.

He *was* sexy.

I thought Camden Burke was fucking gorgeous, but this was the first time I'd allowed myself to think of him in those terms, outside of our night with Melinda.

"That good, huh?" Cam cocked a brow.

"What? No." I shook my head, then stopped. "Yeah. That good." Why deny it? He already knew I'd wanted him, knew I was questioning things.

"I didn't expect you to admit it. You're gonna be the death of me. You know that, right, Beautiful?" Fire sparked in his eyes, and Christ, did I like it. I liked Cam's eyes on me…I liked that he wanted me, which yeah, was not typical for me.

I didn't answer him. Couldn't. Just took him in. The veins in his hands and forearms really did it for me. I liked how strong he looked. His stubble…what would it feel like on my skin?

"You don't stop looking at me like that, and we're not making it to the wedding."

Those words did several things to me. Made my skin flush and my dick perk up. The way he talked to me—his confidence, really—turned me on. And they also snapped me out of whatever the fuck was going on with my brain. Lately, thoughts of me and Cam kept rolling through me, and I really wanted someone to talk to about it.

But the people I talked to were Camden and Rush, and I wasn't sure how much I could talk to either of them about Cam.

"You're blushing." Cam stepped forward and raised his hand. Then, as if reconsidering, he began to lower it again.

"No," I rushed out. "You can."

His eyes sparked again with a heat that singed me. He cupped my cheek, brushed his thumb against my skin. My eyes fell closed, and I just *felt*.

His thumb ran over my bottom lip, my cheekbone. His fingers were rough, callused, a reminder of who this was, even though I couldn't see him. I lost myself in it, melted into his touch that was so damn addicting, I suddenly wondered how I'd ever been without it.

"This changes things," he said, dropping his hand.

"Yeah, I think it does." I wasn't sure there was any denying it anymore. I didn't want to see Cam with Melinda or with another guy. I wanted to experience him for myself. "We should, um…we should go." I cleared my throat.

I turned and grabbed my suit jacket, sliding it on. I was wearing cream dress pants with a white shirt and a cream jacket.

I walked out, closed and locked the door behind me, and got a few feet away before I realized Cam wasn't moving. "What?" I looked back at him.

"You look really fucking hot too. Just taking a minute to enjoy the view."

Damned if my face didn't heat again. I wanted Camden Burke, and now I had to figure out what in the hell I was going to do about it.

THE WEDDING WAS outdoors, at Swift Creek Lodge, about half an hour from Fever Falls. There were orange and red leaves scattered on the ground, white chairs lined up in front of a gazebo, and the creek running alongside it. The twinkling lights around the gazebo almost looked like lightning bugs were there for the day. The whole area was surrounded by trees, by fall, with this soft, romantic vibe that was strong enough I could feel it.

I sat with Cam, Sawyer, Carter, Dax, Jace, Keegan, Owen, Casey, and Steve. Neither Ashton nor Beau had much family—Ash having none at all—but they had this close-knit group of friends, and I found myself getting a pang in my chest. Not that they hadn't pulled me into the fold, because they had. They'd been nothing but welcoming, but I knew the base crew of Ash, Beau, Linc, Rush, Cam, and Sawyer had a special bond between them. Even though Ash came in later, he felt more a part of it than I did, maybe because he was from the Falls and because of what he shared with Beau. I'd never had the kind of friendship they all shared with anyone other than Rush.

I'd never allowed myself to.

With everyone else, when I got close, I ran. It was likely a side effect of growing up with a man who never let himself get close to anyone after we lost my mom.

"You okay?" Cam touched my shoulder.

"Yeah," I replied, surprised he'd noticed I was a little down. I wasn't sure if I should make an appointment to see if I needed to get my medication adjusted, or if it was normal weird moods I'd had lately.

The music started then, and everyone stood. I watched as Rush and Lincoln walked down the aisle together, wearing black slacks, white shirts, and burgundy vests. When they parted in the gazebo, each going to one side, they looked at each other, watched each other, and fuck if I didn't feel how much they loved each other. It radiated off them, this cloud that filled the whole area, and…it was perfect. So goddamned perfect, even though there was still an ache in my chest. Maybe it would always be there, and maybe that was okay.

Beau's brother, Kenny, and Ashton's friend Wyatt were next. Kenny had the biggest smile on his face, and when I looked around, I realized it made everyone else smile too. He had that effect on people.

Then it was Ash and Beau. The two of them came from opposite directions, meeting together at the end of the aisle. From the beginning they had decided they wanted to walk down together, rather than one waiting for the other. They had black and burgundy vests with bow ties, but the rest of their clothes matched those of the wedding party.

My eyes, along with everyone else's, were riveted on them as they shared vows they'd written themselves and Beau's mom officiated. There were rings and promises, and then Beau cupped Ash's face, wiping the tears away with his thumbs. Ash smiled, leaned in, and they were kissing and everyone was clapping and cheering.

When my eyes found Rush…he was looking at Linc, wanting that, wanting what they had with his Red, but then, then his eyes found me, and fuck if I didn't see the sadness there. The truth getting pounded into me that *oh God*, Rush knew I'd loved him…and that he felt guilty.

I shook my head, telling him it was okay. That I

wasn't in love with him anymore, not in the way I had been. That I was ready to move on, and I wanted him to as well.

That we were okay. We'd always be okay.

CHAPTER SIX

Camden

I was so scared, Cam. So afraid of how attracted to you I was. It was electric. I'd never felt anything like it. I couldn't deny it, when I'd spent my whole life denying it with others. - Letter from Henry

THE WEDDING WAS weird in a whole lot of ways.

After the ceremony, we went inside for the reception. Something was going on with Jude. I could feel it, and it had been impossible not to notice the way he'd been looking at Rush all day. I got it, I did. Rush was his best friend. Jude had told me how alone he felt most of his life unless he was with Rush or his family, and fuck, he'd been in love with him, but yeah, it made something strange twist in my chest.

But then…fuck, I'd catch him watching me. He'd been doing it ever since the night with Melinda, but it intensified today. It wasn't the way he watched Rush, with a sort of resignation and fond memories; instead, it was with this goddamned craving I'd been starving with from the moment I first set eyes on him.

Jude wanted me.

I just didn't know if he planned to do anything about it.

And I also didn't know why. Did he want me for me or to forget Rush?

I took a drink of my beer—I wasn't much of a champagne guy—and felt his eyes on me again from across the room. He was talking with Rush, and when I cocked a brow at him, he flushed and glanced away.

"Hey, you." Sawyer took the seat beside me.

"Hey, you. How you doing? Haven't seen you much the past couple of weeks." It was something I was still getting used to, the transition in our relationship. His whole life, Sawyer had come to me, had needed his big brother, and he didn't anymore. And when he needed someone to lean on, he had Carter. Which yeah, I was happy as fuck about. Sawyer's happiness had always been the most important thing to me, but it was still odd. I'd been told I liked to be needed, but whatever.

"I've been busy at Fearless, and Carter and I went to see his mom again, remember?"

"Yeah, I know." I took another swallow, finishing off my beer. It was my one and only drink of the night because I'd have to drive later. "You're all in love and shit." I winked, and Sawyer laughed.

My eyes darted to Jude again. He was leaning against a wall, Rush having left him. He had a beer in his hand, and he smiled at Sawyer and me.

"It's cool seeing Trey look so happy," Sawyer said, pulling my attention from those damn too blue eyes of Jude's.

"Yeah, it is." Rush and Lincoln were speaking to Trey, a teenager Linc had befriended in the hospital while Trey was fighting cancer. Trey wore slacks, and a shimmery shirt he likely didn't get in the men's section of a store. Fucking gender roles. Why were clothes supposed to be men's or women's?

His dad was there too—Tyson, who worked with me. He was a great father, who supported his son even when he didn't understand him. I wondered if Theo would have the same.

Sawyer and I chatted for a few more minutes before Carter came over and dragged him to the dance floor. Sawyer laughed and pretended to fight him off, but he went easily, in a way he wouldn't have done with anyone else. Carter had been the key to Sawyer setting himself free, and I would always be thankful for that.

"You miss him."

I looked up to see Jude. "He's right there."

"You still miss him." He shrugged. "It's okay, ya know?"

"I don't want to talk about my brother. You've been watching me all day, Beautiful. What's going on in that head of yours?"

"I…" Jude started, then stopped. "Follow me." He walked away without another word, and damned if I didn't stand up and do the same. I followed Jude out of the room, down a hallway, and into a supply room.

"Well, you have my attention," I said as Jude moved to close the door behind me. "What's with the secret rendezvous?" I teased. "Or is this like a flashback to high school where we're going to make out in the supply closet and then—*umpf.*" My body hit the wall beside the door, and Jude's mouth was on mine. All I could think was, *Holy fuck, those lips.* I'd wanted to taste them for what felt like an eternity now, so fucking plump and kissable, and now they were on mine, and his tongue was in my mouth, his hands on my hips.

"Shit," Jude said, his forehead against mine, his breaths heavy and rushed against my lips. "I didn't plan to just kiss you like that. I was going to talk to you and—"

"Did you like it? Kissing me?"

"Fuck yes," he replied.

"Talking is overrated." I cupped his face and pulled him in again, this time not being caught by surprise. I led the way, dipped my tongue between those goddamned lips of his, and Christ, I couldn't help moaning in response.

My hands traveled down his back to rest on his hips as I pulled him closer, making us groin to groin, his stiff cock against my achingly hard one. Jude pulled back slightly, and I feared I'd gone too far, that he'd stop this just as I finally got to taste him, but he leaned in so we were forehead to forehead again. "I'm hard," Jude said breathlessly.

"I noticed that. See what you do to me too?" I pushed myself against him, grinding my pelvis to his.

"*Fuuuck.*"

"You like that?" I asked. "I thought I was going to die not being able to touch you that night. Watching you stroke that pretty cock of yours…seeing you shoot your load. I feel like I've been blue-balling for you forever."

"Shit, it's so hot when you talk to me like that," Jude replied before kissing me. I pushed off the wall, wanting him against one, trying to make my way to the other side of the small room so I could press him between me and something else hard.

We stumbled over something, a box or who the hell knew what, which made us laugh while we were kissing, and then he gasped when he hit the wall. I rolled my hips, pushing my dick against Jude's.

"You gonna be okay if I blow you?" I said against his lips. "Is that too much, too fast?" I was jonesing for his dick in my mouth. Wanted to feel it on my tongue as his come slid down my throat.

"Fuck…holy shit, I literally almost came just now. Is that something people do? Say no to a blowjob?"

I smiled and winked. "Not when I'm the one giving it."

I went down to my knees. When I looked up at him, Jude had his head tilted back, staring toward the ceiling as I reached for his pants. "You sure you're okay with this? Maybe we should wait." I wanted him, but I definitely didn't want to be with him if he wasn't ready…or if he was with me for reasons other than his desire for me.

"I—" he started, but it was the only thing he got out before the door opened behind me.

"Holy shit," Lincoln said.

"I knew they had to be fucking!" Carter added.

Sawyer and Rush just stood there watching us, neither saying a word.

I didn't give a shit that they caught me. What I cared about in that moment was Jude. "Jesus Christ. Close the fucking door and act like adults here. Give us some privacy." I stood.

Sawyer reached for the door to do just that. "We weren't trying to spy. They sent us because they needed extra chairs."

"This is who you're seeing?" Rush asked. "You know you could have told me that, right? That you're dating Cam."

Jude cursed, and this was super fucking new to me. I stood still in front of him, then turned to look at him. His eyes were wide and panicked.

"You're dating Jude?" Sawyer asked me.

No…no, I wasn't. At least not that I'd been aware of. Obviously, that wasn't something I could say. But was he dating someone I didn't know about? I wasn't sure I believed that.

My eyes found his again, and his dilated pupils told me all I needed to know. He was freaking out. For some reason, he'd told Rush he was dating someone, and that damn protective instinct I'd always had took over. "Yeah, we are. It's something we were trying to keep to ourselves, though."

"Take it from me, blowjobs in supply rooms aren't

the way to do that," Carter said, and Sawyer rolled his eyes.

Short Stuff looked at Jude, then back to Rush, and I wondered how much he knew about Jude's feelings, and how that made him feel. I knew he trusted Rush. Lincoln knew he was the only person for Rush Alexander, but I had this nagging feeling they were both sort of unsure what to think about Jude, which had to be shitty for Jude.

"Jude?" Rush asked, and I saw their eyes hold each other.

"Yeah…yeah, I'm seeing Cam. Just a few weeks now and, um…it just sort of happened."

A smile pulled at Rush's lips, big and so fucking bright. He was happy for his friend, but also relieved.

"Good for you," Rush replied. "I'm happy for you both. I can't believe you didn't tell me."

"It's just…like Cam said, we were trying to keep it to ourselves for now. It's, uh, new for me."

"Well, I mean, we turned Ash, Jace, and Owen. It only made sense you were next," Linc teased, and I could tell he was trying to make light of it, to make everyone, Jude especially, comfortable.

"We should get the chairs," Carter said, going into PA mode. They all began going for the folded stack against the wall, but Sawyer, he stared at me, and I knew he didn't believe I was dating Jude. Fucking around? Yeah. Dating? No, if only because I didn't date and Sawyer knew me so well. He knew when I was lying and when I wasn't.

"Come on," I told Jude, nodding toward the door, and he gave me a small smile.

When everyone walked out, I whispered, "I think we need to have a conversation tonight. You didn't even officially ask me to go steady."

He chuckled, which was exactly what I hoped for. "Thank you for that, and maybe I was going to officially ask you tonight."

Jude winked and walked away, leaving me dumbfounded…and maybe a little happier than I should be.

CHAPTER SEVEN

Jude

Lost Man befriends Awkward Boy. ~ Theo's comic

IT WAS A hell of a day.

Between the wedding, witnessing what passed between Lincoln and Rush, and my own growing desire for Cam…oh, and then attacking him in a supply closet like a teenager, almost getting my first blowjob from a guy, only to have it interrupted by friends who now thought we were dating. Yeah, one could say it was a hell of a day.

The rest of the wedding was slightly awkward. Sawyer was eyeing Cam, who was eyeing me, coupled with Rush and Linc, who were obviously relieved I wasn't sitting around pining for Rush. I both understood it and hated it.

Luckily, Ashton and Beau were too wrapped up in each other to realize anything else was going on, as they should have been. The last thing I wanted was to be a distraction on their day.

We ate cake, and Kenny, Lincoln, Wyatt, and Rush all spoke about Beau and Ash, how much they meant to them, and they spoke of Ash's bravery and love and Beau's loyalty and kindness.

It wasn't long before they were heading out on their honeymoon to New Zealand and Camden and I were in his truck, silently riding home.

"So…" I started. Fuck, this was embarrassing. How in the hell had I found myself in this position? Especially after knowing Linc and Rush had done something similar, but at least they hadn't been lying to their friends.

"Not now. We'll talk at home, Beautiful. Oh, hey, Beautiful Boyfriend—BB." Cam paused. "Never mind. That's weird as fuck since I call Sawyer BB." It came from Baby Burke since Sawyer was younger.

"Yeah…not sure we have the same relationship." We were quiet again, and my damn pulse was slamming against my skin. Every couple of minutes I fidgeted in the seat. "My place or yours?"

"I figured yours since you're more comfortable there? I mean, not that you're not comfortable at my place, but your condo is yours, and—"

"And I'm delicate and you need to baby me? Come

on, man. Don't do that."

Cam glanced over at me. "I wasn't trying to do that."

No, I knew he wasn't. Camden was just a nice guy, one who took care of people who were important to him. He'd done it his whole life with Sawyer, and somehow I'd found myself in the place where he did it with me as well. "I don't do this, ya know? I don't need other people. I don't let myself get close to other people. Not in the ways that matter, at least." It was something every girlfriend I had over the years struggled with, not that I blamed them. They deserved someone who could fully give themselves to them, but caring meant losing, and losing meant turning into my dad.

"Except with Rush," Cam said, his voice tight.

"Because I've never known a time in my life when Rush wasn't there, or wasn't important to me, but let's be real, I do it with you too. I have from the start. Do you think I would have shared with just anyone that I was in love with Rush? You're the only person I could have said that to." What I didn't understand was why. Camden had shamelessly flirted with me from the start. He'd called me beautiful, something I typically didn't like, but the word didn't bother me coming from him. In fact, it made me feel *good*. I'd befriended him and trusted him and talked to him. Those were things I didn't give to most people. Not in an honest way.

"I know," Cam replied. "I see that. Don't think I don't. Now, let's wait until we get home, and am I allowed to reach over and put a hand on my boyfriend's leg? And just so you know, I also expect you to really ask me to go steady. You can pass me a note and—spoiler alert—I'll check the yes. Do you have a letterman jacket I can wear?"

Shaking my head, I chuckled. There was something about him that was so damn electric, so contagious, in the best way. Even when he was doing what he was doing at the moment, which was simply trying to make me feel better. If it were anyone else, I would brush the attempt aside, tell them I appreciated it but didn't need it. Hell, even with Rush, but I wasn't doing that with Cam.

What I did do was reach over, put my hand on his thigh, the way he'd asked to do to me. "Thanks, Cam."

"Eh, not like it's a hardship. You have nothing to thank me for."

From there we really were quiet all the way back to my condo. When we got there, Cam took off his suspenders and untucked his shirt. "Sorry. I need to get comfortable. I'm not used to this shit."

"No, no. It's fine." I removed my jacket and got us

each a beer as we sat down on the couch.

"You told Rush you were dating someone?"

I appreciated the fact that Cam started the conversation, but I wished we didn't have to talk about it. "Fuck." I ran a hand over my face. "Yeah. It just sort of happened."

"As these things often do in Fever Falls," Cam teased.

"We were talking about the wedding, and fuck, he wants to marry Lincoln. I can see it, but I think he's worried about me. That I'll be alone." Like my father was. We Sandoval men loved hard when we let ourselves do it. Rush and I had that conversation more than once over the years. My dad had spent his whole life alone after he lost my mom. He hadn't known how to be happy without her. He hadn't known how to move on, even for me. "I don't think he believes I'm not in love with him anymore. And I don't know, it likely doesn't make sense to anyone else—Rush worrying about me that way, especially since he and Lincoln are together and in love now. But I know Rush, and I know how he feels."

"So you made up someone you were seeing and he believed it? I mean, not that anyone wouldn't want to be with you, but he thought there was a mystery person no one knew about? And that you would care enough about them you would forget him?"

I knew exactly where Cam was going with that. "Rush believed it because he needed to. Not that I think he even sees that. He's not that kind of man, but he can't stand the thought of me hurting."

Cam nodded, was quiet for a moment, then shrugged. "Okay, so we'll be fake boyfriends."

"That easily?" It meant lying to his friends…to his brother.

"If it'll help you, then yeah, we'll figure it out."

Jesus, he was a good man. Looking at him then, playing his words over in my head, made me realize why I'd connected with him. Because he cared about people. Because he was sincere, and no matter how much he joked or how full of himself he pretended to be, he put others first.

And fuck, he was gorgeous.

Goose bumps pebbled over my arms as a smile tugged at his mouth, as though he could read my thoughts. It was everything I'd just thought about him and acknowledging how much I wanted him that made me say, "Does it have to be a lie?"

Camden's brows rose.

"I mean, not fully. I think I showed you how much I want you. Fuck, it's been driving me crazy since

Melinda. Probably even longer if I'm being honest. I'm not asking you to really be my boyfriend, but…is it a lie if we're fucking around? I think it's safe to say I'm bi. There's no one better to experiment with than someone I trust."

His eyes blazed, and I thought maybe it was a combination of desire and the fact that I'd admitted I trusted him. After how our friendship had grown, didn't he know that?

"You want me to show you what it's like to be with a guy? Is that what you're asking me?"

Well, shit… "When you say it like that, it sounds wrong. Like I'm using you." That didn't feel right, though. I wanted more from Camden than that. I didn't want to use him. I just…wanted him. We'd been leading up to this for how long now? It couldn't be a surprise for either of us, could it?

He looked a little pensive for a moment, then asked, "Do you want me for me or because you're trying not to want Rush? I'm not saying I'd say no either way. I just need to know."

The question slammed into my chest, stealing my breath. I didn't know why I hadn't expected him to ask it or why I hadn't considered it myself, not really.

I thought about the talks Camden and I had…the

laughs, the drinks. Him staying at Fever to hang out while I worked, and our trips to the falls, and the things I told him about my life. The things he told me.

About how quickly he'd been willing to jump in and go see Theo's show, and the way Cam asked about him.

How he always made sure I knew that if I didn't want him to flirt with me, he'd stop.

My eyes traveled down his body. I remembered the muscles in his back and how they moved. Seeing his cock and how I'd been curious about what it tasted like…what it felt like. The way his lips had moved against mine, and his throaty moans, and fuck, my dick was plumping up. Still, I wasn't sure I could say all that, so I simply let out the first words to hit my tongue. "I'm obsessed with your hands…well, and your forearms."

"Come again?"

It was on the tip of my tongue to say I hadn't come at all yet, but it wasn't the time. "I don't know what it is about them. Why I fixate on them, but I do. The veins in your hands and arms…and I wonder about the calluses and how they'd feel against my skin. How strong your arms look and…fuck, how much that does it for me. It's fucking crazy, but there you have it. I'm obsessed with your hands, and I…goddamned if I don't want them to touch me, all the time. My want for you has nothing to do with how I felt about Rush and everything to do with *you*."

It didn't surprise me when he grinned that cocky Camden grin. "Mmm, I think I'm liking where this is going. What else about me do you want? Tell me what you think about my body, Beautiful, and what you dream about."

My heart rate sped up at the sound of his voice, the way it went an octave lower and the things he'd said. It was so strange, how different it was with Camden. I'd always enjoyed sex. I'd had a lot of it in my life. I was confident in the bedroom or wherever else I decided to fuck, but with him it was all new. He'd had experiences I hadn't, and knew what he wanted in ways I didn't. It was like he was leading the way when that was something I was used to, and damned if I didn't find I liked that with him.

Cam leaned closer. "Hold that thought. Can we take this off first?" He signaled toward my shirt.

Without opening my mouth, I knew I wouldn't be able to speak. Instead, I nodded, and he smiled again, making my cock throb.

He worked the buttons on my shirt. When he had it open, he brushed his callused fingers over my chest, gently, so fucking gently, I thought I would die. "Okay, answer the question now. What else about my body gets you hard?"

"Umm…" My brain was short-circuiting. I could feel it misfire. Every time I thought something, I felt him, and the wires sparked, making me lose it.

"Umm, what, Beautiful?" He was hardly touching me at all, but somehow it got my head spinning. He leaned in closer, his mouth next to my ear as his thumb rasped over one of my nipples. "What about me gets you hard?"

"This," I managed to say huskily. "How you're talking to me…and your back…that was fucking hot, watching how you moved. Your smile. How it's both cocky and sweet at the same time."

He sucked in a sharp breath at that, and I wondered if he was as shocked by my confession as I was.

"What am I going to do with you? Something about you really fucking gets to me. Ask me to kiss you, Jude."

This was it. He was giving me a chance to change my mind, to tell him to slow down, to think this through and make sure it was something I wanted. I knew that as well as I knew my own name, and all it did was make me surer. There was no one I wanted to do this with, to experiment with, more than Cam. "What's taking you so long? Hurry up and kiss me."

Cam chuckled, then leaned in and did just that.

CHAPTER EIGHT

Camden

It's just you, I guess. Do you know that about yourself? How comfortable you make people? How something about you just makes people feel safe?
~ Letter from Henry

THIS WAS PROBABLY all kinds of a mistake, but no way in hell could I stop myself. Not after how much and how long I'd wanted Jude.

A shock of electricity ran up my spine as our tongues tangled together. Jude kissed hungrily, with passion and desire woven together with nerves. "I'll take care of you, Beautiful," I said as I kissed my way down his throat. "Don't worry. It's just us."

At that he growled, grabbed me, and before I knew it, Jude was flipping me on my back and hovering above me. "Treat me like you would any other lover. I don't want you to coddle me."

"Say it again."

Jude's forehead wrinkled in this way that was too fucking adorable. "Say what?"

"That you're my lover. Or just the word *lover* over and over again. It's hot hearing you say it. Gets my dick hard." I pushed my hips up to grind against him. He wanted no-holds-barred, and he was going to get it.

"Oh fuck, that feels good. Different but good. And you're ridiculous. I'm not saying lover again."

"Not saying what again?"

"Dickhead…as in you are one."

"Was that supposed to be less hot? I like hearing you say dick too. And I wanna see yours and touch it, so why don't you get those pants off, Boyfriend. That real enough for you?"

I watched his Adam's apple move as he swallowed.

"What are we going to do?" Jude asked, heat flickering in his gaze.

"I'm gonna make you come so hard, you'll wonder why in the hell we haven't been doing this all along."

Jude trembled, and it radiated from him through me. My hands traveled up and down his back under his open shirt. "Do you like it? You said you wanted my hands on you. Tell me what it feels like."

Jude didn't answer me. Instead, he crushed our lips together, sought entrance with his tongue, fast and furious and messy. Like he wanted to feel and not think, and I couldn't help but question how many times in his life Jude tried to turn off his brain.

I sucked his lip, and he rutted against me, buried his face in my throat as I shoved my hands down his pants to cup his ass. He jolted as if I'd electrocuted him, but then whimpered into the crook of my neck. Somehow I knew he needed a minute, that he was gathering his thoughts, trying to wrap his head around this. "You wanna stop, we stop. At any point."

"I know," he said, then gently rolled his groin against mine. "I…I don't wanna stop."

"You okay getting naked for me?"

"You're coddling again."

"Do you know me?" I teased, and something about that made Jude stiffen on top of me, and I didn't mean his dick either. That was already hard as a rock.

"I'm not your brother."

It was my turn to freeze then. "Um…no shit?" My erection began to deflate. Talking about Sawyer when I was with another guy was all sorts of wrong.

"No, I just mean…you wanted to make sure I'm not with you to try and make myself not want Rush, and I want to make sure you're not here out of some hero-complex thing you have where you feel like you have to take care of me. I know it's different for you…Sawyer having Carter now, but I don't want to take his place."

He was right in a way. I was used to Sawyer coming to me. I was used to putting him before everything else, and he didn't need me to do that anymore. But that had nothing to do with why I was with Jude. "Have you been here the whole time you've lived in Fever Falls? Yes, that was clunky, but I don't know how else to say it. Obviously, you've been here if you're here. I've wanted you from the start, and it has nothing to do with anything except you. And I sure as shit haven't spent so much time with you and become friends with you for any other reason than the fact that I like looking at you." It was a joke, and I hoped like hell he knew that.

Jude grinned, reassuring me that he did. "Just because you like looking at me?"

"I mean, your personality sucks, but the rest of you…"

"Fuck you," he replied and then—

"Ouch. You motherfucker. You pinched my nipple." I rubbed my abused chest.

"My personality is better than yours," he countered.

"I feel like we're having a playground fight right now, but instead of pulling my hair, you're pinching me. If you run away afterward, we're going to have words.

Do you want to name-call or have an orgasm?"

Again, I saw him swallow and then…then, fuck if Jude didn't slide down my body and kneel between my legs, one of his knees on the couch and the other foot on the floor. His fingers shook as he opened my slacks. A part of me wanted to jump in and take the lead, because I liked it but also to make it easier on him, but he was right. I did have a hero complex, and that was something I needed to work on.

He hooked his trembling fingers in my pants and trunks, and I said, "Not sure it's gonna work that way."

He nodded, then stood to pull my slacks and underwear down. My dick was already hard as a post again as it bounced against my stomach.

He dropped my clothes on the floor. I pulled my shirt up, spit in my hand, and slowly stroked myself. "Second thoughts?"

"No. Just taking in the view."

"You gonna give me one too, Boyfriend?"

"You gonna call me that now?"

"Eh, we'll see."

Jude rolled his eyes, but a small smile teased those plump lips of his. It was killing me not to jump up and strip him bare, but I wanted him to do it, wanted to give him this moment, because otherwise he would think I was going easy on him when really, I just wanted to rip his clothes off.

He dropped his shirt from his shoulders first, letting it fall to the floor. His fingers still visibly trembled as he worked open his slacks, removing them along with his briefs, and holy fuck, I wanted his dick in my mouth. Precome beaded at the tip. He was long and thick, with dark pubes, and I wanted to devour him.

"Fuck, I gotta taste you." My head was throbbing, and I could swear my damn vision blurred, I was so damn hungry for him.

I sat up on the couch and tugged him forward until he stood between my legs. With my forefinger, I wiped the precome from his tip and licked it.

"Jesus fuck," he gritted out as his cock twitched.

"Jesus fuck?"

"Shut up and suck me…please suck me, Cam."

He definitely didn't have to ask again. I leaned in, nuzzled his balls, and inhaled his musk, which made my dick even harder.

"Do you know how bad I've wanted this? How bad I've wanted you? Christ, it killed me not to get on my knees for you that night. I wanted to make you crazy. Wanted to make you come so hard, your brain turned to mush, and now I get to."

"Oh God, yes," Jude said breathlessly. His hand tangled in my hair, and I looked up at him, held his eyes with mine as my tongue started at the root of his cock and traveled to the tip. His whole body began to tremble then, but I kept going, licked the salt from his skin and swirled my tongue around his glans, and damned if I wasn't shaking too.

A wildfire ignited in his stare. "Suck me," he said again, his voice both pleading and commanding. He held the base of his cock with one hand, his other still in my hair as he angled his cock toward my mouth and nudged my lips.

"Hmm, Boyfriend is demanding, huh? I can work with that."

I opened my mouth and let him push inside, let Jude run the show. He didn't push all the way inside, only halfway, with slow, short, shallow thrusts, like he was testing the waters, testing me, which wouldn't do at all.

"Who's coddling who now? I can take you."

His reserve snapped, I saw it, a rubber band stretched to the limit before it broke. Jude pushed down my throat, and I swallowed around him, held his ass as he fucked into my mouth with tender yet urgent strokes.

"Oh fuck, you're good at this. You're gonna kill me."

He filled my mouth, stretched my lips, but I still

smiled around the cock in my mouth. My own was throbbing and aching, my balls tight and full.

"Camden…holy shit, Cam, Cam…Cam." He dropped his head back, looked up at the ceiling as he said my name over and over as though worshipping me. It made me feel like a god, like he needed to say it so he knew it was me, like maybe he'd wanted me as badly as I'd wanted him.

The fine hold I had broke open, like a dam had burst free. Then it was me leading and Jude following. I played with his heavy balls, stroked and sucked, then licked his balls and took his sac into my mouth. He tasted like salt and need, and it was every fucking thing I craved.

I blew him like my life depended on it, like this was the only time we'd have, because who knew, maybe it was. And when I took him deep and worked the head of his cock with my throat, he gasped out, "I'm gonna come… Oh God, I'm gonna come."

I didn't pull off, wanting to drink him down. His dick jerked in my mouth as he spurted his load down my throat. I pulled back slightly so I could get the rest of it on my tongue, needing his flavor there, and Jude shot again, giving me exactly what I wanted as I swallowed him down.

Before I knew what was happening, Jude pulled free,

dropped to his knees, and spit in his hand. He wrapped it around my aching rod, his spit and my precome lubing me enough so he could work my cock.

I'd already been on the edge, and seeing him there, determination and bliss on his face as he jacked my dick, made my body feel fuzzy and my balls unleash. My eyes rolled back as I thrust into his grip, and my orgasm ripped through me, my come landing on my shirt and running down his fingers.

Jude didn't say anything, just sat there and looked at me as my cock lay against my stomach. I wanted to ask him if he was okay, but I knew it wasn't what he wanted. So instead I cupped his face, leaned forward, and pressed a kiss to his lips. "You taste even better than I thought you would."

Damned if my beautiful fake boyfriend didn't look at me and blush.

CHAPTER NINE

Jude

Awkward Boy's suspicions are confirmed.
~ Theo's comic

I WAS FILLED with conflicting emotions. On the one hand, I'd just come harder than I had in a long time, maybe ever. I'd been coming to terms with my feelings for a while by then. I had been in love with Rush. I was attracted to Camden.

I was bisexual. Full stop.

Maybe a bisexual man who rarely felt that pull toward other men, but I did with Rush and Cam, so that had to mean something.

On the other hand, it was different knowing that, different getting used to it or planning to act on it, than it was actually having an orgasm in a dude's mouth and then jerking him off. I didn't regret it, not at all, but I was sorting through it all in my head.

Cam had blown me. I'd jacked his dick, watched him

come…wondered what he tasted like.

Was a little freaked out, but I didn't want him to go home. And yep, the more I thought about it, the more I wanted to know what he tasted like too. Definitely into men.

"Do you, um…wanna stay?" I asked, vulnerable in a way that made me shift uncomfortably.

"You sure you're okay with that? If you need space, I'd understand."

The second he finished speaking I knew I was, in fact, okay with it. I wanted him to stay. His response was the exact reason—his unwavering, quiet nobility that made him do the right thing, that made him care about others, that had shown me I could be vulnerable with him even when the thought made me want to run.

"There you go babying me again," I joked. I stood and held my hand out for him. Camden looked at me for a second, then another and another, until I began to fear he wouldn't stay, but then he reached for me too, and I pulled him to his feet.

He followed me into my bedroom.

"I can give you some clothes." I went to the dresser, opened a drawer, and got him a pair of basketball shorts.

"Thanks." Cam nodded, then disappeared into the en suite. I heard the sink run as I grabbed a pair of underwear for myself. It struck me then that I was standing there naked as I waited for my male lover, who was also my fake boyfriend, to clean up in the bathroom. A chuckle slipped past my lips just as Cam came out wearing nothing but the navy-blue shorts I'd given him.

"What's so funny?"

"Nothing." I shook my head.

I took my turn in the bathroom, cleaning up quickly, then pulled on my briefs and went back into the room again. Cam was lying in the middle of the bed, blanket pulled up to his waist and his arms bent with his hands behind his head.

Goose bumps pebbled along my skin. Jesus, he really was sexy.

"I didn't know which side of the bed was yours, and are we gonna have to go again? Not that it's a hardship. You're looking at me like it's killing you to keep your hands off me."

Which it likely was, but I also thought maybe it was a bad idea to do anything else that night. "So fucking cocky," I teased. "And I don't have a side of the bed."

"Are you crazy? Everyone has a side of the bed. I think something is wrong with you."

I climbed in beside him. "Something is obviously wrong with me since I like you."

"Aww, you like me?" he said playfully, and I rolled my eyes before reaching over and turning off the lamp.

"No."

"Liar."

"You'll never get me to admit it again."

"I don't need you to. I see it every time you look at me."

My pulse stumbled a bit at that. Damn Camden Burke and his bluntness. For a moment I just lay there, unsure what to do, but then he rolled over and wrapped an arm around me.

"Shh, don't tell anyone my secret, but I'm a snuggler. Is this okay?"

"Yeah. But I'm not sure I'm going to keep your secret. You might have to bribe me."

"Um…were you there for that blowjob I just gave you? It doesn't get any better than that. You owe a shit ton more secrets for that alone."

"And there's the fact that you're willing to be my pretend boyfriend I hook up with. I owe you for that too," I admitted.

"Nah. I get orgasms out of that. Those are thanks enough."

A chuckle stumbled out of my mouth, but then it got me thinking about sex—sex and Camden, and sex between two men… "You're usually a top, right?" I made myself ask. I'd become versed in the jargon since I moved to Fever Falls and started working at Fever.

Cam laughed against me. "Oh God. It's weird to hear you say that." He pushed up on his elbow, and even though it was dark, I could see the outline of him looking down at me. "I always top. I haven't bottomed since—"

"Henry?" I asked, unsure why I held my breath while waiting for his answer.

"No. I wasn't going to say him. It was when I lost my virginity to a guy. I was nineteen. It was a hookup with an older guy. I was scared out of my fucking mind, but I wanted to experience it, so I did it, and it wasn't great. I'm sure it was because I was so tense and he didn't take the time to make sure I relaxed like I should. I topped Henry, and every other guy I've been with, though I do enjoy a little ass play. There's nothing quite like a finger up your hole and hitting your prostate just right."

I rolled my eyes, but damned if my face didn't feel hot.

"I think you're blushing, Boyfriend. I don't have to see you to know that. And if we get to the point where fucking is on the table, if I top, then I promise you, I'll make it good for you. But if that's not what you want,

I'll bottom for you."

His answer was a shock to my system, a jolt through my chest. It meant a lot that he was willing to do that for me.

But…

A tendril of interest curled in my gut. I was curious what it was like to be on the receiving end, but I wasn't sure that was something I could say. It wasn't something I really had time to work through yet, so I said, "Henry…he's different from me. I'm different from every guy I've seen you interested in at Fever." It was something I'd thought many times in the past. I wasn't Camden's type. He went for smaller, twinkier guys.

"My physical tastes run toward a specific look, yeah. But on the other hand, I like beautiful things, and I'm not sure it gets much prettier than you."

My whole body overheated, and a tremble rocked through me. Fuck, did I like that, liked hearing that from Camden. In that moment, I wanted to give him something. I wasn't sure he realized how much he'd given me since we met—friendship, an ear, laughs, making me feel less alone, and he made me feel good, so fucking good.

"I usually hate that. My whole life I've heard how beautiful I am, and it's always made me uncomfortable."

"Shit. I'm sorry. I wouldn't have said it if I'd known. Why didn't you tell me?"

"Because…" Reaching up, I began to stroke his back. "Because I like it from you. I did from the start. Don't know why it was different, but it was. Is." My pulse thudded, and my chest felt tight. I didn't do well, admitting shit like that. Talking about my feelings. That was a Sandoval family trait. But damned if I didn't feel Cam smile in the dark, and that helped.

"Oh, you got it bad for me, don't you? Someone's got a crush."

"I don't know what you're talking about," I countered, needing the levity of the moment. "Most of the time, you make me crazy."

"Crazy horny? Crazy turned on? Crazy in crush with me?"

I laughed. "In crush with you?"

"Don't try and deny it."

"I don't know what you're talking about," I said again, but I was pretty sure we both knew I did. "Now be quiet and go to sleep. I'm trying to get some sleep here."

"Whatever you say, Boyfriend," Cam replied, that stupid, addicting smile still in his voice.

I WOKE UP with Cam's face stuffed in the crease of my neck, one of his arms and one leg slung over me, the weight of his firm muscles heavy on me. His dick was hard against my hip, which obviously was a new experience for me.

My fingers tingled with the urge to reach down and stroke him, to feel comfortable enough to pleasure him, but I was still settling into my bones and wasn't sure where we really stood as we teased the lines of friendship, fake boyfriends, and, well, fuck buddies. So instead I tried to gently ease out from under him, but Cam moaned and held my arm.

"Where are you going?"

"To take a leak," I replied, and he rolled over, watching me as I stood and walked to the bathroom. It was different in the light of day, recalling what we did the night before, the things we said, and having the lingering effects of his hands and mouth on me.

I pushed the door closed behind me and took a quick piss, then washed my hands. When I went back into the room, Cam was sitting on the edge of the bed. He stretched and smiled. "You want some space?"

"No," I answered honestly. "Though I might be a little testy until I have my coffee. I'm not a morning person."

"Okay. Coffee, then we'll cook breakfast. I'm fucking starving."

He was so easygoing. It was like nothing shook him, which was one of my favorite things about him.

I tugged on a pair of sweats, and we went to the kitchen. Cam made himself at home, looking through the fridge while I took my medication and started coffee.

"Bacon, eggs, and hash browns?" he asked.

"Sounds good to me." I grabbed skillets for the potatoes and the bacon, just as there was a knock at the door.

"Go ahead and grab it. I'll get started."

The condo was small, a one-bedroom with the kitchen not far from the door. When I opened it, Theo stood there with his sketchbook under his arm and his ever-present beanie tugged down low on his forehead. "Hey! Sorry to disturb you. If it's too early, I can come back. Or not come back at all if I'm bugging you. I was just hanging out, and I wondered if you were around, which is sort of dumb. Of course you're around. You live here. Do you want me to leave?"

Jesus, this kid. He spoke so fast, it took me a minute to comprehend everything he said, but when I did, it made me…sad. How lonely must he be to want to hang out with some random neighbor guy he didn't know? And he automatically assumed I wouldn't want him around. "No, I definitely don't want you to go. You're welcome here anytime if your mom doesn't mind."

"Are you sure?" Theo asked.

Cam called out, "Get your ass in here for breakfast. We're cooking." I knew it was to make Theo feel more comfortable, and I appreciated the hell out of it, but then it reminded me he was there. It would be obvious he'd spent the night, and we were both shirtless, making breakfast together.

"Oh my God, really? I'm starving!" Theo sneaked past me into the unit. "Hey, Construction Guy. That's fine if I call you that, right? You said I could call you that, but I don't know if you were joking or not."

"Hello, Art Boy," Cam countered, at ease as always. As I closed the door, I told myself it was fine and there was nothing to feel strange about. "And it's absolutely okay for you to call me that. I've definitely been called worse. You like bacon, eggs, and hash browns?"

"If it's food, I like it."

"Speaking like a man after my own heart," Cam replied as I watched them together. He was so damn good at making people feel at ease, at comforting people and making them feel like they had a friend. He'd spent his whole life doing it with Sawyer, and he did it with me, and now he was doing it with Theo too. "You gonna get in here and help me or what, Beautiful?"

Cam eyed me, and my skin suddenly felt a bit too tight. Theo's eyes darted from Cam to me to Cam and back to me again. There was no question there was something between us, which shouldn't matter. It didn't really. It was just…new. But then, I'd asked the guy to fuck around with me and be my fake boyfriend, so it wasn't like I could complain.

"Yeah." I cleared my throat. "Just let me go grab a shirt real quick."

"Can you get one for me too?" Cam asked. "Frying bacon and being shirtless don't go well together."

"I can help too!" Theo said. "Though I mostly just do microwave stuff, so you might have to teach me. I mean, if you don't mind, of course."

"Mind? We would have been disappointed if you didn't help," Cam told him, and damned if Theo didn't glow.

In that moment, none of the other shit mattered.

"I'll go grab shirts, and then we're on." And it was then I realized I was looking forward to it.

CHAPTER TEN

Camden

I needed the safety you provided. If it weren't for you, I never would have made it into the bar that night. I don't even know what I was thinking by going there. ~ Letter from Henry

IT HAD THROWN me a little when Jude was obviously uncomfortable with my attention. I'd been flirty without even thinking about it. After the night we'd shared, things felt different. I didn't know what exactly different meant or what I wanted, but then I'd called him beautiful, and he froze up. I didn't know if it was because of Theo or what he told me about being complimented.

But as the three of us cooked breakfast together, talking Theo through it when he got shells in the eggs and nearly burned the bacon, Jude relaxed. We had fun. Theo too, which was something the kid needed.

He rambled and laughed a lot, and his eyes were

constantly on me or Jude, or me and Jude together, even though I made sure not to touch Jude. The kid wasn't dumb. He knew something was going on between us, and damned if I didn't think he needed to see that it was okay for us, because maybe if it was okay for us, it was okay for him.

So we ate breakfast together, which we discovered was Theo's second one of the day. The first being cereal.

After breakfast we worked on Jude's puzzle for a bit, then went to watch Theo ride his skateboard at Willow Brook Park. From there, we decided on a movie—making sure Theo called his mom to ask permission, which she readily gave, without speaking to Jude or me. She didn't know us at all, but that didn't seem to matter. What did I know about raising teenagers, though? Maybe that was normal at his age.

When the movie ended, I took the two of them home, pulling up in front of the condos. I really wanted to kiss Jude goodbye, or at least make some kind of inappropriate joke about me wearing his clothes all day, but I didn't because of Theo and the fact that I was pretty sure Jude was still getting used to this whole screwing-around-with-a-dude-who-happens-to-be-my-fake-boyfriend thing.

"Thanks!" Theo said. "For today, I mean. It was

awesome, like really, really awesome."

"Well, you were with me, and I'm a really, really awesome guy, so of course it would be a great day. Jude's all right," I teased. Theo laughed, and Jude again gave me the finger.

Jude looked at me for a moment, and I cocked a brow at him. *Somethin' you want from me, Beautiful?*

"So I'll see you later," he said, getting out of the truck.

"Yep." Then Theo got out, and I pulled away.

Once I got back to my place, I took a shower, changed into my own clothes, and tossed Jude's into the washer.

There was still a buzz beneath my skin after the night we'd shared, which was new for me. I didn't typically think about my hookups much afterward, but then they weren't usually fake boyfriends who were basically my closest friend.

I ignored the missed calls from Sawyer, instead calling Trey's dad, Tyson.

"Hey, man. Everything good?" Tyson asked.

"Yep. Everything's fine with work." We chatted a bit about the week ahead before I said, "I have a sort of personal question to ask you."

"Go for it." Tyson was a good man. He'd recently

started dating a new woman, and from what both he and Linc said, Trey really liked her. I hoped for the best for them.

"There's this kid…he's like seventeen, I think? I'm pretty sure he's gay, or at least questioning. I don't know for sure, but I don't think he has anyone he can go to. If it comes down to it, I wanted to see if Trey might be willing to talk with him? Maybe I can introduce them or take them to do something. It might not happen, but I wanted to ask if it's okay, in case the situation arises. I think the kid feels alone, and I want to make sure he has someone his age to talk to." I figured it would be okay, which was why I'd already sort of mentioned it to Theo, but after today I wanted to make sure.

"Yeah," Tyson replied. "I understand that. Trey didn't have anyone until Lincoln, and even after that, no one his age." Now Trey had friends from the LGBTQ center, but it had taken a while. "I'm sure he'd be honored to do it, but I'll talk with him and let you know."

"Thanks, man. I appreciate it."

"No problem. What you guys all did for Trey and me? I'll never forget it. Pay it forward, right?"

"For sure," I replied, before we got off the phone.

Fever Pitch? I texted Sawyer, knowing we'd need to

talk.

Yeah, I can head there now, if you can.

I told him I'd see him soon, then grabbed my keys and made the drive to our favorite restaurant on Fever Street.

My brother was already there when I arrived, wearing his glasses, which he donned much more often now. Apparently, Carter liked him in them. "What's up, Baby Burke?" I slid into the booth, across the table from him.

"Nothing's up with me. I'm not the one with the new boyfriend."

"Carter's not that old. Unless you've been with him longer than I thought?" I teased, and Sawyer rolled his eyes. He had a habit of doing that with me, and I had a habit of enjoying it.

"You know what I meant."

The waiter came over and gave each of us a beer, which Sawyer must have ordered before I arrived.

"You hungry for dinner?" my brother asked.

"Sure. It's been a while since we hung out."

He cocked his head slightly, making me think there must have been something in my voice I hadn't planned. Either that or he just knew me. It was likely the second option.

"Bacon cheeseburger and fries," I said without looking at the menu. Sawyer got the same.

When the waiter left, Sawyer looked at me with a concerned-Sawyer frown I had seen a million times before. "Are we okay?"

"Of course. That's a stupid question. Why wouldn't we be?"

But then, things had been different with us, hadn't they? I figured that was just me being used to being the person Sawyer came to, and I wasn't anymore.

"Because normally I would know if you had a boyfriend."

And he would…except Henry. He hadn't known about him, but then Sawyer had been off at college and I'd been Henry's dirty little secret.

"Yeah, but normally it wouldn't have been this long since you and I had dinner together either." That time I tasted the bitterness on my tongue and felt guilty for it. "Shit. I'm sorry. I don't know why I said that. You know I'm happy for you." Yet strangely, I also felt left behind, which was probably weird, but I'd always put Sawyer first, and now he didn't need me to do that.

"You're right. I'll make more time."

"You shouldn't have to do that."

"I *want* to do that. I also know Jude isn't your boyfriend."

I scoffed, not at all surprised Sawyer didn't believe our little charade. He knew me too well. But I wasn't going to betray Jude's trust. "Did you not see me on my knees for him? I think that's self-explanatory. And you know I've wanted him from the second he showed up in Fever Falls. I just hadn't gotten around to telling you about us yet."

Sawyer shrugged. "You were going to blow him, yeah—and at Ash and Beau's wedding? Really? We'll get back to that in a minute. I do know you want him, but no, he isn't your boyfriend."

"And you know that how?"

"The way we've both always known everything about each other. That hasn't changed."

He was right about that. People often said twins had a special connection. Sawyer and I weren't twins, but we had it. Always had and always would. "I'm dating Jude in all the ways that matter." Which wasn't a lie. We were friends, and we were fucking around. We spent most of our free time together. Was there more to dating than that?

It took Sawyer a moment to reply. I could see the wheels turning in his brain, the way they so often did. Carter helped quiet it, helped Sawyer let loose, and I would forever be grateful for that, but in this moment, he was working through it all, trying to figure me out.

"You really like him, don't you? Obviously, I've known the two of you were close, and I knew you wanted to fuck him, but it's more than that. You care about him more than I realized."

He was right, but still, I rolled my eyes. "Aw, look at you, trying to pretend I'm in love just because the rest of you took the plunge. I'm happy with my life the way it is."

"Who said anything about love?" Sawyer countered.

"You know what I mean, BB."

"Why is it different for you to talk to me than it is for me to talk to you? I come to you. I've always come to you, even with Carter. You don't do the same with me." He took a drink of his beer, a melancholy look on his face. "I guess you were always different from me. You didn't need me the way I needed you."

He didn't say it to make me feel bad. Sawyer didn't work that way. He said it because he believed it was true. He'd always seen himself as weaker than I was, when he wasn't. "Come on, man. You know that's not how it is." I needed him. I missed him, even though he was right there. Hell, part of me was sad he didn't need me anymore, because I did need him. But then, I didn't think he'd ever believed I did.

He looked at me, waiting, like he knew there was more and was giving me the time I needed. I wasn't proud of my thoughts in that moment, but I knew I would share them with Sawyer. There was no biting them back down. "Yeah, I care about him. I'm not in love with him, but I care about him. And there's a part of me that feels a little left behind now…which is some weird-ass shit." I rubbed a hand over my face, hating the way I felt, because Sawyer was happy and that was all I'd ever wanted. "I like to be needed. I'm aware that makes me a bit of a self-important asshole." Because what the fuck? Did I want Sawyer to depend on me his whole life?

"You're looking at it from the wrong angle. It's not that you like to be needed; it's that when you care about someone, you want to be able to take care of them. That doesn't make you an asshole, Cam. It's what makes you the best brother in the world and the best man I've ever known too."

"Obviously. Was there any doubt about how incredible I am?" I thought about how Jude had been confused when Rush and Lincoln were getting together. That was when he'd truly come to terms with the fact that he had been in love with Rush. The situations were different, because yeah, Sawyer and the whole brother thing, but some of the feelings were the same. When you were used to being the most important person in someone's life, when you were used to being the one they came to, it made things different when those roles changed. Maybe I'd always understood that with Jude because I'd known I would experience it when Sawyer found someone.

In some ways, it didn't make sense, this connection we'd had from the start, even when he'd pretended I annoyed him, but maybe this was part of it. We felt the same about people we cared about. "He's special, ya know? I spend all my time with him. I'm not seeing anyone else. He's not seeing anyone else. He's the first person to make me want to date them in a long time."

Sawyer's mouth tugged into an ear-to-ear smile. "Holy shit. You know I recognize this road, right? I'm pretty sure I know where it's headed."

I looked around, wishing I had something to throw at him. "I've been good and made myself avoid drinking the water. I'm not sure what was put in it ever since Ash and Beau fell in love, but I'm not ready for that yet. I buy bottled."

Sawyer laughed.

"We're just having fun, BB." Because the truth was, even if I did fall for Jude, which I was determined not to, I couldn't be someone's second choice, and I wasn't sure he would ever love anyone the way he'd loved Rush Alexander.

CHAPTER ELEVEN

Jude

Sometimes Awkward Boy feels alone even when other people are there. But then, superheroes often carry their burdens alone. ~ Theo's comic

LINCOLN ALWAYS JOKED about "something in the water" in Fever Falls, and I was beginning to wonder if he was right. Maybe not magic gay dust, or whatever he thought it was, turning all the straight boys gay or bi. Regardless, it drove me crazy, because I thought about Camden all the time and I was fairly sure there was a good chance I'd lose my mind.

It had been a few days since he'd stayed the night and we'd hung out with Theo. I hadn't seen him since. We texted back and forth, and I knew he was busy at work, but he usually came to Fever to see me. Even if he wasn't drinking, he'd find a stool at the bar and we'd shoot the shit when I wasn't busy making drinks.

Only he hadn't come in.

And he hadn't been to my place.

All this after I'd had my dick in his mouth—and I knew from hearing him talk that he quite liked dick in his mouth—but maybe he'd realized he wasn't super fond of *my* dick in particular. I'd never had any complaints before. It was a nice cock, if I did say so myself. It had made many women scream in pleasure over the years, and they sure as shit had liked sucking me off. But since he was the first man to blow me, he had my head spinning with stupid-ass shit like, *What if he doesn't like sucking my dick? What if dudes look for something different and my junk doesn't do it for him?*

Then logic would take over, and I'd feel like an idiot for thinking that way, only to have those insecurities worm their way to the surface again later.

I'd miscalculated how weird it would be to screw around and be fake boyfriends with Camden. All I'd thought was: friend, hot, orgasms, experience what it's like to be with a guy, and I'd jumped in. There had never been a time in my life when I'd stressed about sex. I had it when I wanted. I was good at it. It was easy for me to say goodbye to the person afterward.

Camden Burke was fucking with me, and I didn't like it.

Maybe it was the fake-boyfriend thing. I mean, it

wasn't normal behavior, pretending to be someone's boyfriend. But this was Fever Falls, and from what I could see, that shit happened here fairly often.

Fuck. I was obsessing again, which wasn't like me.

It was Thursday night before I saw Cam again. Fever was busy for a Thursday night at eight, but I noticed him right away as he walked toward the bar. He had on a faded pair of jeans with holes in the knees and a black, long-sleeved tee that pulled tight across his chest. Even though he wasn't close enough, I knew it said *Burke Construction* in the upper left-hand corner.

I was making a Long Island as he eased onto a stool down the bar from me. I didn't make eye contact with him, but still felt his stare on me, felt him take me in, so I thought, *Hey, maybe he* had *liked my cock*, while also berating myself for the fucked-up train of thought.

After handing the drink over and being paid, I made my way down the bar. Charlie, one of the other bartenders, was leaning over the counter, talking to Cam. He was a cute, twinky little thing who'd told me more than once he wanted beneath Camden…or on his knees for him. Every time I laughed it off and ignored him, but suddenly I felt my gut twist as I watched Cam laugh at something he said.

"Hey, Beautiful," Cam greeted me as I stood beside

Charlie with my arms crossed.

"Well, that's not fair. You never call me beautiful," Charlie teased, winking at me. The tightness in my stomach increased, and I couldn't figure out why I'd liked Charlie before. It wasn't his fault. I'd told him a thousand times I wasn't with Cam, but dude, did he have to flirt so much?

"You want a beer?" I asked Cam, trying to get myself to chill the fuck out.

"Nah, just some ice water tonight. It's been a long-ass week, and we're topping out a big job tomorrow, so I need to head out early. Just thought I'd stop in and say hi."

There was confirmation as to why I hadn't seen him all week. Why did I still not feel better? This insecure shit was getting to me.

"I'll grab it," I told him just as Charlie said, "You're starting to hurt my feelings, Camden."

Cam laughed as I plopped the ice water in front of him.

"You know you're sexy," Cam said. "You don't need me to tell you."

"And he needs it? Everyone knows he's fucking gorgeous," Charlie replied, and my teeth ground together.

"Yeah, he is, but I'm special, so I'm the only one

who's allowed to call him that." Cam cocked a brow at Charlie before taking a drink of his water. I watched him swallow and I shivered, remembering what his mouth had felt like on me.

I also knew what he was doing, and damned if it didn't make my pulse speed up. Cam was easing Charlie away from giving me compliments because of what I'd told him.

"Oh…*oh*." Charlie clutched his chest. "Does that mean the two of you are finally fucking? I'm stuck between saying it's about time and having my heart broken because I didn't get to have you first."

"Aw, no broken hearts on my watch," Cam replied. "And we're not…" He let the words trail off, looking at me and waiting. He was going to say we weren't fucking, which typically I would have said myself, but the strange annoyance at Charlie wouldn't let me. I wanted Camden to admit it, which was something I had to unpack later.

"Not what?" Charlie asked, and that was like a light bulb going off in my head. Cam was waiting for me to answer because we were supposed to be fake boyfriends, and that wouldn't work if he went around telling people we weren't together, which technically we weren't, but I still didn't like that he was going to tell the truth to Charlie.

"Holy shit! You guys *are* fucking! I thought you didn't play for our team?" Charlie asked.

"He drank the water," Cam replied.

"Huh?" Charlie's forehead wrinkled.

And this was it. It was one thing for our friends to think we were dating, but now we were going to have to tell everyone. My hands trembled, and my throat closed up.

Cam cocked his head, looked at me, then turned to Charlie. "Nosy little thing, aren't you?" he said playfully, almost flirtingly.

"Excuse me, can I get a drink?" a guy asked, and I turned to go do my job. Charlie and Cam were still talking.

Things picked up even more, and I had customer after customer. The next time I looked down the bar, Camden was gone.

CHAPTER TWELVE

Camden

Somehow, you made it better. No matter how much I hate myself for these...desires. You helped me forget. ~ Letter from Henry

I WOKE UP early Saturday morning. Strangely, I'd always been a morning person. I knew Jude wasn't. We'd talked about it plenty, but that didn't stop me from rolling over and picking up my cell to call him.

I felt bad for walking out of Fever without saying goodbye, but things were...weird. I didn't want shit to be weird with Jude. I didn't do weird.

Still, things being off with Jude wasn't something I was willing to put up with, so I called him because it was harder to avoid than a text.

"It's early," was the first thing he said, his voice rough from sleep. My dick perked up a bit, so I reached down and stroked it lazily.

Fuck, I wanted to tell him how hard he got me,

wanted him to know I was touching myself and to ask him to touch himself too, but I wasn't sure where in the fuck we stood; if this was something he was going to be able to do. "Good observation. The early bird catches the worm."

"I don't want a worm," Jude replied, and it was on the tip of my tongue to say something like, *How about my snake?* But that was cheesy, and I was being respectful and all that.

"Get up before I come over there and drag you out of bed. We're going Christmas shopping."

"It's November."

"Again, good observation. I'm not sure if you've looked at a calendar, but this happens to be the month before December, which is when Christmas is."

"Someone is in a mood this morning," he said on a yawn before clearing his throat. "You're one of those people who get their shopping done early? I don't know why that surprises me."

I gasped. "I'm hurt. I can't believe you don't realize the magic that is me at Christmas. I'm the best at giving gifts and getting shit done early. It's weird, but it's my thing, so again, get up before I come and get you up."

Please say something sexy, please say something sexy—

"My door is locked."

That wasn't sexy. Fuck, he really didn't want me anymore. Not that Jude had ever been the biggest flirt with me. That was my job. "Yeah, well, I'm like Spiderman or something. I jump buildings in a single bound."

"That's not Spiderman. It's Superman. Who even are you?"

"The guy who is about to break into your condo?"

"Ugh, fine. I'm getting up."

"You don't sound very excited to see me. You're supposed to be much more enthusiastic about me. You've seen me, right?"

Jude chuckled, this rich, rough laugh that again, my dick liked. I ran my hand over my glans before stroking again. Oh, if he only knew. Would Jude be the type to get dirty with me? Would he let me talk him through an orgasm over the phone? Fucking someone with your words could be almost as fun as doing it literally.

Unfortunately, he didn't tell me he'd seen me and that he wanted me. "Stop talking so I can get up and get in the shower."

"Bossy motherfucker."

"Who called who and demanded they get out of bed?" Jude countered.

"Good point. Be there soon."

Before I did anything, I squirted some lube in my hand and rubbed one out because I was horny as fuck. From there I got out of bed, showered, and dressed in a hoodie and jeans. On the way to Jude's, I stopped by a coffeehouse and got him a large caramel latte because he liked that shit, and then headed over.

The first thing I thought as I walked up was how much this place didn't seem like him. It was Lincoln, that was for sure, but the expensive high-rise just wasn't Jude. He was simpler than that, which made me consider the fact that he hadn't gotten his own place because maybe he didn't plan to stay in Fever Falls. The thought sat heavy in my chest.

"Oh, hey," I heard as I was about to get into the elevator. "You're going to see Jude? Of course you're going to see Jude. What else would you be doing here? Sorry, dumb question."

"It's not a dumb question," I told Theo. "And yeah, I'm dragging him shopping with me, which he isn't excited about."

"Why wouldn't he be excited to hang out with you?"

"Right? That's exactly what I said. He gets a little grumpy in the mornings."

Theo blushed, making me realize how that sounded. It wasn't like I was waking up with Jude very often—

which was a damn shame if you asked me. "Where are you headed?"

"Oh, just this art thing."

"Do you need a ride?"

"Nah…thanks, though. That's really nice. You're always really nice. Jude too. You're both nice."

I couldn't help smiling at him. That was a lot of *nices*. "You're nice too." I paused for a moment, then decided to go for it. "Listen…I volunteer at the LGBTQ center sometimes, and we're always looking for extra help. If you wanted to go with me one day, that'd be really helpful."

Theo's blush burned brighter.

"No obligation, okay? I'm sure you're busy, but like I said, it would help me out a lot, and I know it would help them out too. We're always looking for volunteers."

"Does…does Jude ever go with you?"

Oh yeah. The poor kid had a crush on Jude. I could understand why. I'd had one on him for a long time now. "He hasn't, but I know he would. The three of us could all go."

Theo's eyes darted toward the ground. "I… I don't know. Maybe? I don't know if I can, but maybe. Thanks for asking. I gotta go. I'll talk to you soon. Well, I mean, if I ever see you around here, I'll talk to you, or if I'm able to go with you to the…the place." And just like that, Theo was out the door.

I silently cursed to myself, hoping I'd done the right thing by mentioning it. I wanted him to be around other LGBTQ+ people, though. Wanted him to feel comfortable.

I hit the button again for the elevator and then took it up. Jude answered a few seconds after I knocked, wearing a pair of blue jeans and a long-sleeved Henley.

"I brought you a caramel latte. It might need to be warmed up. I ran into Theo and talked to him for a minute."

"You brought me a coffee?" Jude's forehead wrinkled.

"Um…yes? It's nothing special or anything. Just a normal latte. Warm it up. Let's get going. We have shit to do." I made a point not to call him beautiful. I was caught between a rock and a hard place. He'd said it made him feel good when I said that to him, but he'd been uncomfortable in front of Theo and weird at Fever, so who the hell knew.

"It's fine. I don't need to warm it up. Thanks." He smiled almost bashfully, which was really fucking hot, especially with those damn lips of his. Fuck, I wanted to taste them, wanted to watch my cock slide between them as he sucked me.

When we got in my truck, I asked, "You work tonight?"

"Nah, got it off."

"Good. We're going to Atlanta."

"So if I were working tonight, we wouldn't have time to go? How the hell much shopping do you plan to do?"

"However much it takes," I replied.

"I had no idea you were such a shopper."

"I'm not. I hate that shit. Except this time of year."

I pulled on to the freeway.

"What did Theo have to say?" Jude asked. There was something slightly off in his voice, like he'd just realized he was with me and things were weird between us. We were gonna have to figure this shit out and do it soon.

"He was going to some art thing. I asked him if he needed a ride, but he didn't. I also asked him if he might want to help me at the LGBTQ center sometime. I think he wants you to be there, though."

"Yeah, sure, no worries. Is he…" Jude let his sentence trail off.

"I don't know. Maybe. Only he can figure that out, and it's his story to tell, but I put it out there. Thanks, by the way. For being willing to go if he wants."

"Of course. I don't know why I didn't think about that. That was cool of you—to offer to bring him."

I shrugged. "It's not a big deal."

"Yeah, it is."

I shifted uncomfortably, then started wondering what the fuck was wrong with me because I sure as shit never felt insecure about compliments. I ate that shit up. "What can I say? I'm an amazing guy. Sexy, sweet, a good friend, an incredible fuck…"

"Oh God." But Jude was grinning, and things were starting to feel more natural between us again.

We talked about random stuff as I drove to Atlanta. It took hours to get my shopping done. Jude was a trooper the whole time, except when he made fun of me, which I liked because it meant he wasn't being a weird-ass anymore—and it also meant I could tease him back. Which I did. A lot. It was kind of us. Or me, I guess.

Still, I made a point not to touch him all day. Not to call him beautiful or boyfriend and to let him lead the way, which wasn't in my nature. Damn, this beautiful boy did shit to me. Got me all wrapped up, and I wasn't sure I minded all that much.

We had lunch together while we were out. It was a good day. There was something about spending time with Jude that just made me feel good. And I liked to feel good. I did as much as I could to feel that way in my life.

"There's nothing you need to buy?"

"Nah, not really. I just have Rush and Mama K…probably your annoying ass."

His words made me sad but also caused a jolt of electricity to zip up my spine. Fuck if I didn't want to be special to Jude, if I didn't love being in that small group of people he let into his heart. But even beyond that, I wanted him to have more. "That's fine if those are the only people you exchange gifts with, but you know more people than that care about you, right?" Sometimes I wondered if Jude didn't feel quite part of our friends. Except when Elliott was around, he was the only one who identified as straight, until recently. He hadn't lived in Fever Falls as long as the rest of us, or maybe he felt he was just there because of Rush.

"Don't get all sappy on me, Cam."

I chuckled. "Okay, fine." I understood what he was saying. I didn't want it to feel like pity. "I'm just sayin', some of them might like you more than me."

"Everyone loves you. You're a good guy."

"Do you mind repeating that about eleven thousand more times?"

He rolled his eyes playfully, but I was still stuck on what he'd said. "Everyone loves you too. I mean, you're my bestie, and that gives you street cred right there."

"Street cred? Bestie?"

Okay, so not typical things I would say, but who gave a shit? I just wanted him to know he was as much a part of the Saturgays—and Saturbisexuals?—as everyone else. "I'm serious."

"I know. But I really don't wanna talk about it."

I nodded, but damned if another question didn't roll off my tongue. "You and your dad don't do shit like that?"

"No. It's not really our thing."

And the way he said it, I knew the conversation was over.

CHAPTER THIRTEEN

Jude

Awkward Boy wonders if his secret is out.
~ Theo's comic

I WAS GOING out of my damned mind.

I couldn't stop thinking about Cam and what we'd done together and how things were now. Fever had been frustrating enough, but today he'd been careful around me in a way he never was. It was as if everything was measured, thought out. It had gotten better as the day went on, but it just wasn't the same. I felt it in my bones.

Which yeah, I was aware sounded hokey when that wasn't my thing. And though it made me a bit of an ass, I sure as shit couldn't stop thinking about the fact that he hadn't called me beautiful all day. Or boyfriend. Or touched me. Weren't we supposed to be fake boyfriends who touched each other now? And even when we weren't, he'd always called me beautiful.

But I wanted Cam to touch me. It made me feel special, which was something I could never admit out loud, even if it was true.

I shifted, biting back a groan. This wasn't me…this needy guy I suddenly was for Cam.

It was evening by the time Cam pulled his truck up in front of the condo, and I looked at him and frowned. "Aren't you coming up?"

"Do you want me to come up?"

"Don't you usually come up?"

"Do you wanna have a contest to see how many times we can say *come up* in a row?" Cam asked, making me chuckle.

"Park your truck and let's go."

"Fine, I'll come up." He winked, then drove around to the side of the building where the parking lot was.

We were quiet as we got out and went into the building. Cam pushed the button for my floor, along with the code I had given him.

It was stupid, and I was getting annoyed at myself, but with each second that went by, my stomach felt tighter and my heart rate sped up. I didn't know if it was my depression or some weird insecurity shit that suddenly decided to hit me, but I was bursting at the seams with…fuck, with *everything*: want, fear, confusion...

The second we were in the condo and he closed the door behind us, I twisted around to face him. "You don't like my dick?"

"Huh?" Cam's face squished up, puzzled.

"Shit. That came out wrong. What the fuck is the matter with me?" I ran a hand through my hair. "If you don't want to screw around with me, that's okay. Just tell me. And if you don't want to do the fake-boyfriend thing, we don't have to do that either. I just..."

"You think I don't want you?" Cam pushed off the door and took a step toward me, then another. He reached out, fingered my hair, then rubbed my temple with his thumb. "Christ, you have it all twisted up. I don't know how you don't see yourself clearly, how it's all muddled up in that brain of yours."

"It's not usually like this for me," I admitted. "I don't get it. I've never been this guy, and then with..." I didn't want to mention Rush. Didn't want this to be about him, because it wasn't. I didn't want him anymore. I wanted Cam.

"You can say his name," Cam said, but his voice was tight.

"It really has nothing to do with him. I guess realizing something was missing in my life, realizing I wasn't happy, led me to acknowledging my feelings for him, but this want I feel for you is different. And more confusing, but Jesus, it's potent, and obviously it's making me lose my damn head."

Cam smiled. "We wouldn't want that."

"No, we really fucking wouldn't. Can you not let that make you even more conceited?"

"That's not happening. I want to shout it from the rooftops. Let's get back to what we were talking about, though. You think I don't want you?"

He dropped his hand, but then it was me who reached out, who held his hip. "It's been different since we fucked around, and I don't want that. I don't want to lose you. You haven't touched me or called me beautiful ever since." God, that made me sound like an egomaniac.

He cocked his head, like he was studying me, trying to figure me out. "You're such a contradiction. I can't get my head wrapped around you. Compliments make you uncomfortable, but not from me. You want them but don't believe they're true, and you really think that after craving you all this time, I'd suddenly just stop? You weren't comfortable the next day. I saw it when I touched you in front of Theo and called you beautiful. It makes me nervous to once again be with someone who isn't comfortable with their sexuality."

Because of Henry. Because that had been the only time Camden had been in love.

Jealousy burned through me. Maybe it wasn't something I had the right to feel, but I did all the same.

"There's a difference between adjusting to something and feeling ashamed. I'm not ashamed of being bisexual. I just don't know how to do this." I didn't know how to let myself truly care about someone.

"I think you're doin' just fine." Cam wrapped his arm around my waist and pulled me closer, until we were groin to groin. His erection rubbed against me, and I gasped, trembling at the sensation. Fuck yes, I was bi, and I really, really wanted him. "You feel that? I definitely still want you, Beautiful. Christ, I was stroking my cock just hearing your voice when we were on the phone this morning."

My dick throbbed behind my fly as my whole body flushed with heat. "Fuck, I wish I could have seen it."

"You can. I'll do it for you anytime. Right now, though, I want you to say it. Tell me you want me."

I grasped his hips with both hands, held on to him. Inhaled his scent, which was all masculine, fresh wood and cologne. "You're gonna make me say it?"

"Mmm, you better believe I am. I wanna hear it."

"I want you. Jesus, I want you so fucking much, I

ache with it." The second the words left my mouth, Cam's lips crushed mine. His tongue pushed right in, and I let him, wanted to taste him, and fuck, did I want to be devoured by him. I'd never wanted that from a lover before, but then, Cam was different in every way.

We kissed as we stumbled toward the bedroom. His hands slid under my shirt, rubbing my abs, chest, back, and then around to the front again.

"Goddamn, these lips," he pulled off to say, and then he was kissing me again. We fell onto the bed, Camden settling between my legs, rutting against me and owning my mouth.

And Jesus, did I want that, to be controlled and feel owned by him. It settled into my bones, into the marrow, before truly infiltrating my thoughts. Fuck yes, I wanted this. It was something I'd been missing in every other sexual encounter in my life.

Cam leaned away, and my hands automatically went for him, tried to pull him back to me. Everything felt new, all these sensations I didn't know were possible, and I was hungry for more.

"I'm not going anywhere, Beautiful. Just trying to get these clothes off you."

I hated that he could tell how needy I was for him, but this was Camden, and that somehow made it okay.

He tugged my shirt over my head, then went for my jeans.

He fumbled with the button, laughing. "I'm like a goddamned virgin here."

Without direction from me, my hips lifted, and he pulled my pants and underwear down. My dick sprang free, and for a moment I had a slight shock of *I'm naked in front of a dude again*, but then it simply fell away.

"Shit. Shoes," Cam said as he got to my feet. He pulled those off so he could get rid of my pants, and then he was looking down at me, heat blazing from his eyes and burning through me like wildfire.

Then…then I really did focus on the fact that I was naked in front of him and he was fully clothed.

"You gonna take off your clothes too?" I asked, trying to sound more confident than I felt.

"Only if you ask me real nice."

"You get off on this, don't you?" It was meant sarcastically, but the moment the words left my lips, I realized how serious I was…and that I liked it too.

"Yes. That okay? We don't have to play it that way."

"Will you take off your clothes?" I went to cover my face, surprised I'd asked him, but then I saw his jaw tighten, his control snap, and fuck if that didn't make me want to do it more, to do anything to have him look at me like that.

"I don't think you know what you do to me, Beautiful," Cam said, stepping out of his shoes and pulling his clothes off.

Then he was standing in front of me, naked and looking down at me on the bed. It wasn't the first time I'd seen him like this, but he still stole my breath. My reaction to him, the way my pulse pounded and my blood rushed through my ears, the throb in my cock, were all overwhelming.

"What do you want?" Cam asked, and I answered with naked honesty in my voice, not allowing myself to feel self-conscious, because this was him.

"I don't know."

"Okay." He nodded. "Just tell me if I do something you don't like."

Cam knelt, and I shivered. He hooked his arms around my waist and tugged me toward the edge of the bed so my ass hung slightly over the side.

"I…"

"I'm not gonna put anything in your hole," he answered my silent question. "I might touch it, though, but if you don't want me to, I won't."

"I trust you," I admitted, and I did. The only people in my life I'd ever truly trusted were Rush, his family, and Camden Burke.

He leaned in and rubbed his nose against my sac. I heard him inhale, breathe me in, and damned if my legs didn't start to shake.

"Fuck, you smell good." He ran his callused hands up my thighs, my stomach, before his tongue sneaked out and lapped at my balls. My eyes were riveted on him and his on me as he licked me, then sucked me and buried his face in my groin. It was like he was worshipping me, my taste and scent and masculinity, and damned if that didn't nearly shoot me to the damn stars.

Camden wrapped a hand around my cock, angled it toward his face, and swallowed me down. My hips thrust off the bed, and I almost apologized, before I remembered what he told me last time, and I let myself do it again. He smiled around my dick as I pumped into his mouth. He took it, seemed to want it as he sucked me and stroked me, then played with my balls. His mouth was so hot, so wet and smooth, my brain turned to mush.

When he lifted one of his hands to my mouth, I frowned at him, but then he pushed at my lips, and I understood what he wanted. He slipped two fingers between my lips, and I sucked them, sucked them like they were a cock, as I thrust slowly between his lips.

Then…then he pulled his fingers free, went behind my balls, and I tensed up.

"Just touch," Cam said before swirling his tongue around my glans. "Can I touch your hole, Beautiful?"

I was pretty sure my bones melted then. I didn't know what it was about him or how he spoke to me, but I was positive I would give him anything.

I nodded, and he sucked my cock again before rubbing my asshole with his wet fingers. It was…weird at first. He rubbed it, then tapped it, before massaging it again. And fuck…it felt good, like all these little nerve endings were pulsing and throbbing and needing more.

I moved against him, felt my vision blur. The sensation of his mouth on my dick and his fingers on my asshole had me bucking my hips, lost in this pleasure I'd never ventured into.

I cried out when Cam pulled away from me, off me, wanting him back, wanting to tumble into an orgasm with him.

"Do you have lube?" he asked.

"No. What are you gonna do?"

"You're going to jack us off together, and we're both going to come all over you. Lotion?"

My body jerked as though shocked. Fuck, I wanted that. It sounded hot as hell. "Nightstand drawer."

"Ooh, someone's a naughty boy. You rub one out and think of me?"

"Maybe."

"Tease."

Cam grabbed the lotion and squirted some in my hand. Then he pushed me up, so I rolled and lay in the center of the bed. He held himself over me, hands on the bed. "Lube us up. Wrap your hand around both our cocks together," he instructed, and I did so.

He was so hard, veinier than me, and damned if I didn't like the feel of his dick in my grasp. "Make us come," Cam said, thrusting into my hold, and *ooh fuck*, a tremble ran the length of my body.

"Oh God…fuck, that's good." Two dicks together was a-fucking-mazing.

Camden fucked my hands as I jerked us off, our cocks rubbing against each other. My balls were already full, so damn tight, I wasn't sure how I was holding back.

My eyes locked on him, and he bit his lip. His neck was corded and tight as he fucked me…no, he wasn't fucking me, but it was almost like he was. Did I want Cam to fuck me? It had been a fleeting thought before, but now it was there again, pushing at my consciousness.

"You're so goddamned sexy, and as fun as this is, I'm gonna need you to come before I blow my load ahead of you."

I didn't know why that made me chuckle, but then he leaned in, took my mouth, our bodies skin to skin, sweaty and needy, and my load shot from my balls up through my cock, come splattering on my chest. The second I did, I felt Cam tense. He groaned, and my eyes couldn't move away from his dick as I watched him unload, spilling all over me, his come mixing with mine, before he fell on top of me and kissed me sweetly.

"Tell me that was okay?"

It was such a Camden Burke thing to say—making sure the other person was okay. He was so quietly noble, I thought sometimes it went unnoticed.

I smiled into his neck. "That was everything."

CHAPTER FOURTEEN

Camden

But then...then when we were apart, when I wasn't with you, there was no forgetting.
~ Letter from Henry

"SHOULD WE GET cleaned up?" Jude asked after we'd been lying there for a few minutes.

"No, we absolutely should not get cleaned up. I'm offended you asked. I wanna smell me on you all night and wanna be sticky with your come and sweat. That too much for you?"

"You're not debauching me, Cam. I'm not a prudish virgin."

"You're a little prudish," I teased. "When I asked you to go home with me and Melinda, if you'd have been wearing pearls, you would have clutched them." I rolled off him and onto my back.

"Maybe I just didn't want to share you," he admitted, and well, yeah, I obviously liked that. A thrum of excitement flittered inside me.

"I like the sound of that, Fake Boyfriend."

Jude rolled over onto his side and looked down at me. He stole my damn breath with how beautiful he was. I truly never stood a chance against him. I made it out like it was a joke all this time, but there had always been something about him that got beneath my skin, like I felt him there, deep inside me, from the start.

"Were you scared? Your first time with a guy?" he asked.

"Scared? No. Nervous, of course. But I knew it was something I was curious about, and I also knew Sawyer was gay, and strangely, that helped."

"You're not afraid of anything, I don't think." Jude reached out, set his hand on my chest, and brushed his thumb over one of my nipples. Damn if the sweet contact didn't send a jolt through me.

"Nah, everyone is afraid of something. What are you afraid of, Beautiful?" I cupped his cheek, pulled him toward me, and rubbed my nose against his. Jude chuckled, his breath ghosting over me.

"You really are a cuddler, and you're more affectionate than I would have thought."

"Eh, probably just because I've wanted you for so damn long." Because yeah, I told him I liked to cuddle, and in some ways I did, but I wasn't as affectionate with other people as I was with Jude. I wanted to touch him all the time. Maybe part of me couldn't believe he was really there with me, which was another first.

"I'm sorry."

"What the hell do you have to be sorry for? Not wanting me at first? I mean, obviously, most people do want me because *me*, but there's a first for everything. And you had a lot of shit on your mind. You were in love with your best friend and had never been with a guy before."

"I'm still sorry it took so long. Being with you feels too good not to wish I'd done it sooner."

Well, shit. Hearing that made my chest pump up a bit. "We're gonna be in trouble, you and me."

"I know," he replied, a sort of sadness in those crystal blue eyes of his.

"Are you happy?" I found myself asking.

"Yeah, most of the time. No one is happy all the time, but I feel better than I have in a long time."

All sorts of thoughts muddled around in my brain, little feelings I had about him and his life. "You know…it probably sounds silly to some people, but I always wanted to work in construction. There was never a time it wasn't my dream. It didn't matter that it wasn't something most people wanted or dreamed about. I did." I thought it was probably a career most people just fell into, but not me. It was who I was, what I wanted. To build things. To make something out of nothing.

"I don't think that's a silly dream. I think it's incredible, actually. You've always known who you are and what you want. You don't think you have to be like everyone else. I went into business like my dad and then realized I hated it. I'm bartending because it's what I did in college, and yeah, it's fun and I enjoy it, but it's not my dream."

"What is?"

"I don't know," he answered softly, and my damn heart broke for him. Jude did something to me, had me all wrapped up, and I wasn't sure how to untangle myself—or if I wanted to. But falling for another guy who wasn't settled in his sexuality was a dumb thing for me to do.

"Then I guess we have to work on figuring that out."

He smiled, then leaned down and kissed me. I opened my mouth, and he swiped at my tongue with his. Jude groaned into the kiss, and I swallowed it down…and then, then he was pulling back. "You want dinner?" he asked. We hadn't eaten dinner, just ended up in bed.

I knew the serious conversation was over, and maybe that was best for now. Hell, I wasn't sure why I even went there, made shit all heavy, but again, there was something about him. "Yeah, I could eat."

Unfortunately, we did end up having to clean up. We pulled on pants and ordered Chinese, then ate and watched a movie. We were naked in bed again, with the lights off and the blankets over us, when he said, "Letting people in."

"What?" I asked, stroking his back.

"Earlier you asked what I'm afraid of, and I didn't answer. My dad, he folded in on himself when my mom died. He never recovered from losing her. He spent his whole damn life lost after that, still is, and he's never tried to change it. Never sought therapy or anything like that. I lost him when I lost her. I had no family except Rush's. If it wasn't for them, I would have been alone. I'm scared of being like him. Of letting people in and losing them, and then myself."

Christ, he was truly going to wreck me. My heart thudded against my chest, this chaos of feeling, of want, surging through me. We had that in common, Jude and I, but in different ways. It wasn't tough for me to let people in the way it was for him, at least not as obviously, but I was afraid of losing people I cared about. I'd loved and lost Henry. And I was scared of losing my brother, even though I knew it was a ridiculous fear.

Clearing my throat, I finally managed to say, "You let me in."

At least a full minute went by before he answered, "I know."

Damn, I was honored he'd chosen me. That he'd opened himself up to my friendship, and now... Well, the boyfriend thing was fake, but he was still giving me something he'd never given anyone else. "I won't hurt you, Beautiful. I promise. And you won't lose my friendship. Ever."

"Okay," he replied huskily.

I pulled him close to me, held him tight, and we went to sleep.

I NUZZLED INTO Jude's neck and kissed him. He groaned in response, and not the sexy let's-have-morning-sex way, but in the I'm-tired-leave-me-alone way.

"Wake up, sleepy face."

"No."

"Please?" I kissed him again, but he ignored me, and

I figured he was already out of it. Chuckling quietly, I got out of bed, took a piss, washed my hands, and started coffee.

While I waited for him to wake up, I played some *Call of Duty* in my underwear because it was still my favorite game and being in my underwear was the next best thing to being naked.

A good hour and a half later, there was a noise behind me. I looked over my shoulder to see a sluggish Jude rubbing his face as he walked out of the bedroom, wearing only his underwear too. "Coffee," he grunted.

I couldn't help but take in the view. A half-nude Jude was a beautiful thing. "It's in the kitchen waiting for you—*Motherfucker*," I growled when I realized I died. Tossing the controller on the coffee table, I leaned back and waited for Jude.

He doctored his coffee, then sat on the couch beside me. "Why are you such an early bird?"

"Why are you such a sleepy face?" I countered.

He took a drink of his coffee and moaned, which went straight to my dick, making it plump up. Jude noticed and cocked a brow at me.

"I can't help it. You're fucking sexy. Set the coffee down. I know a better way to wake you up."

He did so without argument, and I got us both naked, then got on my knees, jerked off and blew him. I shot when he did, swallowed his load, and waggled my brows at him. "Told you I was good at that."

"I'm seeing that. I'm pretty sure you sucked my brains through my cock. I, um…wanna try that with you, sometime soon."

"Sucking my brains through my cock?"

He rolled his eyes. "You know what I mean."

"Whenever you're ready."

"Do you wanna go out to breakfast or something?" Jude asked. "My treat."

"Are you asking me on a date, Boyfriend?"

He shrugged, smiled, then said, "Yes."

"Then yep, I'd love to go to breakfast with you."

"Would you have said no if it wasn't a date?" he countered.

"No, but I like it better that it is."

His golden skin was tinged with pink. "I do too." He shook his head. "I don't know what you're doing to me."

"I don't know either, but you're doing the same to me." I pushed to my feet, and his eyes snagged on my cock. "Remember all those times you insisted you were straight? One taste of this was all you needed." Wrapping a hand around myself, I stroked my shaft.

"Oh, fuck you. I haven't tasted it yet, and now I'm

not going to." He stood too.

"Don't be embarrassed. There's just something about me. A sort of magnetism that makes it impossible not to want me."

"Want to hate you? Because I want that real bad right now."

"No you don't. You wanna take me on a date, Fake Boyfriend, so get your ass in the bedroom and get dressed so we can go."

Jude flicked me off, but he did just what I said.

CHAPTER FIFTEEN

Jude

Awkward Boy really thinks he might be gay but is scared to tell anyone. ~ Theo's comic

YESTERDAY HAD BEEN a good day with Camden. We had breakfast, then went back to the condo because I had to work later that night. He stayed with me until I went in, and then I thought about him while I was on my shift…basically the whole damn time, the fucker.

At some point Charlie mentioned him, which ruffled my feathers more than it should, so I continued to spread the lie about him being my boyfriend by confirming we were together…only we weren't really, I didn't think. We'd talked about being fake boyfriends and fucking around, but that was it.

Did I want to be real boyfriends with him? Were we basically already? I wasn't sure.

Jesus, maybe Lincoln was right and Fever Falls really had some kind of magic…something or the other in the water, because I was now thinking about being fucked, giving head, and wondering if I wanted my friend to be my real boyfriend rather than my fake one.

Life was so damn weird sometimes.

My gaze darted to the scenery as I continued my drive to Rush's. We hadn't hung out together in a while, so when he'd texted me last night about going over to ride on his track today, I'd been all for it.

I pulled into his driveway and jumped out. As soon as my arm lifted to knock, the door pulled open and Rush's mom was there.

"There's my sweet boy." She pulled me into a hug, and I closed my eyes, savoring it. She was the only reason I knew what it was like to have a mom.

"Hey, Mama K. How are you?"

"I'm good. Keeping busy with school. How are you?"

Lincoln had talked her into going back to school to become a nurse. She was loving it, and I was so damn happy for her.

"Good," I replied as we headed for the kitchen. "Keeping busy myself."

"Yes, I've heard that. What's this about you having a boyfriend? I always thought you and Rush would be together one day, but he always said you were straight. A mom knows these things."

Ugh. This was awkward. Guilt churned through me, hating that I was lying to the people who were most important in the world to me, but then, was I lying? Camden and I were *something*. "It, um, wasn't something I tried to keep a secret. I just didn't really know, I guess? Until I did."

We were in the kitchen by then, and she reached over and patted my hand. "Things work out the way they're supposed to. You and Rush are the best of friends. More like brothers. I see that now. That boy is so head over heels in love with Lincoln, it's a joy to see. They're perfect for each other, and now you have Camden."

There was a time when those words would have hurt, when I would have wished Rush was with me. But I didn't any longer. Still, Cam and I weren't the same as Lincoln and Rush. "We're not serious, Mama K."

"Hmm…" She smiled. "I seem to remember Rush saying the same thing about him and Lincoln."

I chuckled uncomfortably. "This is different."

"We'll see. Does your dad know?" Her voice was soft, caring.

"No." He wouldn't care if I was gay, bi, or fucking everyone in the world, not just because he'd never been homophobic, but because he didn't care about anything.

It was tough sometimes, thinking about that, because I knew my dad loved me. He had never hurt me. He'd always been there for me and tried to give me what he could. I never wanted for anything other than affection. He loved me, he just didn't *actively* love me because he couldn't actively care about anything.

"Your turn to get Boyfriend Questions 101. I kind of like this." Rush grinned, walking into the kitchen.

"Hey, man. What's up?"

He was already wearing his moto pants and jersey. I'd come over in my jersey but not bottoms because they weren't the most comfortable things in the world.

"Not much. Ready to get out there and ride."

"Yeah, me too." I missed it. We hadn't ridden together in a long time.

"I'll let you boys go. I need to head back out to my house anyway." She was living in the guesthouse on Rush's property.

The three of us walked out together, Mama K to her place and Rush and I toward my car, where I grabbed the rest of my shit. Then we went for the garage. "Have you talked to him lately? Your dad?" he asked.

"Yeah, I call about once a month, same as always. He's still working like crazy, surviving on frozen dinners and his sorrow."

"I'm sorry." Rush squeezed my shoulder.

"Yeah, me too."

"How are you and Cam doing? Christ, that's so weird to say. I can't believe you're seeing Camden fucking Burke."

Him and me both. I shifted, scuffed the dirt with the toe of my shoe. "We're good." Which we were. Not a lie. "I like spending time with him. He makes me feel good." Not a lie again. See? We weren't being dishonest to everyone we knew.

"I'm glad. I feel like things have been a little different with us for a long time now. We pretended it wasn't—or hell, maybe that was me, and I'm sorry about that. You're my best friend. You're like a brother to me. I'm so fucking glad you're in Fever Falls, and I just want you to be happy."

"I know." And I did. There wasn't a doubt in my mind that Rush loved me and wanted my happiness. He just didn't love me the way I used to think I wanted. "I'm figuring shit out. Took care of my depression and enjoying my work." Even if it wasn't what I wanted to do forever. I felt too old not to know what I did want, but there wasn't much I could do about that. "I've got more friends here than I ever let myself have, and I have Cam." I did have him. Even if we were only fake boyfriends, I had his friendship, and that was important to me.

"God, this is weirding me out. Camden Burke and my best friend."

A laugh fell from my lips. "Yeah, took me some getting used to as well. There's something about him. He just got under my skin." I didn't know how, and I sure hadn't expected it, but that was exactly what happened.

"You did the same to him. He was different with you from the start. None of us really understood it. You're not his usual type. I was worried it was a game at first, but yeah, obviously it's not."

And there was that guilt, making me nauseous again. Whether I was lying or not, we were still being misleading, and that didn't sit right with me. "It's not serious, though. I don't want you to get the wrong idea." But saying that, saying we weren't serious, tasted bitter on my tongue. Because Cam truly was important to me. This was such a clusterfuck. Even I didn't understand it. "Anyway, are we gonna ride or what?"

"Fuck yes," Rush replied.

I pulled off my jeans, got my knee braces on and then my moto pants. Neck brace, boots, gloves, helmet. We got on the bikes, that loud *braaap* sound we both loved filling our senses as we did, then headed for the track and rode.

I wasn't as fast as Rush. I didn't jump as high either, and he didn't try to slow down to my pace for me, which I loved. It would piss me off if he did, and Rush knew that.

There was something about riding that made it easy to let go, to forget everything else, which I did, but every time we took a break, I found myself thinking about Cam and what was going on with us. Him asking me if I was happy and me not knowing what I wanted to do. But then we'd ride again, and all that was gone with the scent of gas burning and that sound in my ears.

"I missed this—riding with you," Rush said hours later when we were done. "We need to do this more often."

"Yeah. We do."

He was quiet, looking around before admitting, "I'm thinking about retiring after the upcoming season."

My eyes snapped to his. "No shit?" That…surprised me.

"I'm not sure. I haven't told Red yet, so don't say anything. It's just… I won the championship last year. I've not ridden the outdoors the past two years. Before him, riding was my life, and while I love it, I don't need it the same way. I did everything I set out to do, and I can still ride or be a part of the sport. I just don't know if I wanna keep up with the training and the traveling and all that. Does that sound fucking crazy?"

Before, it would have, but as I looked at him, I realized it didn't. "No, it doesn't. You've never been the type who's scared to go for what you want, and you've also never been the type not to get it. You have your championship. You've had your career, a better one than most riders. Maybe now it's time to do something else."

"Exactly. I knew you'd get it."

I did, and I wanted that for myself as well. To find my thing.

"You should come spend Thanksgiving with us," Rush said, changing the subject. My first thought was Camden. I wondered what he was doing. He'd be with Sawyer, of course, but then, what if he wanted to be with me too? Or hell, maybe I was way off, and they'd go to Florida to see their parents or something.

"Cam is welcome too, of course. Hell, the more the merrier. Ash and Beau will be home. Maybe we should make a big thing of it—*The Saturgays Do the Holiday*."

I laughed. "You sound like Linc." I never had big holidays like that. I'd spent my childhood with his family, but nothing like this large group of friends. "I'm gonna talk to Cam and let you know." Because the truth was, if Cam wanted me to spend it with him, that was where I wanted to be. It was another thing I wasn't ready to unpack the reason of yet.

"Yeah, man. That's good." For the second time that day, Rush squeezed my shoulder, but this time, he smiled.

CHAPTER SIXTEEN

Camden

When I'm with you, I feel like I can fly…but when we're apart, I'm drowning. - Letter from Henry

I GOT RAINED out of work. Sometimes I toughed it out. I wasn't afraid of a little water, but if there was a safety issue, I wasn't putting my employees at risk. We'd made it a couple of hours before a drizzle turned into a downpour, and that was that for the day.

After going home to get changed, I headed to Fearless to see Sawyer. The bookstore was fairly packed, the weather likely having something to do with it, people reading, sitting on their laptops, and drinking coffee.

"Hi!" Lizzy, one of his employees, who was currently making some kind of drink for a customer, smiled at me.

"How's it going?"

"Good. Busy, as you can see. Casey's working the floor. Sawyer is taking care of paperwork in his office."

"Nope. I'm taking a break." My brother came over.

"Do you want anything to drink?" Lizzy asked.

"I'll make them," Sawyer replied, going behind the counter. "What do you want?"

"Surprise me," I replied, and he chuckled.

One of the tables emptied, and I sat down. A couple of minutes later Sawyer brought over two drinks and cinnamon coffee cake.

"I made us both this new recipe we have for caramel apple cider."

That sounded awesome.

"Get rained out?" he asked.

"Yeah, so I thought I'd come say hi. You talk to Mom?"

"Yeah. I can't believe she and Dad are going on a last-minute vacation for Thanksgiving. They're enjoying their retirement entirely too much," Sawyer said playfully, and I laughed. He was right. They were having a blast in Florida, and we were both happy for them. They were great parents and deserved it. "I'm taking Carter there for Christmas. Are you taking Jude?"

Well, shit. I hadn't even thought of that. Obviously, my situation with Jude was different from Sawyer and Carter's. Hell, this whole thing was only happening because he wanted to experiment with me and because he wanted Rush to think he had a boyfriend, which still made me uncomfortable at times. There were moments I thought I got it, but then others, I wondered why in the fuck it mattered what Rush thought. The only thing I could think of was Jude still had feelings for him, and I cared much more about that than I liked to admit.

"Not sure." I shrugged. "We'll see what happens. That's kind of a big step." There was a sort of twisting in my chest, like the words had been wrong. I was pretty sure I wanted Jude to go home with me for the holidays, that I wanted him to meet my parents, which was a shock to my system. I'd never taken a lover home for a holiday before, but I'd never dated or fake-dated someone I considered my best friend either. "Maybe," I tacked on at the end, and Sawyer grinned.

"Oh, wow. Cam has it bad. Camden and Jude sitting in a tree," my brother sang, and I rolled my eyes.

"Fuck you very much, Baby Burke. Are we really going to start teasing each other? Because I'll win."

"Only because you don't play fair."

"I play to win," I countered before taking a drink of the cider. "Holy fuck, that's good."

"That's what Carter says to me every night."

A laugh jumped out of my mouth. The changes in Sawyer were incredible. Carter had helped him find the confidence I'd always known was there. "Eh, must be in the Burke genes. Though I'm sure I'm better at that too."

"Okay, this is getting weird."

"You started it."

We finished the coffee cake and cider, chatting for a while before Sawyer needed to go back to work.

The rain was still coming down, so I jogged to my truck, my pants and hoodie wet when I jumped inside. My cell beeped, and I pulled it out to see a text from Jude.

Lunch?

Now, obviously, I'd just eaten coffee cake, but I also didn't plan on passing up a chance to hang out with Jude.

You really like going on dates with me, don't you, Beautiful?

Oops, sorry. I texted the wrong person!

I frowned just as another text came through.

That was a joke.

I know, I replied, even though I hadn't fucking known…and probably shouldn't care. Jude could go to lunch with whomever the fuck he wanted, but it was better when he chose me.

I can be there in about half an hour, Jude added, and he didn't even have to say where. We were always at Fever Pitch.

See you then. I tossed my cell to the seat beside me and made the quick drive to the restaurant. I would be there early, but what the fuck else did I have to do?

A few minutes later, I was sitting in a booth at the bar and grill.

Should I invite Jude home with me for Christmas? Fuck, I really wanted him there, wanted my parents to meet him and for him to feel part of a family. *He has that with Rush...* Which he did, and that was fine and all, but he could have it with me too.

But then that made me consider that he would be with Rush, Lincoln, and Rush's mom for Christmas. Or hell, maybe he would go home to Virginia to see his dad, though I didn't think so, which was sad. But inviting someone home was a big step, as I'd told Sawyer, especially when the guy in question was your pretend boyfriend.

And yeah, I needed to stop obsessing about this. Jude was making me lose my damn mind.

"Where's your other half?"

My eyes snapped up at the sound of Linc's voice. "Hey, Short Stuff." Rush stood beside him and smiled at me. "Jude's meeting me here in a bit."

"I was talking about Sawyer because you guys are usually here together, but I guess Jude makes more sense.

It's so weird. I can't believe you're going to fall in love with Rush's best friend."

"Who said anything about falling in love with him?" I asked.

"Don't hurt him," Rush said, which rubbed me raw like sandpaper.

"Jude is a big boy. He can handle himself. And I'm wounded. Here I thought we were friends, and now you're accusing me of…what exactly?"

"Shit. I'm sorry. I didn't mean that. I just worry about him."

I nodded, knowing that was the case, but I was still a little pissed off about it. "Jude and I know what we're doing."

"I didn't mean that the way it sounded. I think of him like a brother, and I want to protect him the same way you would Sawyer, but I shouldn't have said that to you. I know the kind of man you are."

"We're cool," I told Rush, because I got it. I would protect Sawyer the same way. And the truth was, I did normally sleep around, and I wasn't usually the guy who was in relationships.

"I don't know why any of us are pretending we're surprised this happened," Linc added.

"Because Jude always said he was straight?" I replied.

"Are you aware what town he lives in?" Linc teased, and the three of us laughed. He was good at breaking tension that way.

"Anyway," Rush said, "I'm sure Jude told you we invited you both over for Thanksgiving. I'd love it if you could come."

No…no, Jude hadn't told me. And he didn't have to, but it still stung. Maybe Jude didn't want me there.

"I'm not sure. I might be heading to Florida," I lied and then reminded myself that I could get caught in that lie very easily since our parents would be traveling and Rush or Linc could easily speak to Sawyer. But I sure as shit wasn't going to be there if Jude felt weird about it, which obviously meant Christmas was out of the question too. "I'll let you guys know soon."

"Okay," Rush said. "But if you don't go visit your parents, you should get your ass to our house."

Then they said their goodbyes, already having eaten.

A few minutes later my pretty fake boyfriend slid into the booth across from me. "Hey. Sorry you had to wait."

"No worries." *Is shit going to be weird with us? Do you not want me at Rush's?* "So, to what do I owe the pleasure of this lunch? Miss me?"

"You wish," Jude countered with a playful grin.

"Aw, it's okay. You can admit it."

The smile slid off his face, replaced by that cute-as-hell bashfulness. "Maybe I did."

"Well, maybe I missed you too." I mean, look at him. Obviously, I had. I also liked the fact that he was admitting he missed me as well.

"Good."

"Fine," I replied.

"What are we doing?" Jude asked, and I laughed.

"I have no idea."

The waiter came then. I'd asked him to wait for Jude when I first arrived. I got water and Jude got sweet tea, and we decided to share a large plate of nachos. When the waiter left, I teased, "Looks like neither of us is bottoming today."

His eyes went wide, and he choked like he had something in his mouth other than his tongue, but I was fairly sure that's not what he was currently suffocating on. Well, that and my words.

"Not something you had to think about before, huh?" I asked.

"No…" He chuckled. "Linc talks about his bottoming diet, and it sounds like a full-time job."

"It'll be fine. It was as a joke. If we get there, it's not something you need to stress about that much. I can do the planning." Which again was me offering to take his cock—and I would. It was him, so I knew I'd like it.

"I think... Never mind, we'll talk about it later. I have something to ask you, but it's cool if you aren't into it."

"Sounds kinky," I replied, and when he rolled his eyes, I added, "Shoot."

"I know we're just screwing around...that this isn't a real relationship, but... Fuck." He rubbed a hand over his face. "And it's last minute, but Rush invited me over for Thanksgiving. I wanted to see what you were doing first. I'm sure you'll be with Sawyer, or maybe you're going to Florida, but I thought—"

Well, shit. Maybe Jude did want to spend it with me. Or it could be something else. "You want me with you and I'm there, Beautiful. I just gotta know first: is it for show, or because it's what you want?" I would accept either answer. It's what I had agreed to, but I needed to be prepared.

Jude watched me, those blue eyes of his holding on to me, until I was pretty sure it turned tangible and I could feel it. "Because it's what I want. I don't ever spend time with you for show."

Damned if my cheeks didn't hurt from smiling.

"You like that answer?" he asked.

"Yeah...yeah, I do."

CHAPTER SEVENTEEN

Jude

Awkward Boy likes boys! He likes boys and that's okay...isn't it? - Theo's comic

TWO DAYS BEFORE Thanksgiving, I came home from an errand to see Theo hanging around my unit. His eyes snapped to me the second I approached. The kid was pacing the hallway, almost like he was jumping out of his skin. He was always nervous, his brain always at a higher speed than other people's, but he seemed extra jumpy then.

My stomach twisted up. "Is everything okay?"

"Yeah, of course. I'm fine. Absolutely fine. Why wouldn't I be okay?"

I couldn't help but smile. There was something about this kid that I just liked. I wanted him to be happy. "No reason. Just making sure."

"Oh...okay. I was just... I mean, I wasn't creeping around or anything, but I was bored and I thought maybe—but then, I'm sure you're busy and all, so I—"

"I'm not busy. I'd love to hang out with you."

His eyes practically glowed. "Really?"

"Yes, really." I unlocked the door and let us inside. Theo swapped his sketchbook from his left hand to his right. I was curious about it but never sure if I should ask to see it. I didn't know how personal it was. When I used to draw, I'd been a little protective of it.

The thought sort of hit me from nowhere. I used to draw and I'd loved it. I couldn't remember the last time I'd done it. Not since college, likely.

"Hungry? Thirsty?" I asked, pushing the other thoughts from my head.

"I'm always hungry, but I don't have to eat if you're not."

I chuckled. "Nah, it's cool. I could eat too."

I began making grilled ham-and-cheese sandwiches for us. Theo sat at the table, watching me. Even when I wasn't looking, I could feel his eyes on me.

"Where's Construction Guy?"

I smiled. "I like that the name stuck. He's at work."

"Is he coming over later?"

"I'm not sure. We haven't discussed it." Putting my back to him, I grabbed some juice from the fridge. I figured sometimes it was easier to admit things when people weren't looking at you. "Did you want him to come over for anything?" If Theo needed someone to talk to, I would make sure he had that.

"No. I mean, it's cool if he does. I like him. He's funny. I was just curious. I like talking to you too, so it's like totally cool, or whatever."

Looking at him, I winked. "Well, I *am* much cooler than Cam."

Theo grinned, then glanced down, picking at the edges of his book.

I finished the food, set our plates and cups at the table, and sat across from him. We were almost finished eating before Theo broke the silence.

"So…is, um…is he your boyfriend or whatever?"

The twisting in my stomach increased, but not for the reason I would have thought. Not because I didn't want to admit I was dating Camden, but because it wasn't supposed to be real. I didn't want to lie to Theo in a situation like this. It seemed…dirty. But then, what Cam and I were doing felt pretty damn real to me. There was a part of me that wanted it to be. How much more real could it get? "Yeah…he is. Are you comfortable with that?"

Theo's big green eyes stretched wide, a deer-in-the-headlights look. "Oh God. Yes. Like super okay with it!"

Then...then he blushed.

"Hey, there's no reason to be embarrassed. I'm still getting used to it myself. He's, um...the first guy I've ever dated." I hoped like hell I was doing the right thing by talking with him about this stuff. I had no experience, and that made me wonder if Cam would be the better man to talk to, but then, if Theo was questioning, I definitely understood that piece of it.

"He is?"

"Yep."

"How come? Were you, um...in the closet?"

I took a drink of my juice and tried to sort through my thoughts. None of it was easy to explain. There was no manual, no step-by-step guide. Everyone was different, which meant experiences were different too. "I wouldn't say in the closet, really. Sexuality is complex, I'm learning. I considered myself straight most of my life. I only dated women and felt attracted to women."

"Oh," Theo said softly, maybe sadly.

"No, no. Wait. I think maybe if I truly thought about it, I'd likely see there were signs earlier than I let myself acknowledge. Maybe I'd notice something about a man, but I'd tell myself it was because my best friend Rush was gay, and I wanted...hell, maybe I wanted to be what he was, or prove I was okay with it. I'm not sure if that's making sense or if it makes me sound like an asshole."

"It doesn't," Theo replied. "You would be surprised at the things the brain is capable of doing. I've read up a lot about it. Plus, like you said, it's all super nuanced."

Damn…he hadn't sounded like Theo there for a moment. He was a smart kid, not that I hadn't known he was before, but he'd seemed very… "You're mature for your age. That was very grown up."

He smiled, blushed, shifted in his seat. "So you thought you were straight, but you didn't care that your best friend was gay? Like didn't care at all?"

"Nope. Not at all." Was he afraid people would care? That his mom or others wouldn't accept him? "So anyway…like I said about Rush. He was always the most important person in my world. Then he moved here, and I was still in Virginia. I was struggling a bit, couldn't find my place in the world. I wasn't happy, and I didn't know why. But I knew I missed him and that he made things better, so I came to Fever Falls. And…he was seeing someone. He'd been talking about this guy for years, and I knew they were right for each other, but I was jealous."

"You? But you're gorgeous!" He slapped his hand over his mouth. "I mean, you're like, attractive or whatever. I bet girls think that."

"Eh, does it ever matter what other people think? What matters is how we feel in here." I touched my chest. "And in here." I touched my temple. "I never felt good about myself, and being jealous didn't help. Rush was my best friend, and I wanted him to be happy. I started to realize that I was...that I was in love with him." Shit. This whole thing was harder to talk about than I expected, but I wanted Theo to know. If it would help him, I'd tell him anything.

"Oh, wow..."

"Yeah, it was a hell of an internal revelation. And it was tough to work through because part of me felt like I was losing him right when I was struggling to know who I really was. So I told myself I was straight and it had just been Rush, which I know makes no sense."

"The brain," he reminded me.

I chuckled. "Yep. And mine does some funny things sometimes. But then, through it all, Cam was there. We became friends, and I talked to him...hell, I talked to him in ways I hadn't with Rush in a long time. He never made me feel embarrassed. He was always there. He became important to me in a way that only Rush had ever been." My pulse sped up, and my hands began to feel clammy.

"You were falling in love with him?"

My eyes snapped to Theo's. "What? No." I wasn't in love with Cam. I couldn't be. Could I? It definitely wasn't something I wanted to sort through right then, so I shoved the thought out of my head. "I just realized I liked him, that I was attracted to him. That it wasn't only Rush, which meant I wasn't straight. I settled on bisexual because it was the closest label to what felt right for me, even if sometimes it doesn't feel like it fits a hundred percent."

"And Camden feels the same. I bet he liked you the whole time. You should see the way he looks at you."

Goose bumps ran the length of my arms, making the hair there stand on end. Camden wanted to fuck me. He'd always wanted to fuck me. That was no secret. And we'd become friends, the best of. We enjoyed each other's company, were attracted to each other and everything, but I wasn't sure he looked at me like I was something special, or that he had the whole time. "Emotions and relationships are complicated. Right now, Cam and I aren't serious. We're just…seeing what happens."

"And it's, um…it's been okay? No one has been homophobic to you or anything?"

Goddamn, this poor kid. I wanted to protect him from the world, but I knew I couldn't do that. "It's been fine so far. No one has said anything, but I'll be honest with you, everyone who knows is either LGBTQ themselves or LGBTQ friendly. I haven't told older friends from Virginia, or my dad."

Which was complicated in and of itself, but considering Cam and I were technically friends with benefits in a fake relationship, I didn't see a reason to tell my father yet.

I continued, "But I think the smart thing is to always do what makes a person comfortable and keeps them safe. If a person feels unsafe, they should be careful. Everyone should be able to choose for themselves who they tell and when they tell them. And there are resources out there. I would do my best if anyone needed me. Cam's also a very good person to talk to, and he knows a lot of people who would help. We have a friend named Trey, who would be a good person to talk to as well. If a person needed it, I mean."

Theo nodded. "Construction Guy told me about him." Then…he set his sketchbook on the table. His hand was shaking as he pushed it over to me.

"You want me to look at it?"

He nodded again.

Damned if my hands weren't trembling too. This was a really fucking big moment, one I was honored to be a part of, and I didn't want to screw up.

I picked it up and…holy shit, he was a good artist. It was a comic about a kid named Awkward Boy. He wore a beanie and carried a skateboard like Theo did. Only he had powers too. He could fly on the skateboard, and he helped people in trouble.

Construction Guy was in the comics too. And…me. I started out as Lost Man, but then became Friendly Man, the kind guy with the sad eyes. Had I seemed lost to him? Did I have sad eyes? Jesus, I wouldn't be surprised if I did.

My hands still shook as I turned the pages, as I saw that Friendly Man seemed lonely like Awkward Boy. That Awkward Boy had noticed it right away, and it made him feel a connection to Friendly Man…but that he didn't seem so lonely when Construction Guy was there. That Friendly Man laughed more then and his eyes lit up. And that it made Awkward Boy wonder if he could feel that way one day too.

With another boy.

But he was scared.

"Theo… I…" I didn't know what to say.

"Is it stupid? Oh God, it's stupid. I'm sorry. I just thought—"

"This isn't stupid. This is maybe the most incredible

thing I've ever seen. You're so talented, and you bled your heart into this. I can feel it. I'm honored to be a part of it, and I feel so damn special that you shared it with me. You can trust me, and I'll try to help in any way I can."

"I know. It's, um…why I told you."

"Am I the only person who knows?"

"Yes."

"Do you feel unsafe telling your mom? I'm not saying you have to tell her at all. I'm just gauging the situation."

He shrugged. "I mean, she wouldn't hurt me. She's not like that. And I don't think she would kick me out or anything. She's never said anything that makes me feel like she's homophobic, but I just…don't want to give her a reason not to love me…more of a reason not to hang around, ya know?"

Jesus fucking Christ, this kid was going to wreck me. "I understand feeling that way. My dad, he couldn't let me in either. He was there physically, he wasn't there emotionally or mentally. I spent most of my life wanting to make him proud, hoping it would help him feel closer to me and let me in, but with him, it wouldn't work. He is who he is, and I couldn't change that with anything I did. He's too lost, and he has to want to become found again. I'm not saying your mom is the same, but that's my situation."

He wrung his hands together in his lap. "Yeah, I think my brain knows that, but my heart is on the fence."

"Hearts are weird like that."

He smiled. "I'm not ready yet to tell anyone else. Just you and… Can you tell Camden for me?"

"I absolutely will tell Cam. And we'll both be here for whatever you need. You're not alone in this." I reached over and squeezed his shoulder. "Do you and your mom have plans for Thanksgiving? Our friends are getting together. I know they would welcome you."

"No plans. She's supposed to take the day off, and we're gonna do something special just the two of us, she says. Hopefully, she'll stick with it. She's not a bad mom. I know she loves me. She's just not good at showing it."

I had experience with that, and it sucked and wasn't fair. "If anything changes, let me know. Even if it's on that day and we have to come get you, we will."

"I… Thank you. I think maybe you're my best friend. Is that okay?"

My lips stretched into a smile. "That's maybe the best title I've ever had."

Theo rolled his eyes. "I wouldn't go *that* far. But can

we like, talk about something else now? Or play a game. We can do some of your puzzle if you don't mind me helping. If so, that's fine. I totally get it. Ooh! Then maybe we can play video games?"

I laughed. There was the Theo I knew. "Perfect—puzzle, then games. I'm on board with that."

And it was exactly what we did. When we were finished there, he sketched and for the first time in a long time, I doodled.

CHAPTER EIGHTEEN

Camden

The truth is…I love you…but I don't want to be gay. ~ Letter from Henry

It was Thanksgiving, and I was picking Jude up like I typically did when we went out. I didn't know why it always worked that way. It wasn't as if Jude couldn't meet me, but it had become a habit we slipped into along the way, like being under your favorite blanket.

I hadn't seen him in a few days, and we hadn't talked much either. It almost felt like he was avoiding me, and all I could think was that it went back to him inviting me to Thanksgiving or saying he missed me that day.

All I knew was I didn't like it.

He was already outside waiting when I pulled up in front of the condo. He jumped in the truck and mumbled a hello.

"Hey, Beautiful. We gonna play this game again?"

"What game?"

"The one where you get all weird and I don't know why."

"It's not a game. I just have a lot on my mind. I'll tell you about it when I sort through it all."

I nodded. "Fair enough."

He was wearing a pair of jeans and a red-and-black flannel shirt rolled up to his elbows. Like always, Jude looked hot as fuck, so I let my eyes linger on him a minute, taking in the view.

"See something you like?" he teased.

Attaboy. I wanted to get back to that. "You know I do."

"Me too," he said as his eyes roamed me, leaving a lick of fire sliding up my spine.

"You're not careful, and we won't make it to Thanksgiving."

Unfortunately, that seemed to snap him out of it, and I wished like hell I could take the words back.

We were mostly quiet as we made the drive out to Rush and Lincoln's. Part of me wondered if it was where we were going that got him all riled up. The Rush thing bothered me more than I liked, more than I wanted to admit, because I sure as shit had never been jealous before.

"Rush texted. Apparently, Mama K, Beth, Kenny, and Lincoln have been cooking since yesterday."

Short Stuff had told me that Rush's mom had been teaching him different things to cook the past few months, so I wasn't surprised that he was in there helping. "They wouldn't let me bring anything," I told him.

"Yeah, me neither."

We pulled into the driveway of Rush's ranch-style home, right behind Dax and Jace. My brother's car, along with everyone else's, was already there.

"Hey, man. How's it going?" Jace asked as we got out of the truck. He had that blond, boy-next-door look going for him like he always did.

"Not bad," I replied. "How about yourself?"

"Good," Jace answered as Dax put an arm around him.

"Are your moms coming too?" Jude asked.

"No, both our moms are in Parlaisa with Keegan and Owen. Owen had some business he had to take care of. Jace's mom wanted to be with him, and who the hell knows what Serena is doing," Dax replied, and we laughed. His mom was…well, she was crazy, but a hoot.

The four of us headed to the door. Jude knocked, then slid it open, reminding me how at home he felt with Rush. Damn that nagging jealousy again.

Rush's mom, Kathy, was walking by just as we came in, and she hugged Jude right away. "So good to have both my boys here today," she told him, and damn it, my chest felt too tight.

"It's good to be here, Mama K. It smells good. You know I love your Thanksgiving dinners."

She said hello to everyone else before going back toward the kitchen. "Most everyone is in the living room," she said, so we headed that way.

Ash and Beau were standing together, looking like a couple of cartoon characters, they were smiling so damn big. They leaned against the back of the couch, Rush and Linc standing in front of them, the four of them talking.

Carter was fiddling with Sawyer's shirt like he was trying to fix it, and Sawyer was grinning at him like he had just provided the answer to world peace or something.

I reached over and grabbed Jude's hand, threading our fingers together. Fuck it. If I was playing his boyfriend, I was going to excel at my part. If he didn't like it, he was going to have to tell me.

For a moment he tensed up, but then his body loosened. He looked down at our hands, then at me, cocking a brow.

"Something wrong, Boyfriend?" I asked.

"No. Just interesting."

"Jude finally joins the cool kids club, but I have to question his taste in men," Linc teased, prompting me to let go of Jude.

I grabbed Lincoln and pulled him into a loose headlock, messing up his hair.

"Ugh! I hate it when you do that to me. Rush is going to kick your ass."

I laughed when he pulled away. "Rush, huh?"

"I'm too pretty to fight," Linc replied.

"Are you saying I'm not pretty?" Rush countered.

"No. You're fucking gorgeous, but obviously not as pretty as me. *Duh*." Linc tried to fix his hair while giving me the evil eye.

"You know you love me, Short Stuff. Hey, BB," I added when Carter and Sawyer approached us.

"Are you picking on Lincoln again?" Sawyer asked.

"Yes, yes he is. He's always picking on me. Control your brother." Linc mock-frowned.

"Can anyone control Cam?" Jude asked.

"You can, Boyfriend." I winked. He flushed. Everyone got quiet.

Rush was watching us, Sawyer smiled, but of course it was Ashton fucking Carmichael who broke the silence.

"Blowjobs every night for a week! Boom. I told you they'd get together!"

"First, did you just say *boom*?" I asked. "And second, you have to make bets with your husband to get your dick sucked? Definitely never getting married now."

"Nope. Who wouldn't want to blow me?" Ash teased. "I've got a great cock."

"After I fixed it," Beau said, and Ash's eyes widened.

"Context, Campbell! I assure you all, my dick is just fine. He's talking about the being-with-a-guy thing." Then Ash looked at Jace. "Fucking amazing, right?"

"Hell yeah," Jace replied.

Elliott, who worked with Dax and Carter, approached us. I hadn't known he would be there. "I wouldn't know," he added.

"Oh, speaking of…we still need to do the ceremony for Jude," Carter said.

"Ceremony?" Jude's brows pulled together.

"Yeah, it's where we welcome you to the club, share the gay agenda and all that with you," Linc answered, and we all laughed.

I wrapped an arm around him, pulled him close, and kissed his temple. "Don't worry, Boyfriend. I'll be with you the whole time."

It wasn't until Jude looked at me and said, "I know,"

that I realized I hadn't said it as part of the charade. Not that there was a gay ceremony, which honestly would be a hell of a good time, but still, if Jude needed me, I'd be there.

🔥

DINNER WAS LOUD, delicious, and perfect.

Rush had added extra tables in the dining room, and we filled them with laughter.

I couldn't help but watch Jude through most of it. His cheeks were pink from laughing so hard as he joked and chatted with everyone. I knew how different this was for him. This had to be the only holiday like this he'd ever had, and I suddenly wanted him to have more of them. Sure, he'd been in Fever Falls for a while now, but this just felt…different.

And he watched me too.

All fucking day.

It was similar to Ash and Beau's wedding a few weeks before. Christ, had it only been weeks? It felt longer. And I could see the wheels turning in his head, much as they had that day. I could see him working through something, and I could only hope I liked whatever he decided on as much as I liked it when he'd pulled me into that storage room and kissed me.

We stayed for a few hours after dinner. There was pie—my favorite was apple, but Jude loved pumpkin, which I didn't understand.

"Pumpkin shit is gross," I teased him.

"You're gross," he countered.

"Wow…are you twelve?"

We both laughed, and I kissed him again, hoping he was okay with it. We were fake boyfriends, after all; it wasn't like I wouldn't be touching him all day.

"You wanna come home with me, Boyfriend?" I asked when we were back in my truck. "I can take you to your condo if you want."

"No, that's okay. Let's go to your house."

We were quiet for the drive.

"I like it here. It's calmer than being right downtown," Jude said as we got out of the truck. The motion detector lights came on. My place was really close to town, but just a bit secluded, tucked away in a mass of trees that were now a variety of fall colors.

"Yeah, I like it too. I've only had it a few years. There was a time when I wanted to just be able to stumble home from Fever," I joked as I let us into the house. It wasn't a big place—three bedrooms, sort of rustic, filled with earth tones. "You thirsty or anything?"

"Nah, I'm good. I could use a shower, though."

I nodded, really fucking wanting to ask him if he would like company, but I could tell he was still having one of those moments when he needed some time and space to figure shit out. But he'd still come home with me, which made me feel better.

"Come on."

I took him to my room, grabbed a pair of basketball shorts from my dresser, and tossed them to him. "There are clean towels on the rack. I'll head out to the living room and see if I can find us a new show to watch."

Jude grabbed my arm as I went for the door. "You don't want to shower with me?"

"Obviously, I want to shower with you. I love naked time."

Jude chuckled. "You're such an idiot."

"An idiot who makes you smile."

His smile grew, and fuck, did I like making him do that. He nodded toward the bathroom, and I went. Like I said, I loved naked time, especially with Jude, but as this one went, there wasn't anything going on other than showering. We cleaned up together, taking turns with soap and shampoo, mumbling *excuse me's* as we swapped places under the spray.

My time with him was so different than when I was

with other lovers. It had only been a few weeks, yeah, but Jude and I spent a lot less time actually touching each other. As much as I loved pleasing him, I understood it. This was all so damn new to him, and he'd chosen me to be his first. Plus, it was just different with us. I liked being with him no matter what we did.

We ended up with Jude in my shorts and me in underwear. He lay on his belly with his head toward the foot of the bed, playing a video game, which as always, he absolutely sucked at. I was on my phone, lying on my back with my legs over his, that pert ass of his calling my damn name, which I was trying to ignore.

It was comfortable, relaxed. Felt like we'd been doing it forever, and we had for a long time, only without the touching and the naked time.

An hour or so later, Jude turned off the game and the TV, then sat on the bed and looked at me.

My heart dropped, tumbled and swooped, then kept free-falling in a way that was scary as hell. My chest ached and I rubbed it, trying to get the pain to go away.

Fuck, I realized I was way too wrapped up in this relationship thing. I was way too wrapped up in Jude, and maybe that was it, just the fact that it was him and it didn't feel like it had been such a short time, because we had been leading up to this since the moment he moved to Fever Falls.

"Am I gonna like this, Beautiful?"

"I hope so."

I reached out and cupped his cheek. "There's always so much going on inside that head of yours. Let me in."

Jude nodded, then turned and kissed the palm of my hand. It sent a little zing straight to my cock. You'd think he offered to blow me.

"I think I want… I think I honestly want us to be together. I know that's not what I asked for, and I know that's typically not your thing, but yeah, that's it. Well, part of it…and why are you looking at me like that?"

I grinned, fucking smiled like I was in a toothpaste commercial or something. It felt like he'd stuck the sun inside me and was lighting me up. "You're asking me to really go steady with you?"

He snickered and shook his head. "You're ridiculous."

"But I make you smile," I said again.

"Yeah…you do."

"I'll be your boyfriend. I think we've been that for a long time."

It was like the sun split, like it separated but was still so fucking bright, only now he had part of it inside him as well. "Yeah, that's kind of how I got here. I was talking to Theo, and—"

"So I have him to thank for this?"

"Shh. I'm telling a story," he teased.

I sat back against the headboard, arms crossed, and listened.

CHAPTER NINETEEN

Jude

Awkward Boy doesn't feel so awkward around Friendly Man and Construction Guy. They help.
~ Theo's comic

I SURE AS shit hadn't planned on starting with, *I think I honestly want us to be together*, but that was what had come out, and I was rolling with it. Cam shook me up, twisted up my thoughts and made me vulnerable with him in a way I'd never been with another person in my life. With anyone else I would have been cocky and made some kind of joke, but not with him. With him I was real.

"You telling me a story, or what?" he asked.

"I'm getting there. Have some patience."

So I told him about Theo's visit and him asking if we were together. "It was tough because I didn't want to lie to him, but then as I thought about it, I felt the same as you. We've been together, Cam. Maybe not with the *naked time*," I teased. "Or with exclusivity. But it felt like we've been together for a long time in every other way. And I...fuck, I want that."

"Naturally."

"You're a cocky bastard."

"Who—"

"Makes me laugh and smile. I know."

"I like that I get to call you boyfriend and it's not a joke anymore, Boyfriend." He grabbed me and tugged me closer. "Hi, Boyfriend."

"Hi."

"I'm going to kiss you now, Boyfriend."

I grinned. "Okay."

"Thank you, Boyfriend," he said against my mouth, and then we were kissing. He tasted of mint and smelled like soap and fresh wood. Speaking of wood, I was suddenly sporting some, my dick hard as I leaned over, kissing him.

"Fuck, you taste good. I used to look at you and wonder what your skin tastes like." I licked down his throat, across his collarbone.

"You can taste me anytime you want."

So I did. I worshipped him the way he'd done to me, savoring every inch of skin as I sucked and bit and nibbled at him. It was incredible, so fucking good, but I wanted more. I needed it.

My lips trailed down his chest. The lower I got, the more my hunger spiked, the more I craved him, wanted to know more of him, but the more my nerves bled in too.

When I reached Cam's trunks, my gaze held his as I hooked my fingers in the waistband.

"You sure?" Cam asked with this cocky half-grin on his face.

"If I wasn't, I wouldn't be doing it. You're coddling me again."

Cam held up his hands in mock-surrender. "I'll be good. Promise—oh wait, I wouldn't want you to be distracted by these. I know how hot you find these."

The conceited fucker lowered his arms, but damned if it didn't cause this light feeling in my chest that wiped some of the discomfort away. "I hate you."

"You're the one who said you're obsessed with my hands. I'm just trying to help you out by not distracting you."

"Shut up if you want me to blow you. This is a first for me."

"It's the perfect dick to start on."

I rolled my eyes and went to grab his underwear again, but Cam stopped me. "Hey," he said softly. "I'm glad it's me...and not for the obvious reasons."

I was glad it was him too.

I nodded, then proceeded to pull his dark-blue trunks down. His cock sprang free, so damn hard and leaking. His balls were full, the hair at his groin cut short, and I remembered how he'd inhaled me, so I leaned forward and did the same to him.

It was soap and salt and sex, and it went straight to my head, making me dizzy. Cam damn near jolted off the bed.

"Fuck, do that again."

"Smell you?"

"Hell yes."

So I did. Lying between Cam's legs, I inhaled his scent again, studied his dick that I'd had my hands on more than once now. Lay there and breathed in this man who had begun to mean so much to me.

Cam.

My friend.

My lover.

My boyfriend.

And for the first time, I didn't want to run, which was what I did any other time shit got real in a relationship.

"Boyfriend 101 lessons are in session," he teased,

then sobered. "Can you lick my balls, Beautiful? Look me in the eyes when you do."

A tremble raked down my spine. Fuck yes, I loved it when Cam talked to me like that.

I looked up at him, and he down at me. So fucking handsome. He had stubble along his jaw and hunger in his stare, and suddenly I wanted to give him everything, wanted to please Camden Burke in ways no one ever had.

Holding his gaze, I licked my lips, then leaned forward and lashed my tongue against his balls. It felt like… Well, it felt like what you would assume a nutsac against your tongue would feel like. I did it again, then again, unsure how I felt, but when Cam's eyes fluttered and he made a throaty sound, I realized I fucking loved it. I wanted more—of his taste, his feel, his sounds. I wanted to please him and know that it was me who was doing it.

"You like it," he said. "I can see it in your eyes."

"Fuck yes." I was high off this feeling, off Camden. His scent and his taste and his noises. The fire in his eyes and the desire for me that I saw escalating, which just made me want more instead of feeling that uncomfortable itch beneath my skin I had gotten with others. "Tell me what to do," I said, not because I couldn't figure it out, but because I wanted to hear him, wanted him to ground me in this moment, to him and how he made me feel.

"Oh, we're gonna have fun together, you and me." Cam grabbed the base of his cock and angled it toward my mouth. "Let me see those pretty lips suck me. Just the tip, so you can get used to it."

I damn near convulsed, I wanted him so badly.

My heart was practically pounding out of my chest as I leaned closer and loosely sucked his crown into my mouth. He tasted like salt, his precome on my tongue. Cam groaned as I nursed him, and fuck if my dick didn't throb as hard as my heart.

"That's it. Fuck, you look so good. So goddamned beautiful. Now just lick it."

Again, I did as Cam said, following his lead, my tongue making circles around the head of his cock. A part of me still wondered how I got there, while the other…the other just felt like *finally*.

"Christ, look at you, so sexy." He threaded his fingers through my hair. "Can you take a little more of me? Not too much, just taste me, experiment with me. Fuck, you can do whatever you want with me."

Everything. I was pretty damn sure I wanted to try everything with him. I felt like I was delirious with lust. Sucking him deeper, I gagged slightly when he got too far back. I'd never had much trouble with my gag reflex before, but I'd never had a dick in my throat before either.

I wrapped a hand around him, stroked his hard length as I sucked him…sucked Cam. He told me how good I was, and I wanted that. He told me how hot I was, and it made me soar instead of holding me down.

"Play with my hole. You're gonna have to get me used to having someone back there if you're ever going to fuck me."

I bucked my hips, damn near shot off the bed. I really fucking wanted inside Cam…wanted him inside me too. Maybe a small part of me was a little more curious about the second part, to know what it would be like to be possessed by Camden.

He spread his legs and grabbed my hand, then sucked my index finger into his mouth, which shouldn't have been as hot as it was.

I slipped it behind his balls, rubbed against his rim as I continued to blow him. It wasn't nearly as skilled as when he sucked me, but his body writhed and his dick jerked in my hand, so it was obvious he liked it.

"Here…let me grab this." Cam reached over and pulled lube out of his drawer. He passed it to me, and my damn hands shook as I opened it, as I wet my finger.

I'd fucked a woman's ass before, fingered her too, but this was different. This was a man. This was Cam.

He was tight, tense, even though he said he wanted me. "Let me in, Cam," I begged, tapping his hole the way he had done with me. I felt him loosen, and I pressed forward. The tip of my index finger slid in, and I lapped at his balls, then sucked him, before pushing farther in. Fuck, it was so goddamned hot and tight inside him.

"Yeah…that's it. Suck me while you rub my prostate," he ordered.

I liked following Cam's direction in the bedroom. It made sweat bead at my brow and tingles run down my spine, this sort of whirlwind of want twisting inside me. "Where?" I asked.

"Oh, you're in for a treat the first time I play with yours. Crook your finger."

I did as he said and found a soft, spongy spot. When I rubbed it, Cam's dick jerked against his stomach.

"Fuck yeah. Right there. Wrap that pretty mouth of yours around my cock while you finger me."

There was this constant ache deep inside me that sort of blew up at his command, expanded as a maelstrom of need surged through me.

I stroked him with one hand as I sucked him and

fingered his ass. Every time I rubbed his prostate, Cam nearly jolted off the bed. I kept going, fueled by his reaction, wanting to give him pleasure and wondering what it would feel like to have him touch me like that as well.

"Christ, you feel so good. I can't believe I'm finally here with you," he mumbled, writhing beneath me. His hand was in my hair, fisting it, as he gently thrust between my lips and rode my hand. I could feel the urgent jerk of his response, each second that went by needier than the last.

"I'm not gonna last. Fuck, I can't believe I'm gonna shoot. If you don't want it, pull off," Cam gasped, and…did I want it? He always swallowed my load, but I wasn't sure I was ready for a mouthful of spunk yet, so I leaned back, kept jacking him and fucking him with my finger, rubbing that spot inside Cam that seemed to shoot him to the moon.

And then he did. His whole body convulsed as he shot, the first spurt landing on his chest, the second hitting his face. When his body went lax, he looked at me and grinned, making my heart stumble in a way that was both frightening and exhilarating. "Best. Blowjob. Ever."

I rolled my eyes playfully. "I highly doubt that."

"Don't," he said and then somehow flipped me. I didn't know how it happened, but Cam was rolling out from under me, twisting me to my back, then dropping to his knees on the side of the bed. "Over here. Ass on the edge. Stay on your back. I'm gonna eat you out, Beautiful, and you're going to fucking love it."

CHAPTER TWENTY

Camden

Being with you isn't something I can ever let myself do. ~ Letter from Henry

"Excuse me?" Jude said, his brow cocked.

"I'm going to put my tongue and maybe my fingers in your ass. Unless you don't want me to? If not, I'll blow you. You know I love sucking your cock, but I think you'll like this too." I had a feeling that if Jude just let go, he'd fucking love it. I wanted to be the one to rock his world that way, the first one to ever have something inside him.

"I…yeah. Okay."

"I know it's different being on the receiving end."

"I can't say I ever imagined I'd have a guy even looking at, much less licking, my asshole."

"We don't have to. It's not something you have to check off the list because you're bi. If you don't think it'll be your thing, we won't do it." The last thing I wanted Jude to think was that he had to do anything. Ass play wasn't for everyone, no matter what their sexuality was.

"I want to," he replied, then cleared his throat. "Get your tongue in my ass, Burke."

"Yes, Boyfriend," I teased. "And that was new—calling me Burke. Aren't you supposed to have a sweet nickname for me now that we're official? Like baby or sweetheart, or you know, sex god or something like that. I'm rather fond of the last one."

"Okay, Big Head, are we doing this or not?"

"Cock compliments work too!"

"That's not what I meant." But he was smiling, and I fucking loved that smile.

"Shh. I'm concentrating," I teased. "Been wanting this for a long time." That part I was serious about. I ran my hands up his thighs and watched goose bumps pebble across Jude's tanned skin. "Bend your legs and hold them back some. Can you do that for me?"

"Yeah," he replied sort of breathlessly, and damned if that didn't push me even closer to the edge. I'd already blown my load, but my dick was hard again. Just looking at him did that to me.

"This is awkward," Jude said, but he still began to do it.

"Do you want to lie on your stomach? I thought this way it would be easy for me to get to your dick too." Said dick bounced against his belly. "Someone likes that."

"I trust you," Jude said, and his response made pride surge through me.

"Thank you." There was an unexpected amount of emotion seeping through my words. This…what was happening with us…was big. Different. Real. At least on my end. I should have known it from the way I reacted to him from the start.

I looked down at his heavy balls, at his tight hole tucked between his cheeks. Fuck, it was going to kill me to be inside there, this unbreached piece of perfection that I wanted all to myself.

"Christ, Jude. I think this is going to end up my favorite place to be." My finger brushed back and forth against him, and he clenched. "I can't wait to taste it."

"Do it."

I cocked a brow at him. "Ask nicely."

"Please, Cam…"

Damned if that didn't almost make me come again right then. I leaned in and flicked my tongue across his hole. Jude cried out, and I did it again. He tasted like the soap we'd used in the shower and slightly of musk from our time together in bed. It was heady and sexy, and I could have gotten drunk off him. I did it again and again, teased his opening, tasted it, savored it. Jude was making little gasping sounds, his breaths heavy and deep.

I sucked on my finger, then spit on it as I moved up to suck his balls. "Not gonna get enough of this," I told him, and when his body damn near melted into the bed, I pushed the tip of my finger inside him.

Jude tensed up slightly.

"We okay? Want me to stop?"

"Your tongue again…I want that too."

So I gave it to him. I wasn't sure there was anything I wouldn't give Jude. I pulled my finger out and ate at his hole again, feasted off him like I was dying and he was my last meal. When he loosened up enough, I pushed my tongue inside him and he hissed, before begging for me. "Please…please…"

"What do you want, Beautiful?"

"I don't know…anything…everything…"

"I think I can handle that."

I alternated between tonguing him and giving him my finger, rubbing and tapping, slipping the tip inside. I wanted to unravel him, take him a-fucking-part like no one had ever done with him before.

He was sweating and gasping and begging,

"More…Jesus, I want you, Cam…"

I was a fucking king in that moment. "You have me. I'm right here. Not going anywhere."

With trembling hands, I plucked the lube from the bed and wet my fingers.

"Look at me," I told him, and he did, so damn easily. He looked blissed out, his pupils wide, sweat on his forehead. "You gonna let me inside this tight hole of yours?"

"Yes…fuck yes…"

I licked his balls because Jude seemed to like that as I worked a finger inside him. I took it slow, teasing as I sucked on his sac, then leaned forward to swallow his cock down. The second I was in, I curved my finger, found his prostate, sucking and rubbing and doing my damnedest to blow his fucking mind.

"Oh fuck!" Jude cried out.

"See? I knew you'd like it." As soon as the words left my mouth, I was back to work again. Taking him deep, letting him fuck my throat like he was so good at, as I slid my finger in and out of him, teasing him and touching him.

Jude bucked his hips, then pushed his ass back toward my finger. He was riding it like a fucking pro, and I could see how much he wanted it, how much he liked it as his eyes held me, wide and needy and satisfied.

"Cam…" he said when I massaged his prostate again. This time, I didn't let up on him, and he was crying out and thrashing around before, "Fuck…I'm gonna lose it," but I kept going because I really wanted his load.

Jude's dick jerked in my mouth, and he tugged my hair as he shot, filling my mouth. I swallowed him down, and he shot again before his legs fell and his arms dropped. He just lay there breathing, and I let him, pulling my finger out, kissing one inner thigh, his nuts, then the other thigh.

"That was… I don't have words for what that was. How did I not know how incredible that could be?"

"It's part of the gay agenda. We keep it a secret," I teased, then crawled up so I lay on his stomach. "It was really okay?" Looking down at him, I traced a line from his temple to his chin.

"I've never seen you be unsure."

"I'm not, usually, but this was…" This was Jude. "Different."

He blinked up at me a few times, those ice-blue eyes of his completely open to me. "Yeah…yeah I get it. And I loved it. I might want you to do it all the time. I can't believe I've gone through my whole life without a finger up my ass if that's what it does to you."

I laughed and kissed him. Christ, I had fun with him. "I'll finger you every damn day if you want."

This time, he leaned up and pressed his lips to mine. I was surprised, wondering if he would shy away from my mouth because of what I just did to him, but he didn't. We kissed as we maneuvered our way up the bed to lie with our heads on the pillows, and we kept kissing while we lay together. It was like we couldn't get enough of touching each other, like if we parted, we'd never do this again, so we wanted to treasure it.

"God, your mouth. I used to dream about those lips."

"Used to?"

"Aw, does Boyfriend want a compliment?"

"Shut up," Jude said, before our lips forged together again. We kissed until my jaw hurt. When we finally managed to separate our lips, we were still tangled up together, wrapped in each other when he said, "Theo is gay—or questioning, at least."

"I know. I figured. Did he say you could tell me?"

"I wouldn't have if he hadn't said I could."

I nodded because I knew that.

"He said he's not ready for anyone else to know, but he wanted me to tell you. He's drawn this whole comic. He's Awkward Boy, and we're in it too. You're Construction Guy. And it's...helped. We've helped him. I think it shows him that it's okay, two men together. He's nervous."

"That's normal. We'll just be there and support him. Show him how fucking incredible it can be. If he needs us, we'll be there. That's all we can do."

"I..." Jude cocked his head slightly. "Who are you?"

I both knew what he meant and didn't. He knew me, but then I figured he meant where did I come from in his life and how did we get to where we were. "Your boyfriend. I haven't been someone's boyfriend in a long time. I hope I don't fuck it up."

He laughed. "Well, I've never had a boyfriend before, so I hope I don't fuck it up."

"It's easy, really. You just suck his dick every day. Play video games with him. Tell him how sexy he is, and...yeah, that's about it."

Jude laughed, and it vibrated through me, settled deep in my chest.

"So that's what you'll be doing with me every day too?" he asked.

"Yep." I nuzzled his throat. "Boyfriends are the best."

I just hoped like hell he felt the same.

CHAPTER TWENTY-ONE

Jude

Awkward Boy gets more comfortable in his skin.
~ Theo's comic

"Watch out! You're gonna shoot me!" Theo shouted.

"Then back up and let the expert handle this," Cam said playfully, and I couldn't help but roll my eyes at them as they went back and forth. Camden was fiercely competitive, and I was learning Theo was too. They'd been glued to the thing for who knew how long, and I hadn't had a turn in over an hour. Strangely, I didn't mind. It was nice listening to them in the background while I doodled on scrap pieces of paper. Ever since the day I'd seen Theo's comic, I'd been drawing some myself. It reminded me how much I'd enjoyed it when I was younger, and it was something I hadn't done in years.

It was good for Theo—having us, being here and

spending time with us as he had for the past few days. Cam was at the condo every evening after work, and Theo was too. Yesterday, he'd sat at the kitchen table to do his homework, I think maybe just because he wanted to be around someone.

He hadn't mentioned being gay again or even talked to Camden about it, outside of when he asked me if Cam knew. I said yes and confirmed it was okay, and he'd told me it was. We didn't want to push him; just wanted Theo to know we were there, that we wouldn't treat him any differently, and to let us talk to him when he was ready.

"Oh my God! Stop!" Theo said as shots rang out on the TV. Camden laughed.

"Are you sure you're not thirteen?" I teased Cam, but really, I enjoyed that he was sometimes like a big kid.

"At heart, Beautiful, and you like it—*Goddamn it.* I died." He looked over his shoulder. "You killed me."

"How did I kill you?"

"You distracted me and…wait…you did that on purpose, didn't you? You're on Theo's side," he said playfully, tossing the controller on the table.

"Of course not," I replied, but then looked at Theo and made a big deal about winking at him.

"I knew it!" Cam groaned, then stood, walked over,

and pressed a kiss to my lips. "You guys want a soda?"

It was such a *boyfriend* thing to do and we were so new that it still threw me sometimes. But I guessed it shouldn't, since he *was* my boyfriend and all.

"Yes, please," Theo said, smiling at me, then pretended to make out with his hand. I flicked him off, then silently cursed myself because I wasn't sure I was supposed to give the finger to a seventeen-year-old. Cam was rubbing off on me.

Oh, that thought made me blush slightly.

"I'm good," I finally replied. We'd been…enjoying each other ever since the other night. I'd sucked Cam off every night since, and I was getting better. I also discovered that I really liked giving head. Receiving was fucking awesome too, of course, but it was…empowering, driving Cam wild. And I fucking *loved* having my ass played with.

He handed a soda to Theo, who opened it right away and immediately sucked the whole thing down. He was a bottomless pit, though I guess I had been at that age too. Mama K had always teased Rush and me about it.

"We need to figure out dinner." Cam ran his fingers through my hair. I might have groaned deep in my throat, and he winked at me. Fuck, I loved touching him and being touched by him.

"What about Chinese? Do you guys like Chinese? It's totally my favorite." Theo's cheeks turned pink. "I mean, if I'm invited. I didn't mean to invite myself. You guys probably want alone time or whatever to like... Oh God, not that! To like eat or whatever."

"I wasn't thinking *that*," Cam said, and I nudged him. "I'm kidding." He looked down at me. "I'm always thinking that." Then to Theo. "You're always invited."

The appreciation shined brightly in his eyes. God, this kid was so needy for attention, it broke my damn heart.

"Chinese it is." I stood.

"Wait...what about that place? That other one you guys go to? Fever Pitch on Fever Street? I've always wanted to go there."

If Linc were here, he would say something about Fever Street being the gayest street in the gayborhood, which was likely why Theo wanted to go.

"I'm always down for Fever Pitch," Cam said, and I nodded.

"Yeah, me too."

Cam and I grabbed our jackets. Theo seemed okay in his hoodie, even though it was drizzling out, and then we were on our way. The condo was close enough that we could walk, which made it slightly strange that Theo had never been there. Maybe he had, but he just felt different going with us.

As much as I wanted to be there for him, I got a sort of tightness in my chest. I was still figuring stuff out for myself too, and this fear kept clawing at me, that I'd screw up with him…that I'd say or do the wrong thing.

Theo chatted our ears off the whole walk to Fever Pitch, the way he was so good at doing.

Just as we went inside, a lesbian couple walked out, holding hands, and Theo smiled. Then we were seated, and a familiar dark-haired guy approached us.

"What's up, Keeg? How's your prince?" Cam asked.

"Oh my God! You're the guy who's dating a prince?" Theo asked. "And you guys like, know him? Oh my God. Do you guys know everyone? Do you all like, hang out all the time and stuff?"

Cam and I both chuckled. "Well, it's not like a thing. We don't hang out with every LGBTQ person in town, but we do have a large group of friends." The words settled in my chest, making me feel warm. I liked it, having these guys as friends, belonging with them.

"It's basically because we're really fucking cool. Everyone wants to be friends with us," Cam told him. "And now you're friends with us too."

Theo grinned.

"Keegan, this our friend Theo—Theo, this is Keegan, who really is dating a prince," I introduced them.

"Wow…that's…wow. Do you have a title?"

"Prince Owen's Super Hot Boyfriend?" Keegan teased, and we all laughed. "It's nice to meet you, Theo." Keegan's eyes darted between Camden and me, obviously wondering what was going on. "Can I get you guys a drink?"

Cam and I both got water, and Theo ordered another soda. Keegan asked if we were ready to order or needed more time. By now, we basically had the menu memorized, but Theo didn't, so we asked for a minute. We all ended up getting cheeseburgers with fries.

"I can't believe he's dating a prince. I want to date a prince one day." Theo's hand slapped over his mouth like he couldn't believe he'd said what we had.

"Who doesn't want to date a prince?" Cam replied, not missing a beat. "I mean, not me. My boyfriend is hot, but it's a good goal."

I rolled my eyes, but really, I liked it.

"Did you like…always know?" Theo asked softly, without looking at us.

"I think so. I finally admitted it to myself and put myself out there to experiment with a guy because I knew my brother was gay. I know that sounds weird. I've always joked about doing it because of Sawyer, but I think knowing that he liked boys, even though he'd never actually told me, made me feel okay inside about being attracted to them myself. I've always drawn more strength from Sawyer than he realizes."

My pulse went a little crazy hearing him say that. Cam always came off like he didn't need anyone—want them, yes, but not need. I knew that wasn't true. He needed his brother more than anyone in the world.

I reached over and grabbed his hand. It was the only time I'd done something like that in public.

"I bet that helped…" Theo said, "it being both of you."

"It did," Cam replied. "I don't want to push you, and if you don't want to talk about it, you can always tell me to shut up, but there's a holiday party coming up in a few weeks at the LGBTQ center. I got tickets for the three of us in case either of you two knuckleheads wanted to go. Again—no obligation, but the offer is there."

Well, damn. I hadn't known he'd done that. But I wasn't surprised. It was such a Camden thing to do. "That sounds fun. I'm down if you guys are." They'd all opened my eyes to so many different things since moving to Fever Falls. I'd never been involved in so many charity events or organizations as I had since meeting Camden and their crew.

"I… Can I think about it?" Theo asked.

"No," Cam replied, but thankfully, Theo chuckled and shook his head. He knew Cam as well as I did.

"Thank you."

"Nothing to thank me for, kid."

They brought our food after that, and the three of us sat together and ate. We laughed and talked, and Theo ate all his food and some of our fries. We'd just finished when Cam's cell rang. It sat on the table beside him, and he picked it up, looked at it, and frowned.

"It's Henry," he said.

Honestly, I hadn't even known the two of them spoke enough for him to know Cam's phone number, but then…maybe Cam had had the same one for years? And really, why did it matter either way?

"Who's Henry?" Theo asked.

"An old friend," Cam replied. "I'll be right back. I'm going to grab this real quick. I want to make sure everything is okay."

He stood and answered, saying hello as he walked away.

"Who's Henry?" Theo asked again.

"One of his friends."

"Old boyfriend?"

I wasn't sure they'd ever used that title, but what I did know was that Camden had loved him…and that Henry had loved Cam too.

"I'm not sure." I shrugged. "But it's fine either way." And it was. Hell, I was best friends with the only person I'd ever been in love with.

My stomach clenched, this sort of wrongness slamming into me.

Oh God…I didn't know what made it hit me right then, but I realized I felt wrong because my thoughts had…because Rush wasn't the only person I'd ever loved.

I was pretty sure I might be in love with Camden Burke…and maybe I had been for a long time.

CHAPTER TWENTY-TWO

Camden

I can't be with you...for real, at least...even though it's you I'll always love. ~ Letter from Henry

IT FELT STRANGE waiting in the Italian restaurant for Henry.

We hadn't done something like this in years—actually, we'd never done anything like this before. When we'd been together, any time we spent with each other had been behind closed doors. We'd done it in hiding. Henry hadn't even wanted anyone to know we were the kind of friends who hung out, this fear inside him that people would take one look at us and know we were together.

I'd been understanding at first, then resented him, been angry with him, but I hadn't left him. I loved him and wanted to support him. That was what you did when you cared about someone. And coming out, or hell, even admitting to yourself, was so damn personal. I couldn't push Henry into it even if I hadn't understood the need to hide.

"Hey, sorry I'm late," Henry said, and I looked up just as he sat across from me. His blond hair was styled, sort of off to the side with gel. He wore a vest with a long-sleeved shirt underneath it, which was cute as hell, and he knew I secretly liked that shit. But he also liked it himself, and he had a wife, kids, and another kid on the way, so I wasn't assuming he did it for me.

"No worries," I replied.

"You like Italian, right?" Henry asked.

Did he not remember? "Yeah. And it's your favorite. You used to always pick it up for us before we would hide from the world." There was a sharp bitterness on my tongue I hadn't expected.

"I know. I don't know why I said that. I remember. I didn't know if you would."

"What are we doing here?" It wasn't that I still had feelings for Henry at all. Those had ended a long time ago. Even if there wasn't a Jude and he didn't have his wife, I knew Henry wasn't the one for me, but I also wasn't sure I wanted to be friends with him. Wasn't sure I wanted to hang out with him, especially not knowing where it was coming from and how he felt, considering he had a wife.

The waiter approached, and Henry ordered a bottle of wine I had no plans on drinking. Hell, I didn't even like the stuff. I was more of a beer guy myself. I asked for water, and then the waiter gave us bread and oil before asking if we'd had time to look over the menu.

"Do you know what you want?" Henry asked.

"I'm simple. Just spaghetti for me."

He ordered something I didn't know how to pronounce, and the waiter disappeared again.

"How's Dee?" I asked about his wife.

Henry frowned slightly, this sort of panicked look in his eyes. "She's, um…great. Kids too."

"Has the new baby come yet?"

"No. She's due in February." He still didn't look at me, his eyes darting around like he wasn't sure what to do with them. "That's actually why we're here. Dee and I need to have some work done on the house. We're looking to remodel and add another room. We thought maybe we could hire Burke Construction for the job."

Ah, hell, this was not a good idea. Not a good idea at all. Something felt…off about it. Again, not because I had feelings for him, but because at one time, we had meant something to each other. We'd meant everything to each other, and he'd broken it off with me to be with her, and told me it was me he wanted to be with, that it was me he would always love, but he needed to marry a woman. "Why isn't your wife at this meeting with us?"

"She wants me to handle the hiring."

"I think you should look for someone else," I said honestly.

Henry frowned. "Why? I need a service, and you can provide it. There's nothing more here. That was…that was a long time ago."

"Even still." Hell, I probably shouldn't have come, but I'd been curious why he wanted to meet, and I'd also wanted to make sure he was okay.

"How is that guy…Justin? Was that your boyfriend's name?"

I was pretty sure he knew Jude's name wasn't Justin. "He's doing great, thanks for asking. He's…" I wasn't even sure what to say. He was confident, yet insecure too. He was beautiful but didn't see it. He was funny and kind and sucked at video games but liked puzzles.

"Oh God…" Henry cut into my thoughts. "You're in love with him?"

I figured I was, but that sure wasn't something I should tell Henry before I told Jude. Or hell, I wasn't sure it was something I should talk with Henry about at all. "He means a lot to me."

"I…" Henry started but didn't finish right away. "I

think about it sometimes…us. Do you ever think about it?"

Christ, this had been a really bad idea. My heart ached for him, but I was angry with him too. I hated that he was living a lie, but I also didn't want to be pulled into any deception of his wife. She didn't deserve that. "As you said, that was a long time ago. I don't know what we'd get out of talking about it. I'm with Jude, and you're married with children."

Henry closed his eyes, and damned if I didn't wish I could fix it. I hated to see anyone hurting. "There's nothing wrong with who you are, Henry. Don't you know that by now? You don't deserve to live a lie, and your wife doesn't either."

"The kids… I… It's fine. I'm happy. I don't feel…*those things* anymore."

"I think I should go. But if you ever need me, you know how to get ahold of me. Not for doing a remodel on your home, but if you…need a friend or need help working through things, I can help you find someone."

It was as if he cut his emotions off. He looked almost blank, staring through me instead of looking at me. "That's not what this was about. I don't know why you turned it into that. I just wanted work done on my home."

My chest hurt, and I felt…heavy. So fucking sad that he was so in denial, filled with so much self-hatred. I felt it for his wife too, because as far as I knew, she had no idea.

"Take care of yourself, Henry." I pulled money from my wallet for the food I wouldn't eat, and set it on the table. He didn't try to stop me as I walked out.

My body was jittery. It was a little hard to breathe, but I didn't know why I was responding that way.

I climbed into my truck, and before I realized what I was doing, I was pulling up in front of Jude's condo instead of my house. I didn't want to be alone, but there was no one else I wanted to be with either. Even if Jude didn't know what happened, he would be there for me. Just being with him would help.

I knocked on the door, my bones feeling too heavy to hold up. My hands gripped the doorframe. He opened the door and smiled, and damned if that didn't ease some of the ache inside me.

"This is a surprise—hey, what's wrong?"

"I missed you, Beautiful. I'm allowed to miss my boyfriend, right?" I grinned, trying to shove all that other shit to the background.

"Yeah, but you're also a liar. At least, you're lying right now." Jude put his hand on my hip, dipped his finger under my shirt and rubbed his thumb across the bone there. I loved that he felt comfortable touching me whenever he wanted now. Fucking loved that he *wanted* to touch me at all.

He pulled me forward, and I came willingly, eagerly. He closed the door behind me just before my forehead dropped to his. "This is already better," I admitted. There was no sense in trying to deny it. I was so fucking gone for him, probably had been for months, even before our game of boyfriend charades.

"What's wrong, Cam?"

"I met Henry for dinner tonight."

Jude tensed against me, his body almost turning cold suddenly. Like my words had somehow sucked the heat out of him.

I walked over to the couch, and Jude followed me, his eyes distant and leery. "He wanted to hire me," I tried to reassure him. "To do a remodel on his house, to add another room for his child."

"What did you tell him?"

"I said no, that I didn't think it was a good idea. He asked if I still thought about us. It was just…fuck, I don't know." I rubbed a hand over my face, not sure what else to do.

"Do you still have feelings for him?"

That got my attention real quick. I dropped my hand and looked at Jude. "Huh?"

"Are you still in love with him? I know it's been a long time, but…" He looked away, but it was too late. I saw it, the fear that I would choose someone else over him, that I would love someone else more than him. It was crazy to think about, that someone as beautiful, both inside and out, could doubt himself. That someone who came off so confident on the surface could feel so alone. Like somehow his father had chosen his sadness over Jude, and that it meant he was less worthy, when that wasn't how any of it worked.

"No, I'm not in love with him. I feel sad for him. I hate that he's lived his life in denial. That he has so much self-loathing inside. I feel bad for his wife and the whole situation, but I don't have feelings for him. Don't you know I'm fucking crazy about you? Ever since you and those goddamned lips of yours came to town, I don't see anyone else."

"All because of my lips?" The corners of said mouth curled up in a smile. It felt intentional, both of us attempting to keep this light.

"Well…not just your lips. Those fucking eyes too. So blue…and your hair. I like it even better now that it's your natural color."

"What…what else?" Jude asked, sucking in a deep breath, then moving toward me, straddling me on the couch.

"Oh, I see what this has turned into. You just want me to compliment you." My hands made a journey up and down his arms. "Your skin. The way it always looks like you've been kissed by the sun." Wrapping my arms around him, I tugged him closer, buried my face in his neck, licked the skin there. "This spot right here."

"That one spot, huh?" he asked breathlessly.

"Well, all the spots." I pushed his shirt up, tugged it off him, splayed my hands over his chest. "I like all these spots too. I like all of you…and I know how much you get off on my hands. Want me to rub you all over with them? It's the least I can do since you let me crash your night."

"The least you can do?" Jude chuckled.

"Or I can just hold them up in front of you if you want. Tease you with them…let you look but I don't touch? I never thought I'd be used for my hands."

"Your arms too. I like those as well."

"Jude gets off on arm porn. Who would have thought?"

"You forgot your back…I like that. Your whole damn body. I look at you and wonder if I was looking for you all along."

I sucked in a sharp breath. I didn't know if he meant me specifically or men in general, but I sure as shit wanted to believe it was the former.

My hands settled on his waist as I looked up at him. "I'm glad you found me, Boyfriend."

Jude leaned forward. This time it was him pressing his forehead to mine. "I want you…but I'm nervous too."

My grip on him tightened as my pulse sped up, and my body felt too sensitized. "There's no reason to be nervous. If you want me, you can have me, but if we never do more than what we do now, that's okay too. There are no expectations here. It doesn't make you more gay to put your cock in my hole than it does my mouth."

It was supposed to be a joke, an attempt to lighten the mood…I thought. I wanted to say it playfully, but I wasn't sure that was how I felt. I didn't like not having control over my emotions, over my feelings in that way.

"That's not what I meant, but now that you said it, how gay does it make me if I want…if I want you to do it to me?"

A groan slipped past my lips, deep and rumbling with the intense hunger I felt for him. Christ, to be inside him... I wasn't sure I would ever be able to leave. But then, I also didn't want him to do this for me because he knew I usually pitched. "Jude..."

"Fuck you, Cam. If you're going to coddle me, then I think it's time for you to go. I know what I want. I've been thinking about it...maybe I've even thought about it before you. But I want it to be with you. If I don't like it—"

"Oh, Beautiful. I can promise you you're going to like it. I'm very, very good at this."

"I don't believe you," he said with a grin, then slid off my lap and stood. "I guess you're going to have to prove it."

"I guess so."

CHAPTER TWENTY-THREE

Jude

Awkward Boy really loves being a part of something…and it's all because of Friendly Man and Construction Guy. ~ Theo's comic

I SHOOK MY wet hair off my forehead, having just gotten out of the shower when Cam arrived.

My damned hands were shaking.

It was one thing to think about this, to admit to myself it was definitely something I was interested in giving a go, and a whole different story to be like, *Hey, Boyfriend, will you fuck me?* Especially when I'd never had a cock in my ass before. My brain was shooting off all sorts of second thoughts, but the rest of me…there was this eagerness building in my gut, this slow buildup of desire that had been brewing for much longer than I'd been willing to admit, telling me, *Yes, you want this. You've always been curious about it.*

The mind's a funny thing. Theo had been right

about that.

"You can change your mind at any time," Cam said as we stood beside the bed.

I thought about the way he said he hadn't seen anyone other than me since I arrived in town. I knew he didn't mean sleep with. Cam had hooked up. He meant *see*, know, crave, and damned if I didn't feel the same about him. It had been so gradual, our friendship…the laughs, the trust. How one day I realized it didn't hurt not to have Rush anymore, that I didn't want him that way, and that maybe, just maybe, I wanted Cam.

The maybe had percolated over time, grown and morphed into this unstoppable need that I wondered how I'd denied for so long.

"I know," I finally managed to reply.

Cam pressed a quick kiss to my lips, then began to unbutton and unzip my jeans.

"You're shaking," I said.

"Shut up." He grinned. "I haven't been nervous to fuck someone since…well, ever."

"It's just me."

"There's no just about it." Then he was pushing my pants and underwear down. My dick was so fucking hard, aching. He knelt as he took my clothes the rest of the way off, then looked up at me from his knees.

"Christ, Jude. You take my damn breath away."

I hissed when he leaned in and kissed one hip bone, then the other. "You make me feel beautiful. My whole life people have said it, but I've never felt it until you."

"I'll tell you every damn day, then," Cam replied. He pushed to his feet and pulled his shirt over his head. It wasn't something I'd admit out loud, but my damn knees went weak, so I sat on the edge of the bed.

I watched Cam as he took off the rest of his clothes, his cock long, stiff, and leaking…and it was going to go inside me. He was going to fuck me.

"Impressive, isn't it? I mean, no matter how many times you've seen it, my dick is still unbelievable."

I laughed. He couldn't have said anything more perfect to ease my nerves.

I grabbed his hand and pulled him closer as I moved backward, situating myself the right way on the bed.

Cam leaned over me, cupped my cheek. "You make me lose my damn head." He smiled, and then he was kissing me. His tongue swept my mouth, familiar and so damn right. I knew his taste and his scent, knew the feel of him, and I savored it all.

Cam gave me his weight, pressing down on me, thrusting his cock against mine as we kissed like this was the last time we would taste each other. My hands traveled up and down his back, taking in the hardness and the muscle there as he moved on top of me. Finally, my journey stopped on his ass.

Eventually, I'd want him too, but I didn't know what it was, why I needed Cam to show me the first time, needed to feel him in a way I'd never felt another person.

"I'm gonna spend a lot of time playing with your hole," he said, and I grinned against his mouth. I was definitely okay with that.

He reached over and grabbed the lube and a condom, setting them on the bed beside us. "Easy access." He winked, and I rolled my eyes but really fucking loved it. Just being with Cam made me feel *good*. "Get on your hands and knees for me, Beautiful."

Cam moved out of the way, and I did as he said. This was slightly embarrassing for me, sitting there with my ass in the air, but it was him, so that made it better. He ran his hands over the curve of my ass, and an excited tremor ran down my spine. Fuck, I wanted this. I really did.

"I'm glad to hear it," Cam said, making me realize I'd spoken aloud.

When he spread my ass cheeks, I had a moment of humiliation, silently acknowledging that someone was looking at my asshole, but then his tongue swiped across my rim. This guttural moan fell from my lips, and I pushed my ass closer to him. Pleasure shot through me, wave after wave cascading through me as he continued to swipe his tongue over my hole.

Fuck, this felt good. Why in the hell did it feel so good?

There was a lot of spit. I felt it as he ate my ass, and then there was a finger pushing in, and more licking and fingering, and oh…there went another one, stretching my hole.

I closed my eyes and just felt, pushed back against Cam as he talked to me. "So fucking beautiful. I can't believe you're with me like this, that I get to see you like this. That you're mine."

I felt like I belonged to Cam in a way I'd never experienced in my life. Like I was his. His tongue swiped over me again.

I whimpered—Jesus, he made me fucking *whimper*—when his tongue was gone. Cam poured lube down my crack and over my hole, and *oh God*, he had three fingers inside me.

"We good?" he asked, keeping still.

I breathed in and out, trying to relax, to settle myself before I nodded. "Yeah…keep going."

"You're hungry for it," he said, sliding his other hand

around me and stroking my cock.

"Fuck yessss." I was. I so fucking was.

Cam kept stretching me, kept fingering me as he jacked me off. Every time I got close to coming, he would stop, would drop his hand and let me come down before he worked me up again.

"Fuck me," I begged after what felt like an eternity, like days and nights had passed and we'd never left the bed. I knew what he was doing, edging me, making me as needy for him as I could get, and while it felt really fucking good, I also wanted him inside me.

"I want it to be good for you," he said, leaning over and kissing between my shoulder blades.

I knew he was saying that because of the obvious—he wanted it to be good for me—but also because his first time hadn't been. "It will be because it's you."

He growled against my skin, then moved to lie under me. I scooted over as Cam went down on his back. He grabbed the condom, ripped it open, and slid it down his cock.

"Let's try it with you on top. It might be easier for you to take it."

I nodded as Cam lubed up, pouring it down his shaft. When I straddled him, my nerves slammed into me full-force. I was sitting on a guy's lap, about to take his cock in my ass.

"Hey…it's just us," he said. "You can do it, Beautiful, and if you don't want to, we stop."

That easily, the tension slipped out of me. "Tell me what to do," I said, even though I hated that I had to ask.

Cam held the base of his cock and angled it toward me. "We're gonna go real slow. We have to work our way in, okay? You can control it. If it's too much, you stop or pull off. Let yourself get used to me inside you."

"Okay."

"When I first start to slide in, I want you to push out. I know that sounds weird, but it will open you up, and the biggest thing outside of that is to try and relax."

Again, I nodded, doing what he said. I lowered myself some, the head of his cock pushing at my rim. I pushed out, tried to open myself up, which was embarrassing as hell, as I slowly went down, trying to take him in.

The initial breach was intense, this pressure and burn as he started to push in.

"Fuck…*fuck*," I gritted out.

"Ease off if you want. You're in control, remember?"

So I did, before we tried again…and again. Every time I'd begin to lower myself, take him inside me, it was nothing but discomfort, and I wondered how in the hell anyone could like this, want this.

"Do you want to stop? You can fuck me, or we can do something else. There's no rush, Beautiful."

I didn't want to stop. I wanted this, wanted *him* more than I'd ever wanted anything in my life. "I don't want to stop. I just…want you."

"You're in control," Cam said again, and the second he said it, I knew that was what it was. I didn't want to be in control in that moment. I wanted Cam to take me, fuck me, make me feel wanted.

"What if I don't want to be?" My voice shook as I said it, but I had never been more sure of anything. Cam's dark eyes flared with heat, and his lips pulled into a sexy fucking grin.

"That can definitely be arranged." Before I realized what was happening, his arm was around me and he was flipping me. Suddenly I was on my back and Cam leaned over me, his mouth crushing mine in a searing, bruising kiss I felt in my soul.

I reached for him when he pulled back, but he said, "I'm not going anywhere."

Cam rolled me to my side, told me to bend my top leg and raise it up toward my chest. I did so as he lubed himself more, then his fingers. When he pushed them inside me, rubbed my prostate, I damn near melted into the mattress.

He was spooning me from behind…and then it was Cam in control, Cam slowly pushing in, trying to penetrate me. I wasn't going to lie and say it didn't still hurt, but then with the tip of his cock inside me, he reached around me, his arm across my chest, and grabbed my face, tilting my head back toward him, and kissed me…and fuck…fuck, that helped.

His tongue took possession of my mouth as his dick worked its way inside me. I felt dizzy with lust. Protected by him, wanted—no, *needed*—and damn, did that feel good. Before I knew it, his groin was against my ass, and I felt full, so fucking full.

"Christ, this is my favorite place to be. We might need to do this all the time…like all day every day."

I chuckled, and he gasped. "You're going to make me come. You're so damn tight around me."

"Are you planning on moving?"

"Patience. I waited this long for you. You can wait too."

He kissed my lips, the back of my neck, and breathed. He was obviously trying to get himself under control, and then he grabbed my cock, stroked me as he pulled out slightly and thrust forward again.

Cam took me slowly, tenderly, working me up and making me crazy for him. I'd never felt so connected to another person. I licked my lips and tasted my own sweat, and he was wet with it too. He jacked me as he slowly fucked me until I was trembling and begging him to make me come.

Cam fucked into me harder, our bodies slapping together. "So good...so damn good, Beautiful. Christ, this ass. I'm never going to get enough of it."

I cried out when his teeth bit into my shoulder. My orgasm crashed into me, my eyes rolling back and my body jittery as I emptied my balls all over his hand and the bed.

"Oh fuck," he gasped, and then he slammed in, his body tensed, and he moaned, no doubt filling the condom with his own load, as our breaths mingled.

It was uncomfortable when he pulled out of me. He rolled over to drop the condom in the trash, and then his arms wrapped around me again, his mouth close to my ear. "Was it okay?" he asked, vulnerable.

"It was incredible."

"*Duh.*" He buried his face in my neck. "Go to Florida with me for Christmas."

My heart nearly beat out of my chest, too many thoughts to focus on just one, spinning around in my head. "You want me to go to your parents' house for Christmas? You want me to meet your family?"

"Why wouldn't I?"

Because I'd never had a family outside of Rush's.

But then I thought about my dad, about him spending another holiday alone, and damned if that loneliness didn't transfer to me. "I, um…can I talk to my dad first? I don't want him to be alone."

Cam nodded, but I could tell he was disappointed. He understood, obviously, but still. "He can come too. The more the merrier."

"He won't." We would get him to Rush's when we were kids, but that was about it.

We didn't talk after that, just lay there holding each other, Cam only pulling away to turn out the light.

CHAPTER TWENTY-FOUR

Camden

So, I'm finally going to end this.
~ Letter from Henry

"It's Saturgay, bitches!" Lincoln shouted like he was known to do.

"Why does he insist on saying that every month?" Beau asked.

"Because it gets on your nerves, Husband," Ash replied.

"I'm kind of jealous I don't get to say it," Carter added.

Lincoln countered with, "Back off my shit. I'm the resident twink in this group!"

"Lord help us," Sawyer said, and I chuckled.

"Lord help you guys. My boyfriend is normal." There was a swell of pride in my chest at calling Jude my boyfriend, and ya know, it being real now.

"Aww, Camden hearts Jude! Isn't that so sweet,"

Linc joked, and I grabbed him, ruffling his hair because I knew he hated it.

"Shut up, Short Stuff!"

"Ugh! I hate you!" He jerked away from me. "Rush! Get him!"

"You're on your own, Red," Rush answered, and everyone laughed.

I wished Jude were with us. He was already at Fever working, but luckily he was getting off earlier tonight, so at least he wouldn't be behind the bar the entire time. It was early December, and our last Saturgay before the New Year and before Rush would miss it since he would be racing. I knew Linc missed him while he was gone. It was something I'd often teased him about, but now I got it. I'd sure as shit miss Jude if he had to leave every weekend for months on end.

"Are the rest of the guys meeting us there?" Ash asked.

"Yeah," Carter answered. "Dax had a late meeting, and then he had some stuff to take care of with Jace, which I take it to mean fucking."

We made our way into Fever, heading straight to the bar Jude was always working behind. It was busy, a crowd of guys around it, but his eyes shot up and landed right on me.

"Holy shit. It's like he suddenly just knew you were here," Sawyer said, and I winked at him.

"That's because we're good like that, BB."

Sawyer pretended to puke, you know, just a normal night with our crew.

"The party started. We have arrived!" Dax said as they approached.

"Do we know you?" Carter asked. "And that sounds like something I would say…or have said. Stop trying to be like me."

"He was just showing you how ridiculous it sounds," Jace said.

Dax looked at him. "Thanks…wait. I think. Are you saying I sounded ridiculous?"

"If the shoe fits…" I teased.

"God, I love us. I hope we never change. Dear Gay Jesus, never let our group change!" Lincoln threw his hands in the air as if praying.

Everyone began chatting after that, but my eyes found their way back to Jude. He was taking money from someone, and then a group walked away, so I headed over to take their spot. "Hey, Beautiful."

"Hey, Boyfriend," he replied, and I clutched my heart.

"Aww, you have a nickname for me now. I mean, it's

one you stole from me, but still. Best boyfriend ever."

Jude laughed and shook his head, and there was more fake-vomiting, which told me Sawyer and the rest of the crew had approached.

We all ordered drinks and chatted for a little while. Linc and Rush danced and had a crowd around them—all eyes on the duo, which Linc loved and Rush loved to give him. Linc was a bit of a praise slut, always had been. Luckily, that got Rush off too.

Jude was busy and didn't have a lot of time to talk. I couldn't help but wonder what was on his mind. We hadn't spoken about Christmas again, but it had only been a few days since I'd asked him. I still couldn't believe he'd asked me to fuck him. You could have knocked me over with a feather, I'd been so surprised. And the way he'd responded… *Christ*, the way he'd responded was every fucking thing. He'd been sore the next day and was embarrassed, but I'd spoiled him and he'd let me. The damn man made me crazy in the best possible ways.

"Um…hello? Earth to Cam?" a female voice said from beside me, snapping me out of my Jude trance.

"Hey, Mel. How's it going?" I gave her a hug, which she returned. "Sorry, I was spacing out."

"Looking at the pretty boy."

I grinned. "Yeah, something like that."

Jude caught eyes with us then and walked over. "You guys need anything else?"

"You?" I teased, and he blushed.

"Be good, Boyfriend."

Oh, I liked that. Apparently, he was going to use the name more often now.

"Oh wow," Melinda said. "This is new."

"I finally wore him down."

"I put up a good fight," Jude replied.

"Aren't you guys the fucking cutest," Linc said. "Well, not as cute as us, obvi!"

I shook my head and looked at Melinda again. "What are you doing tonight?"

"I'm meeting up with someone. You aren't the only bi-guy in town who likes to have a little ménage fun."

A glass dropped from Jude's hand and shattered on the floor.

"Nooooo!" Linc said. "Jude, you naughty boy!"

"Eh, I don't need threesomes anymore. I have my own sex beast," Carter said.

"Jude didn't have a threesome with Cam and Melinda," Rush added, and we hadn't, but it surprised me that he knew it.

"How do you know?" Jude asked him.

"Because I know you?" Rush replied.

And yeah…he did. I was uncharacteristically jealous of that.

"And I know you too." Rush looked at me. "You've wanted him too much for too long to share him."

Well, shit. That was nice. And he was right. Sure, I'd invited Jude home with us that night, but it would have been strange for me to see someone else touch him. I sure as shit didn't want anyone's hands on him now, and since Rush didn't know when we were talking about, it made sense.

"Can we stop talking about my sex life now?" Jude asked.

Which we did. Jude cleaned up the broken glass and then had another round of business at the bar. We all laughed and drank, but I couldn't keep my eyes off him. I never could when he was around.

Eventually, he got off work. He went to the back to clock out, and then I felt him beside me.

"Hey," I whispered, leaning in and kissing him.

Jude put his arm around me. "Hey."

"Get a room," Ash teased.

"Fuck off." I gave him the bird.

Linc was right. We were awesome. I hoped our group never changed.

"You wanna dance with me?" I cocked a brow at Jude, and he paused for a moment, then nodded. Taking his hand, I led him over to the dance floor. I pulled him up behind me and pushed my ass against his groin. His hands automatically went to my waist and held on as he moved against me.

"Mmm, I like this," Jude said.

"We can do it naked too."

"Yeah? We will. I…liked it the way we did it last time as well."

Oh, Jude was going to be a hungry little bottom. How in the fuck did I get so lucky?

"We'll do it again. We need to give you a little time first."

Jude nodded, pressed his cock against me, and we danced. Through song after song we stayed out there. I'd never danced with him like this before, and I sure as shit didn't want it to end anytime soon.

He moved like he felt alive, like he was confident, and hell, almost like he was putting on a show. When a few guys looked at us and made comments, I was nervous he would stop, but he didn't. It just fueled him on more.

Eventually, we made it back to our crew.

"That was hot," Carter said.

"Um…you're aware that's my brother, right?" Sawyer asked.

"Your hot brother and his even hotter boyfriend," Carter replied, and Sawyer laughed.

"What am I going to do with you?" Sawyer leaned in and kissed him, obviously crazy about Carter.

"Can we go back to the part where you said Jude is hotter than me?" I teased.

"I think Linc and I are going to head out in a minute," Rush said. "But while we're all together, I wanted to see if you guys wanted to do something for Christmas like we did for Thanksgiving? Have the whole crew, families and all, out at our place?" He looked at Jude. "Mom called your dad to invite him. I was shocked he said yes."

Well, I guessed that answered my question about Christmas. Jude wouldn't go to Florida if his father was in Fever Falls.

"Sawyer and I are going to Florida," I replied, disappointment heavy in my chest.

"I'm going with Sawyer," Carter added.

Rush turned to Jude. "Oh shit. Were you going to go to Florida too? Maybe we can do something early, before Christmas or something? Mom just didn't want your dad to be alone, and she assumed… Fuck, we shouldn't have assumed." There wasn't a doubt in my mind that it had been a simple accident. Rush was used to holidays with Jude. Rush's mom knew Jude's dad. They *were* family, but again, that didn't stop the disappointment from working through my veins, heavy like mud.

"I was going to talk to Dad first." Jude looked at me, and I could see it—that he felt stuck, not wanting to hurt my feelings.

"It's fine. We'll figure it out," I replied, and Jude grabbed my hand.

"Let me get back to you," Jude said to Rush, who nodded.

We all went our own ways from there. Jude and I walked back to his condo, and I wished for some reason that we were staying at my place. I liked Jude around my things.

He locked the door behind us and went to the kitchen. "Want some water?"

"Sure," I replied as I looked down at the table. There were drawings there. Hell, probably about twenty of them, characters I didn't recognize, and logos. "What's this?"

"Oh, it's stupid. I used to draw a lot when I was younger. I considered going to school for it, but then with my dad…I just followed in his footsteps. Seeing

Theo's comics inspired me. I've been playing around, just for fun."

"Jude, you're really fucking good," I told him, and he was. I sure as shit couldn't draw like he did.

"You think?"

"Hell yes."

"Eh." He shrugged, and then surprised me when he wrapped his arms around me and leaned his head against my chest. "I want to be with you for Christmas. Hell, I want to be with you all the damn time. You know that, right?"

And honestly, I did. Realistically, I didn't doubt that. Sometimes my emotions got in the way, though. "Yeah, I know. But…?" Because I knew there was one coming.

"I don't know if I'm ready to come out to my father. I know that sounds crazy. I'm a grown-ass man. It shouldn't matter, but this is so new, so right, and there's this strange part of me that isn't ready to open that up yet. It's like I want to protect it."

"You're open with me in public all the time."

"Yeah, around our friends or at a gay bar or on Fever Street. Or hell, around people I don't know, but this is different. This is…"

His father. His family. And it was a big deal. I got that. I really did. Even people who knew their parents would be okay with their sexuality, sometimes were scared to come out. It wasn't something you could explain to people who hadn't experienced it. It was letting someone in to the most intimate part of yourself and knowing they might judge you for it.

Jude added, "Maybe we can do two holidays, like Rush said."

I shook my head. "That's silly. It's not a big deal. Do I want you there? Yeah. But do I get that you're not ready? I do, and obviously your dad would wonder why you were inviting him to Florida with my family. My parents would take one look at us and know. They aren't the best at keeping secrets."

"I feel like I'm letting you down…hell, like I'm letting me down."

"Cut yourself some slack. No one is rushing you here."

He nodded, then pressed his forehead to mine. "Do you know how incredible you are?"

"The best," I teased.

"I'm being serious."

"I know you are."

"I don't know what I would do without you. From the moment I moved here, you've been there for me."

"I'm not going anywhere."

"Well…why would you, when I'm so much hotter than you?" he teased, and I fucking loved it. Jude needed to own that shit. It meant a lot to me that he felt comfortable enough to do it around me.

Still, I wasn't going to let that go. I swatted his ass. "Take it back."

"I can't help it if I'm beautiful." Jude waggled his eyebrows at me.

I reached for him, and he began to run. I went after him, playfully tackling him to the bed. I straddled his hips and held his arms down, not that he was fighting me.

He looked up at me, and there was something different in his eyes. Something deep and intense that reached out and grabbed at my chest. "You're beautiful," he whispered. "So fucking beautiful, it steals my breath sometimes. I'm so lucky you're mine."

We stripped out of our clothes and sucked each other off.

And as we held each other, naked and sweaty and sated, there was no doubt in my mind anymore. I was in love with Jude Sandoval.

CHAPTER TWENTY-FIVE

Jude

Awkward Boy feels…hopeful. And like he's ready to take on a new challenge. ~ Theo's comic

"How's Cam?" Theo asked me as we sat at the table in my condo, drawing.

"He's good." And he was. It had been a few days since we'd had our talk about Christmas, and I hadn't stopped thinking about it. The truth was, I *did* want to spend the holiday with Cam, and I felt like I was letting him down, but fuck, I was nervous too. About making it real by telling my father, and meeting his family, and opening myself up to all sorts of shit I'd never let myself risk before. Opening myself up to losing someone I loved and being even more alone than before. I wasn't good at that, didn't really know how to do it, but I wanted to, for him.

I added, "The holiday party at the LGBTQ center is this coming weekend."

"Oh…cool. What do you think of this?" Theo pushed over his sketchbook and showed me a bit of Awkward Boy's newest adventure. He was making a decision about something that could either be the best thing to happen to him, or could end in disaster.

"I think it's great. Does this have anything to do with the party?"

"Maybe," Theo replied, which I thought meant yes. "What if I see someone I know? Or what if it gets out? What if Trey hates me, or what if my mom asks where I'm going, or what if she hates me too?"

Fuck, this shouldn't have to be so goddamned hard. "There are no easy answers, Theo. I wish there were. I still haven't told my father about Cam and me. Part of me doesn't even understand why I'm not doing it. It's not like he plays a big part in my life or like he's ever had a problem with Rush. Hell, I'm not sure he knows how to care about anything anymore."

But part of me was scared I would make it harder for him to start caring about me, as fucked up as that was.

"I know. I get it. We really need to figure this shit out."

I cocked a brow at Theo for his curse word.

"Stuff. Figure this stuff out."

I couldn't help but laugh. "Yeah, we do." There I

was, trying to work out how to come out, and discussing my relationship with a seventeen-year-old kid.

"I think…I think I want to go. To the party, I mean. I don't know if I want to tell my mom yet, but the party…that will be with other people like us. Or who are allies to people like us."

"Yeah, yeah it will. And if you decide to go, you'll go with Cam and me. And if you want to leave at any time, we'll leave. But I only want you to do it if you want to."

Theo nodded but didn't answer right away. He looked down at the motocross piece I was working on, maybe something for a T-shirt or something like that. "You're good."

"Thanks. I'm thinking about curving the wording around the bike, like a circle, but make it look like a tire. What do you think?"

Theo grinned as though it meant something to him that I'd asked his opinion. I knew it had, and I valued what he had to say.

"I think that would be awesome."

We began drawing again for a little while. I lost myself in what I was doing, enjoying something I'd shoved away years ago. Why hadn't I drawn more? Why had I stopped?

I had no idea how much time had passed, when

Theo asked, "Are you spending time with Cam for Christmas?"

The question was like a knife sliding into my chest. Jesus, I still felt like shit about that. "We'll do something together either before or after. I'll be at Rush's for the holiday. My dad is coming down."

"And you're still not ready to come out? Do you think you might at Christmas?"

I sighed, trying to decide how to answer—or hell, if I even knew what I thought or what I was doing. "It's not that I don't want to come out. It's not even that I'm ashamed or anything. It's hard to put into words. What I have with Cam is different from what I've had with anyone, and not even just because he's a man. And I'm…shit, I'm afraid of losing that."

"How does being public about it mean you'll lose it? And might you lose it since you aren't coming out?"

Damn it. He was on a roll with difficult questions today. "Cam understands." At least for now he did. I hoped he did. "I'm figuring out everything still. And maybe I'll tell my dad over the holiday. I don't know."

I could see Theo still had questions. So I waited, nodded at him so he'd know it was okay.

"Are you like…in love with him or whatever?"

My heart swooped, and one word came to mind: *yes.*

I was so fucking in love with Camden Burke. What I felt for him was different from what I'd felt for Rush. Loving Cam was something my body knew I needed like food or air. "I am, but I haven't told him yet."

"So even after you're in love with someone it's hard to come out? I'm screwed."

His question sort of hit me, slammed through this wall I had inside me. A wall I'd built myself. Theo was right in so many ways. I had Camden, and that was the most important thing. There were others who had nothing. Not someone they were in love with or the kind of friends I had.

I'd spent so long feeling alone and like I didn't belong, but I knew I belonged with him. I wanted to protect what we had, but how did I do that by hurting him? By denying us to the only family I had? "Shit, kid. You're pretty smart."

"I've heard that a time or two," Theo teased.

"I think…I think I'm going to talk to my dad when he gets here. I'm going to tell him about me." That still meant spending the holiday apart, but I felt like this was something I should talk to my dad about in person. I also didn't want him to be alone on the holiday, and I knew he wouldn't go to Florida.

"Wow…I'm good."

"Shut up." I ruffled his hair and felt like Cam when he did the same to Lincoln. "Thank you for talking me through this."

"Yeah…I thought everything automatically fell into place when you became an adult."

I laughed. "I wish. It's okay to struggle. We all do, no matter how old we are."

Theo was quiet for a moment, then looked at me and said, "I want to go to the party for sure—like for sure, sure."

"Are you sure?" I asked, then realized how many times we'd used that word and smiled.

"Yes. I don't want… I don't want to feel alone anymore. I mean, you and Cam are great. You're like totally the best, but I want…"

"Want to know kids your own age who are like you. There's something to be said for community. It's understandable. And I'm very proud of you."

"I'm proud of you too!" he replied, and I laughed.

We continued to draw. I ended up with a new piece of paper, and before I noticed what I was doing, my hands were sketching a cartoon Camden…then a cartoon me. It was silly, and yeah, I was slightly embarrassed, but I kept going, let myself enjoy creating.

"It's good," Theo said after a while. "You should give

it to him."

"I can't give this to him." I wasn't twelve.

"Why not? Would it be silly if I gave you my comics?"

What was with him today? The more I thought about it, the more I knew he was right. In so many ways, Cam was always the one putting himself out there with me. If it hadn't been for him pushing it, we likely would have never become the kind of friends we had.

"Okay. Maybe I will. Do you think he'll laugh at me?" I teased, making Theo chuckle.

"No, he won't laugh at you. If he does, I'll meet him in the hallway after school."

That made me grin, and as I looked at him, it hit me how much he meant to me, how much I enjoyed spending time with him. I'd always wanted siblings, wanted a family to feel less alone, and now I had that, not only with our friends, but in Theo as well.

"Hey…thank you."

Theo's nose wrinkled. "For what?"

"For being my friend…for being like a little brother to me. I always wanted a little brother, and now I have one."

I worried his face would split, his smile was so damn big. "I…I always wanted a big brother too."

"Come here, kid." I stood and pulled him into a hug, which he returned. It took a moment, but then I noticed he was crying softly. Theo wiped his face and pulled away, obviously embarrassed.

"I should like, go or whatever. I have this…thing I have to do."

"Okay. I'll be in touch about the party."

Theo grabbed his stuff and headed out.

My thoughts automatically went to what I'd told Theo. I wanted to tell my dad. Cam was worth the risk, but I wasn't sure I should tell Cam that. Would it only disappoint him if something went wrong?

That made me realize I missed him, that I wanted to spend as much time with him as I could. I didn't let myself overthink it, just put on my jacket and grabbed my keys, phone, and the drawing, and went out the door.

CHAPTER TWENTY-SIX

Camden

I have to end it... ~ Letter from Henry

I WAS BEAT.

It had been a long-ass day at work. One of my men had been sick, and we were working on a tough job. My mind hadn't quite been in the game as it should have been either, hadn't been since Saturgay, as frustrating as it was. I didn't want to be upset with Jude in any way, but I thought maybe I was. Which made me feel guilty because I didn't believe in pushing anyone to come out, and he was spending a holiday with his father. How could I be upset with him over that?

God, I wanted to spend the holiday with him, though. I wanted to cement what I had with him because I was so damn scared he didn't feel the same...or scared that even if he did, he would decide this wasn't something he could do. That it was too much. That no matter how he felt, he wouldn't want to be with a man, be with me. It wasn't like that hadn't happened to me before.

Usually I ended up at his condo after work, at least for dinner or something, but I just didn't have it in me that night. Not because I was angry or didn't want to be around him—the fucker. I always wanted to be around him, but again, I was exhausted. It had been a long day.

I was looking in the fridge, trying to decide what to eat before I went to take a shower, when there was a knock at the door.

The only person who typically showed up without being expected was Sawyer, so I closed the fridge, and assuming it was him, pulled the door open. "What do you want—oh. It's you," I said when I saw Jude standing there. "I figured you were my brother."

"Thank God I'm not." He cocked a brow at me, then held out the pizza in his hands. "Have you already eaten?"

"No, and I'm fucking starving. You're a lifesaver." I let Jude inside, and he went straight for the table, setting the pizza on it. "This is a surprise."

"It is, isn't it?" His forehead wrinkled as if he was putting more thought into this than what I'd meant for it. But the truth was, Jude rarely came to my place, and he certainly didn't just show up here the way I sometimes did with him. "You look tired."

"I am. I had a long day."

"Do you want me to go?"

"Are you crazy? I'm taking advantage of this shit," I teased.

"Sit down. I'll grab beer and plates."

"There are paper plates on the counter next to the toaster if you want to make it easy." I had no idea what had gotten into Jude, but I sure as shit wasn't going to turn down a little spoiling. "I'm going to clean up real quick. I'll be right back."

I was dirty and needed to get my ass in the shower, but I was also hungry as hell, so I took my shoes and socks off, then went into the bathroom and washed my hands and arms. When I made it back out, Jude was sitting at the six-person farm-style table, with the pizza box open and a plate with slices in front of him and one for me. He'd grabbed us each one of the IPAs, which sounded really fucking good right about then.

"Thank you for this. I was probably going to eat stale bread if you hadn't shown up."

"Or ordered dinner."

"Yeah, but doesn't it feel better if I make it sound like you saved the day? I always like it when people do that with me."

Jude chuckled, that rich, earthy laugh I liked so

much.

"How was your day?" I asked.

"Good. I spent a couple of hours with Theo. He wants to go to the party with us, by the way."

"No shit?" I took a bite of my pizza.

"Yeah, we had a good talk, figured some stuff out. Jesus, he's a good kid."

I nodded. I liked Theo a lot too, and I was glad he'd found Jude. Hell, I was glad Jude had him as well. "And you're still okay with it? Going to the center?"

The question made Jude frown. "Why wouldn't I be?"

I'd been thinking all sorts of thoughts lately. It was a lot, and maybe he wanted to go back to a time when he didn't have to *come out* just because he was dating someone specific. It wasn't something he would have to do once either. He would have to do it over and over again, for as long as we were together. Fuck, why did shit have to be so complicated? Why the hell couldn't people just love whoever they wanted without having to explain themselves?

"No reason," I said. "Just making sure."

We didn't talk much as we ate. When we finished, I stood and stretched. "I really need to get my ass in the shower. I probably stink. I might not be the best company tonight, but I'd like you to stay."

"You're always good company."

"True." I grinned, then pressed a kiss to his lips. "I'll be back."

"Does that mean I'm not invited?"

Oh, well, hello there. Someone was in a naughty mood. "You're always invited. I love Naked-Jude time."

He chuckled and said to get started while he put the pizza away. I went to my room and turned the shower on before stripping out of my clothes. I was just stepping inside when Jude joined me in the en suite, pulling his shirt over his head as he did so. "I think this suddenly is my favorite day," I teased, making Jude's cheeks tinge pink.

"Shut up and get in the shower, Boyfriend. I'm gonna take care of you."

"Yes, sir. That's definitely something I can get behind." I had no idea what had gotten into him, but I liked it. Maybe I'd been overreacting. Maybe Jude and I were fine and he was already working through things.

He joined me a moment later. My eyes scanned his body, his tight six-pack abs. His cock, which was slowly growing, nestled in the short, dark hair at his groin. All that golden skin and those eyes and those lips and… "I'm suddenly not so tired anymore." I wagged my eyebrows.

"Be good."

"But it's no fun to be good."

"How am I supposed to spoil you, then?"

Crossing my arms, I pretended to pout. "Fine."

Jude just rolled his eyes at me before plucking my sponge off the hook on the wall. "Sponge?"

"I like my sponge, thank you very much."

He reached for my bodywash next, poured some on the sponge, and began soaping me up. I savored the feel of him, watching him as he concentrated like he was taking care of something treasured.

Jude finished with my chest and stomach before kneeling and washing my legs, thighs… I hissed when he got to my groin, as he rubbed the sponge over my balls and my quickly hardening cock. "Wanna suck it while you're down there?" I teased.

"I thought we were being good?"

"You told me to be good. I never agreed."

He chuckled and stood, and I pouted playfully again. Jude finished, and I stood under the spray to rinse off. From there he went to shampoo, washing my hair.

"Are we going to have naked time now?" I asked when he turned off the shower and we got out.

"You're relentless."

"You're beautiful."

"And I'm trying to be a good boyfriend here. You do a lot for me, and I wanted to make sure you know I care about you too. I want to make sure I'm giving you as much as you give me."

My pulse slammed against my skin as we stood there naked, dripping water all over the floor. "Hey." I hooked my thumb beneath his chin and turned his head so he faced me. "We're okay. You don't have to try and prove yourself to me." Maybe it wasn't all ideal, but I just wanted him. I'd take him any way I could have him.

"What if I want to do this? What if it feels good to give you something?"

Damn it. There was no way I could keep from smiling. "Then I would say why aren't you drying me off yet?"

Jude laughed, which was what I'd been hoping he would do.

"This doesn't mean you can get bossy."

"Ugh. Fine. Whatever."

So I stood there and watched him as he dried me off. I really wanted to know what was going on in that head of his, because it was obvious there was something. When he was finished, I said, "Naked time in bed. We can watch *The 100*. Have you seen it? I've heard good things."

"Nope, I haven't. Sounds good to me."

My bed wasn't made because I didn't trust people who made their beds every day. We walked over, and that's when I saw a piece of paper on my bedside table. "What's this?" I asked, picking it up. I knew exactly what it was—him and me, standing together, little cartoon versions of us.

"Something I was doodling earlier. Theo said I should give it to you. I thought it made me sound twelve."

I studied it. He was good, of course I noticed that, and it was sweet and so damn simple, but it made me feel like a fucking king or something.

"You're not talking. Why aren't you talking?"

I smiled. "I think this might be the coolest thing I've ever seen. I love it. Theo was right. Thank you."

"Oh God. I would die if anyone else saw me right now."

But he didn't die that I saw him.

Jude walked over and wrapped his arms around my waist. He leaned his forehead against my chest. "I know I'm a bit of a mess with all this. I'm sorting things out, making some decisions, but I want to wait before I say anything about it. I really want us to be okay, though."

"We're okay. Whenever you're ready. I'm staying right here."

This was different from what happened with Henry. Jude wasn't ashamed. Jude didn't hide me away. I could wait for him.

"Come on. Let's get in bed and watch this show." Jude climbed into my bed.

I grabbed the TV remote, turned off the light, and followed him.

CHAPTER TWENTY-SEVEN

Jude

With Construction Guy and Friendly Man by his side, there's nothing Awkward Boy can't do.
~ Theo's comic

CAM AND I had had a long talk about Theo and the party at the center. I'd even gone to Mama K for advice because we weren't sure what to do about the fact that Theo didn't want his mom to know he was going.

While we understood his reasoning, we didn't feel comfortable straight out lying to her or allowing him to lie to her with our knowledge. No matter what, he was a child and she was his mom. On the other hand, we had to protect Theo's best interests. We couldn't risk him being forced to come out when he didn't know how she would react. He didn't believe she would disown him or anything like that, though he didn't know for sure. But being around other LGBTQ kids was good for Theo's mental health.

In the end we decided he needed to tell her where he was going. He didn't have to say why. I told him I could speak with her if he needed me to. Cam had offered the same. We could say he was volunteering at the event with us, which was still a little white lie, but the truth too. Cam was helping out, and Theo would be helping Cam.

Theo hadn't wanted us to talk to her with him. He'd wanted to do that on his own.

There was a knock at the door, and when I opened it, Theo stood there with his mom, who looked slightly flustered.

"Hi, I'm Jude. This is Cam."

She shook both our hands. "Annie. Nice to meet you both."

"Thanks for letting Theo go with us. He's a great kid."

"He is a good kid, isn't he?" She looked at him and smiled, making me soften up a bit toward her. Maybe she was like my father. She loved her son, just didn't do a good job showing it.

"It's been really neat to get to know him. He's a wonderful artist, and he got me back into drawing as well. I always wanted a kid brother," I told her, and received another genuine smile.

"Theo always wanted siblings too. He said you're like a big brother to him. I appreciate you spending so much time with him. Video games aren't my thing." She laughed before continuing. "He doesn't get along well with his father and never wants to see him. It's good for him to get out more."

Maybe you should get out with him more…spend more time with him…

And hell, I hadn't even realized Theo's father was in the picture. He never mentioned him.

Her phone began to ring, and she looked at it. "Shit. I have to take this. I gave Theo some money. Thank you again." That simply, Annie was gone.

"She's in a hurry. She's always in a hurry," Theo said, his jaw tight.

"Yeah, but she let you come with us. I'm glad about that."

"It wouldn't have been the same without you, kid." Cam smiled at him. "Looking handsome, by the way."

Theo blushed. He was wearing black jeans, a white button-up shirt…and his beanie.

"You guys look nice too," Theo replied.

"I look great. Jude looks okay," Cam teased.

Cam looked fucking gorgeous in a vest and bow tie, and the way he couldn't keep his hands off me earlier, I was pretty sure he agreed with my similar outfit.

The three of us left after that, taking my car for the short ride to the center. I parked around back, and we sat in the car for a moment.

"You doing okay?" I asked Theo.

"Yeah…I'm scared as shit, though. I mean, I'm scared. Just scared. What if I talk too much and people think I'm weird or no one likes me or…"

"Everyone will like you," I told him.

"Trey is excited to meet you," Cam added. "All our friends are as well."

"And again, if you want to leave, we leave. It's that simple."

Theo nodded, but I wasn't sure he believed us.

Camden said, "Hey, you're doing great. This is a big step. Cut yourself some slack, okay? Awkward Boy is the best, and a whole lot less awkward than he realizes. Everyone will see that. Just ask Construction Guy. He's smart as fuck."

That made Theo laugh and me fall a little more in love with him.

Cam looked at me next. "Do I need to give you a pep talk too, Beautiful? Because I will." He reached out and cupped my cheek. "You good?"

"Rock steady. It's safe here." It felt different in this

environment and with our friends than it did with others.

He frowned slightly, making me think I said the wrong thing, but then he grinned and dropped his hand. I must have imagined it.

"Okay, let's do this, gentlemen," he said, and he was the first to get out of the car.

I looked back at Theo one more time and gave him a reassuring smile before we got out too.

There was a single rainbow flag hanging off the building with a sign out front. Theo walked quickly, with his head down, and my heart went out to him. I was sorting shit out in my own head at my age. It had to be even tougher at seventeen.

Camden held the door open and signaled for us to go in. When we gave the tickets to the woman at the front, Cam said, "Aren't I lucky? I'm escorting the two most handsome men tonight." Then winked. Theo blushed, and I rolled my eyes, but really, he turned me all gooey inside.

We heard music in the distance, and Cam led us through the room and down some stairs, to a large open space with a DJ, food, drinks, and tons of people singing and dancing. There was a large Christmas tree at the front of the room, which Cam had told me about before.

They had a list online where you could buy gifts for LGBTQ teens. They were all stacked beneath it, and damn, there were so many of them. It made me proud that our town had stepped up, or at least part of it had, but also sad, wondering how many of those kids were homeless or couldn't be out in their personal life.

"Oh yay! Cam, Jude, and Theo are here!" Linc said as he, Rush, and Trey came toward us.

Theo clutched my arm.

"We good?" I asked him, and he nodded.

"Well, don't you guys look nice. Not as good as me, except you." Linc looked at Theo. "You look fab. You must be Theo. I'm Lincoln." They shook hands. "This is my boyfriend, Rush, and our friend Trey."

Trey had his nails painted red and green for Christmas with matching glitter around his eyes, which popped against his smooth, brown skin.

"Hey. It's great to meet you. We've heard a lot about you," Rush said. "This guy can't shut up about you." He pointed to me, and Theo smiled.

"Yeah, I've heard a lot about you too!" Trey told him. "I've been really excited to meet you. I'm glad you came tonight. Do you hug? I like hugs," Trey added, and I was pretty sure Theo was going to burst out of his skin, the way his eyes sparked and excited energy radiated off him.

"Yeah. Hugs are cool," Theo replied. Trey wrapped him up, and I couldn't help but feel warmth in my chest as Theo returned it. "I like your stuff…like the glitter? It looks really cool. I've never done something like that. I don't know if I want to, but I like it on you. I mean, not *you*, you, just anyone. Not that I don't like it on *you*, you, it's just—Oh my *God*."

Cam put his hands on Theo's shoulders and gave them a squeeze. "I like the glitter too," he said, and again, the support made my chest swell.

"Thanks. I used to totally be nervous to wear stuff like this. I was bullied a lot at school and didn't know any other queer people, but then when I was in the hospital fighting cancer, I met Linc. He showed me it was okay to be who I am."

"And you're pretty damn fabulous," Linc concurred.

"Wow, that's…amazing. You've been through a lot," Theo said.

"Do you want to go get something to drink? Then we can find a table to talk?" Trey asked him, and Theo turned to look at me.

"You can go. We'll be around."

"Thanks, Jude!" And then the two of them were off, and it was…pretty fucking incredible.

"It's a good thing you guys are doing," Rush told us.

"He's a great kid," I replied. "Like the little brother I never had."

Rush reached over, wrapped one arm around me, and gave me a squeeze. He knew I'd wanted siblings when we were kids, a bigger family. "It's funny how things work out sometimes."

Yeah, it was. When Rush and I finished embracing, I reached for Cam. "Thank you."

He frowned. "What are you thanking me for?"

"Everything." I tugged on his hand. "Let's go dance."

Cam nodded. "Lead the way, Beautiful."

We danced for a little while, but both of us were more interested in Theo. We kept watching him and talking about him.

"Oh, he's laughing!" I said.

"He does that a lot," Cam teased.

"He doesn't laugh with another boy his age who likes boys, though, does he?"

"No, I guess he doesn't."

The two of them didn't dance, but they did talk the whole night. When the rest of the crew showed up, I introduced them to Theo and they said hi to Trey, but we left them alone. It was good for Theo, getting out like this, and I wanted to make sure he had all the time he could.

We all chatted about the holidays and made final plans. Rush asked Cam, Sawyer, and Carter if we should plan something another day for all of us, but Cam said it wasn't necessary. I was a little surprised by that, but then Cam and I would be spending time together regardless, so I figured that's why he'd said it.

"Mom tried to get your dad to stay at my place, since your condo is only one-bedroom, but he wouldn't have it," Rush told me.

"Are we really surprised? I told him he can stay with me too, but he wanted a hotel. Likes his space." Which meant his solitude. I didn't know if we even knew how to talk to each other anymore, or what we would say. He didn't know me. Didn't know why I left Virginia or that I'd been depressed or that I'd hated my job. All he knew was I'd lived there and now I lived here and was a bartender. He didn't ask questions.

We stayed until the party ended, and as we were saying goodbye, I saw Trey and Theo putting their numbers in each other's phones. I nudged Cam, and he wrapped his arms around me.

"I see it. You did good," he whispered close to my ear.

"We did good," I replied.

The second we were at the car, Theo threw his arms around me. "Thank you! That was seriously like…the best night of my life. There were so many people there, and Trey…he's awesome. And so confident. I mean, the nails and the glitter and like…I don't even know."

"You don't have anything to thank me for," I told him. "What are friends for?"

And Theo was that. Regardless of his age, he was my friend.

I looked at Cam over Theo's head, at my boyfriend whom I loved, and smiled.

CHAPTER TWENTY-EIGHT

Camden

I'm going to get married, and I'm going to try and forget you. ~ Letter from Henry

"OH, IT'S SO good to see my boys!" Mom hugged me.

"It's good to see you too, Ma."

"And my sweet Sawyer." He was next as Dad hugged me, and then Mom added, "And this must be Carter. Welcome to the family."

"I… Oh, wow. Thank you. I'm so happy to be here," Carter replied, and I was reminded again how great my parents were. They would accept anyone we brought home, no questions asked. I wondered if Jude's father would be the same. He had no problem with Rush, but sometimes it was different when it was your own child.

"It's a shame your young man couldn't make it," Dad said, and I tried to ignore the way his statement stabbed me in the gut.

Yeah, it was a shame. I was trying not to be bitter about it, unsure if I had a right to be upset at all. Jude was with his family, with his dad and Rush…whom he used to be in love with…but who was my friend and happened to be in love with Lincoln…and I wasn't a jealous guy. I really fucking wasn't, and I trusted Jude, but Christ, I wanted to be with him.

"Yeah, but he's with his dad, so it's understandable. Maybe we can plan something soon."

"You know his father would be welcome here," Mom said, and the last thing I wanted to tell her was that Jude had never been with a guy before me and wasn't ready to announce his sexuality to his family. She'd worry and have a thousand questions I didn't want to deal with.

"Do we get to open a gift early?" I asked, changing the subject.

Mom swatted my arm. "You're always the worst about that! Oh my God, Carter, we used to have to hide the gifts at a friend's house or Camden would find them. He'd find Sawyer's too and then get too excited and spill the beans."

"I bet Sawyer didn't search for his gifts," Carter said.

"That's because I'm the good one," Sawyer teased, but he was looking at me funny, like he knew exactly what I'd done, and he probably did.

"You're the suck-up one," I said playfully, and then we all went back and forth on the subject of gifts and holidays past as we moved into the living room, because this was serious conversation and we all needed to sit down when we got to all the trouble I'd gotten into as a kid.

Carter was great. He fit right in, and as I watched Sawyer with him, I was both so damn happy for my little brother and slightly jealous. I wanted Jude with me. I wanted Jude to look at me the way Carter looked at Sawyer.

Fuck, I was so damn lost over the man.

It was December 23, and we always did this sort of lead-up to Christmas. Not with gifts, of course, because my family hated me and didn't support my need for *now*. But we did have a tradition when it came to food. Tonight we would go out as a family and have Italian. We weren't Italian, but we all loved it, and that was what we always did. Ice cream always followed.

Christmas Eve, Mom would make a roast and potatoes, which would be phase two of the Burke Family Foodmas, and then we'd have chocolate-chip cookies and watch *A Christmas Story* because it was the best holiday movie there was.

And this was the first time Sawyer would have someone home for the holiday.

All through dinner I watched Carter and Sawyer and wondered what it would be like to have Jude there…wondered what he was doing. Were he and his dad having a good time? Was his dad enjoying seeing Jude's day-to-day life? Did he even know Jude had a friend named Cam?

We hadn't talked all day. I thought about calling him but didn't, and I didn't know why. But then, Jude didn't call me either.

It was late that night and I couldn't sleep, so I went out to Mom and Dad's sunroom with a snack. Everyone else was asleep, but I wasn't surprised when I heard footsteps less than five minutes after I got there.

"You got into the cookies already?" Sawyer asked.

"Nope. It was…Santa…?"

"They're on your lap!" he countered, falling down into the chair beside me.

"It's Foodmas! I can't help it."

Sawyer chuckled, and we were quiet for a moment before he asked, "What's wrong, brother?"

I didn't bother to question how he knew something was the matter. I also didn't let myself think before I answered, just let the words fall out. "I know you think you've always needed me more than I need you, but that's not true."

"You needed me to feel like you had someone to take care of. You've always been a caretaker. Those were our roles."

That made me frown. "Yes and no, but you're a caretaker too, and you do as much for me as I've always done for you. I felt…lost when you were away at college. No one knew it. I didn't tell anyone—especially you because I wanted you to enjoy it—but that's how I felt."

Sawyer gasped, but I didn't wait, just kept going. "And as happy as I am that you're with Carter, there's a part of me that's jealous…that feels like I'm losing you. Sort of fucked, right?" Christ, I couldn't believe I'd admitted that.

"What? No. It's not fucked. You've always been and will always be my very best friend. You're one of the most important people in my life. That will never change. Why didn't you ever tell me?"

I shrugged. "You said it yourself—those weren't our roles."

Sawyer nodded, then reached over and plucked a cookie from my lap.

"Those are mine!"

"Mom is going to be pissed. I'm blaming it on you."

"I'll help her make more."

We were quiet for a moment, just sitting there eating our cookies that we were supposed to eat the next day, before Sawyer said, "But Jude helped…having him. That made you feel less alone? If that's even how you felt."

"Yeah," I replied. "It was, and he helped."

"You're in love with him." Sawyer didn't ask, simply told me, and I nodded.

"Yeah." There was no reason to try and deny it. Not to Sawyer.

"You've never felt this way before."

I didn't know why all these years I never told Sawyer about Henry. I'd never told anyone about Henry other than Jude, but I wanted to tell him now. "Yes and no. I've never loved anyone the way I do Jude. He's it for me, BB. I know it. But there was a guy when you were away at college. He's still local, so I can't tell you his name."

Sawyer's eyes widened. "What? Holy shit. What happened?"

"He hated being gay," I admitted. "He felt it was wrong…still feels that way. He'd feel like shit after we were together, but then he'd call me and want to be with me. We were never seen in public together. Hell, he didn't even want anyone to know we were friends, but I loved him and knew he loved me. Not enough to want to be with me, though. He broke it off with me and promptly asked a woman to marry him. They're still together, have a few kids. You know how the story goes." It was like a weight had been lifted off my chest, telling Sawyer that, opening up to him.

"Wow...I'm a little shell-shocked here. I don't know what to say. You deserve better than that. You deserve every damn thing you want. I want to kick this guy's ass, and I'm not a fighter."

I chuckled. "Nah, it's not worth it. He's the one suffering. I just feel...so fucking sad for him..."

"Especially after having Jude," Sawyer finished for me, and he was right. Henry would never know something like what Jude and I had. "But you're afraid too, right? Because Jude hasn't been with a man before, and sure, he's fine and comfortable in our little gay bubble, but what about the rest of the world? What about his family? His dad?"

"I can't believe you said gay bubble. Carter is rubbing off on you, and ew, that sounds gross, but you know what I mean. Jude and I are bi, remember? So wouldn't our bubble be bi? Or an LGBTQIA+ bubble if it's for all of us?"

"Stop trying to change the subject."

I sighed. "Yeah, I am afraid of that." There was really

no sense in trying to deny it. Jude would never want to hurt me, but then, I didn't believe Henry had either. Those things happened, and things didn't always go the way you wanted them to.

Sawyer was quiet, and I knew him well enough to know the wheels were turning inside his brain. Finally, he said, "There was someone for me too…in college."

"Excuse me, what? Why didn't you tell me?"

"Why didn't you tell me?" he countered.

"Because… I obviously didn't think this through. Because I said so?"

Sawyer rolled his eyes. "He wasn't…he wasn't good to me."

My whole body tensed, and my heart pounded against my chest. If someone had hurt my brother and I didn't know…I would never forgive myself. For not knowing, for not being there for him. "Wasn't good to you how?"

"I'm getting there. I know now that I didn't love him, but I thought I did. He wasn't physically abusive, but he would…say mean things to me. He made me feel horrible about myself. Cheated on me time and time again and told me no one would want me. I believed him for a long time."

I was pretty sure I was about to be sick. My stomach

cramped, and my vision went blurry. Heat flushed through me from head to toe. "Who the fuck was he? Why didn't you tell me?" I seethed.

"Because I knew you'd react like this. At the time, I couldn't see past Julian and the fact that I believed he wanted me when no one else would. When it was over, I was too embarrassed. That's not the point, though. It's not why I told you. I told you because I was so afraid of being with Carter because of shit with Julian. I could have lost the best thing in my life because I was afraid of being hurt again. Don't let yourself be afraid of getting hurt."

I sighed. He was right, but… "Our situations are a little different. I'm not running. Hell, I'd be anything Jude wanted me to be in a second. He's the one I'm afraid will run." What if he realized this wasn't what he wanted? What if he wanted easy and it would always be easier to be with a woman? He would never have to come out.

"Have you told him how you feel?"

Oh…well…

"That's what I thought. Cam…you're the bravest person I know. Tell him how you feel. Give him all the information before you worry about what might happen. And it sounds like he's already made more progress than the other guy. Jude doesn't deny you."

I closed my eyes…breathed…confessed. "What if it's not me he wants? Do I want to put myself out there again with someone I love? Especially someone who's never been with a guy other than me?"

"How will you ever know if you don't tell him? And if he doesn't, then you walk away. Give him a chance before you decide how he'll react, but also, you should never accept less than what you deserve. If Jude can't give you everything you want, then he's not good enough for you."

"Yeah…I know." But it wasn't that easy. I loved him, more than I'd ever loved anyone. And I knew he was worth it. I just hoped he wanted me as badly as I wanted him.

CHAPTER TWENTY-NINE

Jude

Awkward Boy is tired of feeling alone…
~ Theo's comic

MY DAD AND I had nothing to talk about. It was…awkward spending time together. It was Christmas Eve, and we'd gone out. I showed him around Fever Falls, we'd grabbed some lunch, and yet we rarely spoke. The silence was heavy, as if we both knew that wasn't how it was supposed to be but neither of us knew how to do anything about it.

Or maybe that was a lie. Maybe we just didn't want to do anything about it.

Now we were back at the condo, with the plan to do…who knew what. Watch a movie? Hell, we probably should have just spent the day at Rush's today too. At least there would be other people and activity around us.

My cell rang. I looked down to see Cam's name on the screen, and as crazy as it sounded, some of the tension seeped from my limbs. Just seeing his name somehow helped.

"Hey," I answered, just as my father came out of the bathroom. "I'm going to go out on the balcony to speak with my friend Cam," I told him.

"Yeah, sure," Dad replied.

Cam was quiet as I went outside and sat on the chair there.

"How's your visit with your parents?" I asked.

"Okay, I guess," he replied. It wasn't how I would have expected him to answer at all. That wasn't the Camden I knew.

"Is everything okay?"

"Yeah, of course. Why wouldn't it be? Just talking to my friend."

My jaw clenched, but guilt twisted inside me at the same time. "Hey, that's not fair. You know he doesn't know." I should have told him already, but that was the thing with us—we didn't know how to talk to each other, and I was afraid of making it worse.

"It still sucks being called your friend. I'd rather just be called Cam than your friend."

My chin dropped to my chest as I closed my eyes. "Shit. I'm sorry. You're right."

"No. Fuck," he said, and I knew without being with

him that he rubbed a hand over his face. "I'm the one who's sorry. I don't know what's gotten into me. I'm overly emotional or some shit. Maybe it's the holiday."

"Yeah, I know. It's weird here too. My dad looks so much older than the last time I saw him. He's graying more. And he's so damn locked inside himself, I don't know how to deal with it."

"I'm sorry, Beautiful. I wish there was something I could do."

Come home ran through my brain, which was a ridiculous thing to think. Cam and I weren't together because of me. Maybe it was the holiday for me too, but I was feeling overly emotional as well. "Talking to you helps," I admitted.

"I'm glad."

But then…then we were just quiet. "My brother is yelling at me. We have some Burke family tradition things to do. You should see Carter. I've never seen him so happy. I think he likes this, the family thing."

Cam's words were sharp against my skin. I knew he hadn't meant them to hurt me. He was just making conversation, but they hurt all the same. I wanted to be there with them. I wanted to know Cam's family. What in the hell was I doing here?

"I need to run. I'll talk to you soon, okay?" Cam

said, and I wanted to ask him to wait, wanted to know what Burke family traditions I was missing.

"Okay," was all I said. Cam sighed into the phone for a moment, then hung up.

My breathing sped up, and my chest felt too tight. Anger bubbled over inside me, lighting a fire in my veins. I was so pissed—at myself, at my father, at the whole goddamned world.

My brain turned off. All my worries and the years of holding back just…gone. I shoved to my feet, pushed into the condo…to see my dad at the table, working on my puzzle in silence. It struck me for a moment because I'd forgotten he liked puzzles too. That I'd gotten my love of them from him. He didn't even look up when I came inside.

"Why wasn't I enough?" rushed out of my mouth before I could stop myself.

"Huh?" He looked up at me, his brows pinched together. "What do you mean?"

"After Mom died. It wasn't like that before she passed away. I remember, and it's like, when she died, you did too. Why wasn't I enough to make you happy?" I shook my head. "That's not fair. I know it's not. That's not how depression works, but don't you want to feel better? Don't you want a relationship with me? I know you love me, I do, but it's like you…let go. Gave me to Rush and his family because it was easier, but you're my dad, and I needed *you*. I still do."

"I…" He hesitated. "I guess I didn't know what I had to offer you. I was so lost."

"You're my dad. That's all you needed—to be present. That's all. It hurt me too, losing her, and then I felt like I lost you at the same time. You checked out. You only cared about work. I spent holidays without you and went on vacations with the Alexanders. Sometimes it felt like you didn't want me around at all." It was as if now that the words were coming out, I couldn't stop them. Years of hurt bled from me as I stood in front of him.

Dad's eyes pooled with tears. "Your mother…she loved you so much. Christ, you look so much like her. You remind me of her—humble but proud. People used to compliment her all the time, whether it was her looks or her humor or how she would do anything for those she cared about. But she never saw it. She never saw it herself. I used to try and remind her of it every day so she would know, and…I should have done that with you too. I love you, son. There is nothing in this world I love more than you, and I just…I don't know how to let myself do it."

"Try, Dad. That's all I need you to do. *Try*. We

don't even know each other. Did you know I hate finance? I went into it because it was what you did. I moved to Fever Falls because I was depressed. I see a therapist and take medication."

His eyes went wide, his chin quivering. "I didn't know."

"And that's my fault for not telling you. We both need to try harder. I know that, but it's not just that." I pulled up the chair opposite him. "Dad, you need to find a way to work through your pain. You haven't lived since Mom died. I know you loved her, and Jesus, I loved her too, but she wouldn't want this for you. You don't laugh. You don't have friends. Hell, maybe you'll fall in love again one day."

He scoffed and rolled his eyes. "That will never happen."

"Maybe not, but maybe it will. The only way to know is to get out there and *live*. I…" I wrung my hands. "I met someone. It wasn't something I ever expected to happen." And I knew then this was the right thing to do. That if I didn't, if I didn't put myself out there, that one day, I could be just like my father. I was telling him to risk his heart, but I needed to as well. "We were friends first. He…he helped me through a lot."

"He?" Dad asked, and I nodded.

"I don't know if that comes as a surprise—"

"It's not a surprise, son."

Oh. I hadn't expected that.

"I always thought you and Rush… Did you think I would care?"

"Not really. Not logically, but I guess I didn't know? Hell, we don't talk to each other now. I was afraid it would be one more thing standing between us, if that makes sense. I don't know if it does. I know you've always been good to Rush, but…"

Dad put his hand on the back of my neck and held me so I looked at him. "I will always love you. I don't care who you love or anything else. You're my son, and that's all that matters. I'm sorry I haven't done a good job showing you that. It was so easy to just check out, and the longer I did it, the less I knew how to come back."

"You can't do it anymore. You have to get help. Maybe…maybe you can move here, be around family. Me, Rush, Mama K, Lincoln, and Cam…he's my…"

"Boyfriend?" Dad filled in for me.

"Yeah. He is. He's…everything to me, and I hurt him, I think. He wanted us to go to Florida and spend Christmas with his family. Then he offered to stay here with me, but I told him I wasn't ready to tell you yet."

Dad frowned for a moment as he watched me, his eyebrows pinched together. "You love him?"

"Yes," I replied, and Dad stood. "What are you doing?"

"What your mother would have done." Then he smiled, maybe the biggest smile I'd seen him give since she died.

CHAPTER THIRTY

Camden

Please don't contact me…not for a while.
- Letter from Henry

On Christmas Day, I got out of bed at six o'clock in the morning.

It didn't matter that I was a grown-ass man and there were no kids in our family. This was Christmas. That called for getting your butt out of bed early, opening gifts, drinking hot chocolate, and spending time with family.

There was a pang in my chest when thinking about family. I wanted Jude to have a family. To have traditions and laughs and joy…but I wanted us to share that together too. And holy shit, falling in love around the holidays made me really fucking sensitive. But I mean, my boyfriend was hot, so who could blame me?

I took a quick leak, washed my hands, and brushed my teeth, then pulled on a pair of flannel pajama bottoms and a T-shirt.

I frowned when I heard voices in the living room because no one was ever awake before me at Christmas. I was already being a miserable bastard, and they were going to take this away from me too?

"I'm not sure if you guys are aware, but this is my thing. I'm supposed to wake you all…" My words trailed off as I rounded the corner from the hallway into the living room and… "Jude? Holy shit. What are you doing here, Beautiful?"

Great. I was fucking sleeping. That had to be what this was, a goddamned dream, but really I knew it wasn't. I just couldn't believe he was there.

"Surprising my boyfriend for Christmas," he said simply.

Mom, Dad, Sawyer, and Carter were all in the room already. My eyes darted around until I saw another man, who had to be his father, drinking a cup of coffee and leaning against the wall.

He'd told him. Jesus fucking Christ, he'd told his father, and they'd come to Florida. "Best. Boyfriend. Ever. You totally passed Boyfriend 101," I said, when what I really wanted to say was, *I fucking love you so much. Let's hide in my room so I can sink inside you all damn day.*

Jude stood as I moved to him. I cupped his face in my hands and paused for a moment. I mean, he'd obviously told his dad he was bisexual and had a boyfriend. They'd come to Florida, so it couldn't have gone badly, but I also wasn't sure how he would feel about kissing in front of him, or my family, for that matter. "Hi."

"Hi," he replied. Then Jude dropped his forehead against mine and pressed a kiss to my lips. "I'm sorry," he said softly.

"Shh." I shook my head. "There's nothing to be sorry for. Nothing else matters right now. You got me the best gift…until you see what I got you. No one chooses gifts as well as I do."

"Camden Matthew Burke!" Mom huffed.

"What, Ma? Everyone knows it's true."

"You got me something better than showing up on Christmas Day?" Jude cocked a brow.

My heart sped up, and my chest felt so damn full. Christ, what this man did to me. "No," I replied. "That'll always win."

I caught his eyes, trying to show him how I felt, trying to ask if he was okay because as glad as I was that he was here, I'd never wanted to rush him. You could want something and miss someone and hurt—which I had—those things were normal, but this was still always Jude's show. He always decided when.

He nodded and gave me a small smile.

Breath puffed from my lungs because I'd needed that smile, needed to know he was okay.

I let go of him, walked toward his father, and held out my hand. "Camden Burke. It's nice to meet you, sir. I can't thank you enough for this. It means a lot to me." I still had no idea how this had even happened, and apparently my family must have known ahead of time.

"Raymond Sandoval. Please, call me Ray. It's a pleasure to meet you too. No need to thank me. Coming meant a lot to Jude, so it meant a lot to me as well." We shook hands. I wanted to hug the guy, find some way to thank him properly, but I could also tell he was slightly uncomfortable with the attention.

"Well! Now that the whole family is here, shall we open gifts?" Mom asked.

"Hell yeah!" I replied. Everyone either rolled their eyes at me or laughed.

Ray was quiet most of the time. He and Jude apologized for not having gifts for everyone, but then, no one had any for them other than me for Jude, which I happened to have with me. I didn't know what made me put it in my suitcase while packing, but I had.

I got my parents a canvas of their wedding photo from when they were eighteen and nineteen years old. For Sawyer I got a first edition of a book he loved and for the both of them together, a plaque that said *Sawyer & Carter* for their apartment.

Jude opened his last. I went to the room to get it, and when I came back, I handed him an envelope. Those familiar wrinkles appeared between his brows as he took it from me.

"This is a lot of pressure," Jude said, everyone watching him as he opened it. "It's a certificate that's good for three classes at Fever Falls Community College and…" Jude pressed the paper against his chest, obviously not wanting to read out loud the part I added about blowjobs, rimming, and thorough fuckings. "You got me college classes?"

"Prepaid art classes." I sat on the coffee table in front of him. "If you're not interested, we can do something else, but I was thinking you could take some…hell, I don't know. Digital art or graphic design or whatever. Even if it's just for fun."

"You're drawing again?" Ray asked, and Jude nodded without turning away from me.

"You deserve to have your passion, whatever that ends up being. I do what I love, and I want that for you too," I told him.

"I can't believe you did that."

"You wouldn't have done it for yourself."

"I…" Jude started but shook his head. "I don't know what to say. Thank you, Boyfriend."

I smiled. I really fucking liked Jude calling me that in front of his father. "You're welcome, Beautiful." We both knew we'd talk more later. There was a lot to say, but now wasn't the time for it.

Carter said, "Swoon," just as Sawyer began making fake-vomiting noises. Carter swatted Sawyer's arm and griped, "Sawyer!" as Mom, Dad, and Ray laughed. I tackled my brother, knocked over a glass of water, and held him down until he said uncle. You know, a typical family holiday.

"Camden, you're in charge of cleaning up the mess," Mom said.

"But Sawyer started it!" I teased.

"Are you twelve?" Sawyer asked.

"At heart."

After letting Sawyer up, I did as Mom said and cleaned up the mess. We always had donuts for breakfast on Christmas morning because obviously my family loved sweets and didn't want anything too heavy before the big meal.

Mom played holiday music, and the house began to fill with the scents of turkey, stuffing, and all the other goodies. I'd discovered that Jude had called Sawyer, who gave them our address and assured them it was okay to come there.

Ray was quiet, sort of keeping to the sidelines.

At one point, I noticed he had disappeared. Jude was busy talking with Carter and Sawyer about something or other. I kissed Jude's temple and went off to find him. This couldn't have been easy on Ray. I knew how uncomfortable he was around people, so I wanted to make sure he knew how much this meant to me.

I found Ray on the sun porch. He looked over his shoulder toward me when I walked out. "I don't mean to interrupt."

"It's fine," he replied with a warm smile. "I'm sure Jude told you I don't do well around a lot of people. Keep to myself."

"He did. That's, um…why I wanted to come out and thank you again. This, having you both here, means a lot to me. I've never felt this way, and I wanted to share it with him. I want to share everything with him—my family, my life."

"I was never good at giving him family."

"That's not true. He loves you. He respects you. You

did your best, and you're here when I can tell you'd rather be anywhere else."

Ray chuckled. "It's nothing personal. You have a really nice family. I just don't know how to let people in anymore. I haven't let myself do it in a long time, but I'm going to try and be better. Jude deserves that."

I put a hand on his shoulder and squeezed. "You deserve it too."

His eyes snapped to mine as if he hadn't expected it. He stared at me for a moment, then nodded. "Yeah, maybe I do. It's time."

My hand fell away, and we stood there in silence for a moment together before he said, "It's good to see my boy happy."

"You don't mind that it's with a man?" I asked, needing the answer.

"No. Who am I to judge anyone's form of happiness? I haven't had my own in far too long to want to deny anyone else theirs."

His words did something to me. Hit me in the chest and filled me up. I'd wanted that so badly for Jude—for this to all be okay. A smile stretched across my face, and Ray's brows pulled together the same way Jude's did. "You're in love with him."

"Very much so. But I haven't told him yet. I was a

little scared, and I'm not usually scared of things." Or if I was, I pushed through.

"Don't be," Ray replied. "Fear will eat you alive if you let it."

I knew he was talking about his fears since the death of his wife. "You raised a good man, the best one I know."

"He's like his mother that way. There was just something about her. The moment I saw her, it was love at first sight. She was so damn beautiful, she stole my breath. I wasn't sure I deserved her, but I knew I would love her until the day I died, knew she was it for me. Always knew she was special. All it took was one look to know she'd be in my life, and it grew from there."

I sucked in a sharp breath. I hadn't known from the beginning that I would love Jude, but I'd known he was special, had been inexplicably drawn to him the way it sounded Ray had been with Jude's mom. From that first time I saw him, I'd known Jude would be in my life somehow. "Yeah…I can relate," I replied, and Ray gave me a rich, hearty laugh. It was so damn happy and contagious that I hoped he could find it in himself to do it more often.

"Hey…what are you guys doing out here?" Jude stepped up behind us.

"Just getting to know your young man some, son. He's a good one." Ray nodded at Jude.

"Yeah, he is," Jude replied.

"I'll leave you guys to it. Maybe Janet needs help in the kitchen."

Jude's eyes snapped to his father's as if he couldn't have been more surprised.

"I'm trying, son. They're family." And with that, Ray walked back into the house.

"I can't believe that. I don't even know what to say." Jude stood beside me.

"He loves you. I know you know that, but you've also doubted it. He loves you, Beautiful, and...I'm crazy fucking in love with you. Did you know that?" My chest tightened, felt heavy as though someone sat on it.

His eyes swirled like liquid steel. "I love you too."

"Yeah?" I asked, feeling like I could breathe. "Obviously."

Jude chuckled and rolled his eyes.

"I'm sorry if you felt like I was rushing you. That wasn't fair of me. I just...fuck, I've never felt this way, and I was afraid of losing it. Afraid you would realize I wasn't what you wanted."

"You didn't rush me. I wanted to be with you. Yeah, I was nervous about telling my dad, but you're it for me,

Cam. You're what I want. That isn't going to change. I'm not Henry."

"I know." I'd thought I loved Henry all those years ago, and I guess I did, but it wasn't this kind of love. The kind you felt in your damn soul.

"And you're not Rush. I need to make sure you know I see that. Yeah, when we started talking I was hung up on him, but it's you I love. Even if there was no Linc, it's you I'd want."

My knees nearly gave out. Fuck, I'd needed to hear that more than I'd realized. "Mine." I pressed kisses to his lips. "My boyfriend is the best."

Jude laughed, and then we kissed. "I feel like I'm part of a family today. Like my family is growing. There's Rush and Mama K, and now Sawyer, Carter, Janet, and Bob."

"There's no like about it, Beautiful. They are your family."

He nodded, and we went back inside after that. Football was watched, and laughs were had. Then dinner was ready, and we all sat around the table together to eat.

Dad raised his glass in a toast. "To family. It's a parent's dream to see their kids happy and with good people. Cam…Sawyer…how'd you guys score them?"

We all laughed, and it was obvious Jude and Ray

hadn't expected that. It was so my dad, though.

We ate, and afterward I was in the kitchen with Mom to clean up. "I've been wondering for years when my boys would bring someone home. Why am I not surprised you both fell in love the same year?"

I shrugged because it wasn't a surprise, I guess. It was just Sawyer and me.

"He's a good man. You did good, Cam. Sawyer did too. It's nice having two more sons."

Grabbing her, I pulled her close. Hugged her. Knew how damn lucky I was to have the parents I did, and now Jude would have them along with Ray and Rush's mom too. "I love you."

"Aw, I love you too, sweet boy. That's always been you. You try to come off tough and like you don't feel anything, but you are fiercely loyal, and I'm not sure there's anyone in the world who loves like you do. Whether it's your brother, friends, or us. Hold on to that, and I'm so damn happy to see someone else giving you some love too."

"Thanks, Ma." I pulled away, then went to the other room to find my man.

CHAPTER THIRTY-ONE

Jude

Awkward Boy takes a page out of Friendly Man's book. ~ Theo's comic

"So it was fine? Like absolutely okay? It wasn't weird or anything and your dad didn't care like, in any way?" Theo was doing his thing where he rambled and I could hardly keep up with him.

We'd gotten home from Florida the day before. One of the first things I'd wanted to do was let Theo know I'd told my dad about Cam and me. I knew he would want to know, and it was important to me that he saw it was okay. No, I couldn't guarantee he would have the same response, but I figured he needed to see it was possible.

"I mean, I was nervous, yeah, but I was also angry and hurt. I just sort of said it, but I'm glad I did. I feel like it's brought my dad and me closer, and I feel better myself, ya know? I hadn't realized I'd needed to say it to him until I did."

"Wow...that's so awesome. I can't even imagine doing that," Theo replied, his sketchbook sitting on the table in front of him, long forgotten.

"You will when you're ready. And if you're not, that's okay."

He nodded. "So then you and your dad just went to Florida?"

Jesus, I still couldn't believe we'd done that. Luckily, Sawyer had been a lot of help. He'd spoken to his parents and assured us it was okay. It had been one of the best days of my life—being with Cam and his family. Being accepted, and feeling a part of something, and being able to share it with my dad too.

He was still in Fever Falls, surprisingly. I'd half expected him to head right back home, but he'd said he was trying, and I saw he was. We'd had lunch together earlier today as well. I still wished he was staying at the condo with me, but we were making steps in the right direction.

"Yeah. When Cam woke up in the morning, we were already there." I found myself smiling, thinking about it, about him. "It was a great holiday, but I want to hear about you. How was your Christmas?"

Theo shrugged. "It was all right, I guess. Mom stayed home, which was like, amazing. I mean, I guess she can't really work on Christmas. I had to spend a couple of days with my dad, and that's always awkward. I've been talking to Trey a lot, though. He's like, *so* freaking awesome. And he's so totally confident in who he is. Like with makeup and stuff. It's crazy! I don't know if I'll ever be that confident."

I reached over and squeezed his hand. "You will. Cut yourself some slack. Hell, look at me. I was nervous too. It's not always easy telling people intimate parts of who we are."

Theo nodded, and then chatted a bit more about Trey and the holidays. I told him about Camden's gift to me, and he teased me and made kissy faces. The kid was a riot.

We drew for a bit before he had to head home. I was expecting Cam soon, as well. He was coming over after work and staying the night.

A GRIN AUTOMATICALLY split my lips when there was a knock at the door. I pulled it open, and Cam was standing there with wet hair from a shower and Japanese food for dinner.

"Hey, Boyfriend." Cam wagged his eyebrows at me

as he came inside.

"Hey, Boyfriend."

"Oh my God. Say it again. That's so hot."

"You're such a dork," I said playfully, but damn, did I like it. Hearing things like that from Cam always did something for me.

"A hot, sexy dork who brought you dinner and who you said you loved." He nodded toward the couch. "I'm starving. Let's eat."

We ate at the coffee table in front of the TV, watching ESPN. Cam chatted about his workday and the new library they were building. I told him some of my conversation with Theo.

"Tyson said Trey has been talking with Theo like crazy, and holy shit that's a lot of *t*'s. How have I never noticed that before?"

"I don't know," I teased, and he rolled his eyes.

After we finished our teriyaki chicken, rice, and California rolls, Cam looked at me and said, "I'm gonna brush my teeth in case there's kissing going on later."

Laughter bubbled up in my chest. "You're ridiculous." But then I brushed my teeth too because I was hoping there would be a lot more than kissing going on. I wanted him again. We'd only fucked the once, and that definitely wasn't enough for me.

Luckily, Cam seemed to have the same thoughts. After cleaning up, we didn't make it out of my bedroom. Cam grabbed me, pulled me close, and his hand slid down my body and cupped my cock, which was already beginning to stir to life. "I missed this, Boyfriend."

"Fuck." I trembled. "Great minds think alike."

"Oh, you want me too?"

"Always."

"Good. Because I really want to suck you."

It wasn't what I originally had in mind, but how could I turn down head from Cam? He was so fucking good at it.

He went down to his knees, and I tugged my shirt off as he went for my jeans. He had them unbuttoned, unzipped, and halfway down my legs before I knew it. Then he leaned in and mouthed my cock and balls through my underwear. "Fuck, I love being on my knees for you. You smell so goddamned good."

He inhaled just as my hand went to his hair. My fingers tangled there as he worked my boxer briefs down. The second the head of my cock popped free, Cam had it in his mouth, sucking me as he finished pulling my clothes down.

I stepped out of them, my whole body sensitized, feeling so damn treasured by this man I loved.

"You gonna fuck my face?" Cam asked.

"Nah, I'm good," I teased.

"Oh, fuck you very much, Boyfriend."

I looked down at him, grabbed my dick, and angled it toward his lips, then pushed in. I did as Cam wanted—like that was a hardship?—because I wanted it too, and let loose on him. He let me go at my own pace, giving him what we both wanted in this primal sort of way that was somehow raw, passionate, and beautiful.

Then Cam pulled off and nuzzled my balls. My eyes rolled back in my head because it felt so goddamned good, I couldn't believe I hadn't come already. My orgasm was flirting with me, about ready to burst free when I gasped and pulled away from him. Cam's dark-brown eyes looked up at me in confusion, but then I said, "I want you."

"You have me." He nodded as if he understood, and I knew he did. Cam always understood me. "You want me in your ass again, Beautiful? I'm dying to be there, but I have to admit, I want you inside me too."

"I thought you didn't like it."

"That wasn't with you."

His words were a shock to my system, lighting me up. I grabbed Cam, tugged him to his feet and slammed my mouth down on his.

CHAPTER THIRTY-TWO

Camden

Maybe one day we can be friends.
~ Letter from Henry

I REACHED FOR the bottom of my shirt, but the second I did, Jude pulled my hands away. "No. Let me do it."

"Yeah, okay." I hadn't planned on asking Jude to fuck me. Hell, we'd only had anal intercourse once, and while he'd said he liked it, and it had felt like he fucking loved it, I second-guessed myself. All I wanted was for this to be good for him, for it to be what he wanted.

He hadn't made a move to take me, even though I'd offered my ass to him from the start, and while I loved fucking, I would have been okay with that. If we only sucked cock and jerked each other off for the rest of our lives, I'd be okay with it as long as I had him. But this…this, I really wanted as well—to have Jude this way.

He tugged my shirt over my head and dropped it to the floor. His eyes never left mine as he took care of my jeans, loosening them and yanking them down my legs. He knelt and helped me as I stepped out of them, and then he wrapped a hand around my cock and stroked.

"Oh fuck, Beautiful. So damn good." I cupped his cheek and looked at him as he jerked me. "Still can't believe I get you here with me." It was so damn true. I didn't lack for confidence. I was pretty sure that was obvious, but Jude…he was different, and I didn't think I ever really believed I'd be lucky enough to have him.

"I hope you know I feel the same way about you," he said, and somehow I did.

Jude swirled his tongue around the head of my cock, then licked at the precome on the tip. My damn eyes rolled back and my knees went weak, it felt so fucking good.

"Get on the bed for me. I want to try something," Jude said, and I nodded. I went to lie on my back, but he shook his head. "No, not like that. I need your ass in the air."

Oh…I was pretty sure I knew where this was going. "Kinky." I wagged my eyebrows, trying to keep things light. It wasn't every day a guy licked another guy's asshole for the first time.

Jude gave me a small smile, which prompted my admission. "Wanna know something? I've never been rimmed. I've eaten a lot of ass and fucking loved it, but no one has ever done it to me."

His big, blue eyes went even wider as he took me in. He gave me a quick nod, understanding what I was telling him. I might have had a whole lot more experience with men than he did, but in some things, we were the same. I'd only been fucked once, and he would be the first guy to have his tongue inside me.

"Guess I better rock your fucking world, then."

"I have no doubt you will." I climbed into the middle of the bed, looked over my shoulder at him, and wiggled my ass. Jude rolled his eyes, but like it so often did, a smile teased at his lips.

"Jesus, your body." He knelt behind me and danced his fingers down my spine. "I remember watching your back that first night, with Melinda. Now the idea of you with someone else makes me want to rage."

"Never again. I'm sorry it had to start that way."

"It was just the push I needed. And we're here now."

Jude's hands slid down to my ass, where he planted them on my cheeks, then spread them. "Fuck, baby. It looks so tight."

I really liked that, liked being Jude's *baby*. "Waitin'

for you to open me up."

He growled low in his throat.

The first brush of Jude's tongue against my hole sent a shockwave through me, this sort of electric current that fried my brain. All I could do was feel as he licked, sucked, and probed my ring. "Fuck yesssss." I was pushing back against him now, begging for more as his skilled tongue, coupled with the brush of his stubble against my ass, turned me to mush.

Why in the hell hadn't I been doing this? I knew both men and women alike lost their fucking minds when I did it to them, but Christ, feeling Jude there was basically the best thing ever. "Finger me," I pleaded.

Jude leaned forward and pushed his fingers into my mouth. I sucked them, got them slick, and then he was there, pushing a finger inside while he still used his tongue to tease and torment me. When his finger brushed against my prostate, I nearly jolted off the bed.

"Like that, do you?"

"Stop talking, and get your mouth back on me," I gritted out, and Jude laughed. His tongue was there again, though, and he gave it to me, gave me what I asked for, licking me out and finger-fucking me.

I was riding his digit like I hadn't known what I was missing, and soon his tongue fell away and he lubed up, pushing two, then three fingers inside to loosen me up.

I'd been penetrated with fingers plenty of times, both mine and other lovers', but it had been a while. The first sting was a shock, and then it melted into the familiar as I reveled in the fact that it was Jude giving me this pleasure.

"I need inside you, Cam. It's killing me to wait."

"Then don't."

Jude let loose another growl, which was hot as fuck. I had to admit, I liked this side of him.

He grabbed a condom out of the drawer and suited up. He used lube on his cock and my hole, then said, "I want to look at you when I fuck you. Is that okay?"

A breath escaped my lungs, making me realize it was more than okay—it was what I needed too.

I rolled over and shoved a pillow under my hips. My aching cock bobbed against my stomach as Jude looked down at me, danced his fingers against my balls and up my shaft. "You are so fucking beautiful," he said softly, almost bashfully.

"Right back at ya, Boyfriend."

Jude lifted my legs and put them over his shoulders, and then he was there, the head of his cock pushing at my rim. Our eyes were locked on each other's. I wasn't breathing. Hell, I didn't think he was breathing either as our gazes held and he slowly, so fucking slowly pushed his way inside.

My back arched as that first stretch and burn set in…but then the head was inside, and he trembled and smiled, and goddamned if it wasn't the best feeling in the world.

"Oh fuck, I don't know if I'm going to last."

"You better get me off first," I teased.

"If I don't, I'll make it up to you."

But I knew he would. We were just good at playing games like that.

Jude leaned over and kissed me, working his way inside inch by inch. When I felt his groin against my ass, felt him buried to the hilt, I rolled my head back so we could look at each other again.

"Good?" he asked.

"Perfect," I replied.

Jude kissed the tip of my nose, and I don't know what it was about that small gesture, but it hit me right in the chest.

He fucked me slowly at first, long deep strokes as we watched each other. My body began to tingle, and every time he hit my spot, I nearly lost it. This was nothing like the other time I'd done this. I was pretty sure I'd want Jude's cock in my ass just as often as I'd want inside his.

"More," I begged, then winked. "Fuck me like you mean it."

"That sounds an awful lot like a challenge," he replied, but he pulled almost all the way out, then snapped his hips forward again. My cock jerked, leaking precome on my belly.

"Fuck yes." I spit in my hand and wrapped it around my rod. Jude did as I said, fucking me like he meant it. The bed hit the wall, and our bodies slapped together. I felt like a slut for him, and I reveled in that. My balls were tight, filled with a heavy load. I jerked off and pushed toward him, watching the corded muscles in his neck and the wrinkles by his eyes when he tightened them.

"So good, Cam. So goddamned good."

He leaned forward and took my mouth, kissed me like he was dying and needed my breath to survive. My body sort of went haywire. All this fire and want and need building to the point where I couldn't hold it back anymore. My orgasm washed through me, my load shooting from my balls and through my cock, one spurt, then two, then three between our bodies. Jude cried out above me. Thrust in again, his cock jerking inside my hole as he filled the condom.

He fell on top of me and pulled out. I cradled him between my legs, carded my fingers through his sweat-wet hair as we breathed against each other.

"It was good for you?" he asked, similarly to how I'd asked him.

"So good, I'm already wondering when we're going to do it again. Think we can find a way to never leave this bed? Just take turns fucking each other for the rest of our lives?"

Jude laughed, his chest vibrating against mine. "I love you," he said a few minutes later. "This…you…it's more than I ever thought I'd have, more than I ever realized I wanted."

"Fuck, Beautiful. Me too. I love you so much. Think I somehow have since that first time I saw you."

He laughed it off, but I wasn't joking.

Then…with his cheek against my chest, he whispered, "Yeah…me too."

CHAPTER THIRTY-THREE

Jude

Awkward Boy strikes again! ~ Theo's comic

"You killed it the past two weekends," I told Rush as we sat in his garage, working on a project bike.

"Did you have doubts?" he teased, making me roll my eyes.

It was mid-January, and the Supercross season had started. The first race was always in Anaheim—A1, since they raced there twice. Rush had finished first overall in both of the two races of the season. He was riding like he had fire in his veins, like he had something to prove.

"This is it for you, isn't it?" I asked. He'd told me once that he was thinking about retiring, but he'd never mentioned it again. There was something about the way he was riding, about the look in his eyes, that told me it really was going to happen.

"Yeah, I think so. I don't want to tell Red yet,

but…yeah, I think I want to go out on top. Then find something else, ya know?"

It made sense. Rush had conquered the sport he loved. He wouldn't lose that love if he stepped down from racing. Hell, maybe he would love it more without the harsh training and time away from the man he loved. "I hear you, man."

He nodded. "What about you?"

I shrugged. "Next week I start the classes Cam got me. The whole thing—going back to school—feels weird as fuck in some ways, but I'm excited too. Who knows if it'll go anywhere, but it'll be nice to have something that's mine. Something I do just for me."

"Yeah, I get it. I always thought you should have done something like that anyway. In fact, I believe I told you more than once when we were younger." He cocked a brow. "But I guess it's different when it comes from the man you love."

The wrench I'd been using fumbled from my hand and hit the ground. My chest felt tight all of a sudden, this need I never thought I would feel to tell the truth, teasing at my mind. "You know…I thought I was in love with you. I know we talked a bit in your gym that one time, but my brain was all fucked up. I didn't know what I felt, but then…then I did."

Rush looked down, almost guiltily. "Yeah, man. I know. I hated hurting you."

"I know you did." Part of me also realized he had to have known. Rush and I were too close for him not to.

"But Cam helped."

I nodded.

"And now what you feel for him, you know that's real. I'm not trying to minimize what you felt for me, but it's different with Cam, isn't it?"

There was no hesitation on my part. No doubt. "Yeah, it is. I never knew I could feel this way—and that's how you feel with Linc. Things are the way they're supposed to be." I paused for a moment, then let myself keep going. "And Cam and I? We weren't really dating when you caught us at the wedding."

Rush rolled his eyes. "No shit. I know the signs of a fake relationship. Did you forget about me and Red? Though I guess neither of us was ever really in a pretend relationship—we just told ourselves we were."

I laughed, figuring he was close to the truth.

"You're my brother, my best friend, and you always will be."

"Always," I confirmed.

"Wanna hear some crazy-ass shit?"

"Do you have to ask?"

Rush rubbed a hand over his face. "Your dad and my mom…they've been hanging out quite a bit. She says they're just friends and he's going through some stuff, so she's just being there for him. I can see it. They've known each other forever, but…I don't know. It's just weird."

"Holy shit. He hasn't said a word." I shook my head, still trying to process. If Rush mentioned it, he must have seen something there.

"Right? I mean, I could be wrong… Who am I kidding? I'm never wrong."

We laughed, and it felt good to do that with him, like we had nothing between us anymore. It had felt like it, whether it was my feelings, or Linc, or my lie about Cam, but now we were just Rush and Jude, like we'd always been. "How weird would that be?"

"Nah, I think it would be kind of perfect. It's time we all have our bit of happiness, ya know? Fever Falls has a way of doing that with people."

He was right. Ash and Beau. Rush and Linc. Keegan and Owen. Carter and Sawyer. Jace and Dax.

Me and Cam.

And maybe my dad and Mama K.

Lincoln had been saying it for a long time—there was something in the water. Of course, he thought that something turned straight men gay, and we knew that was impossible, but maybe that wasn't it. Maybe it was something else—happiness, or love, or…holy fuck, I was going crazy.

"What?" Rush asked. "You're smiling."

"Nothing." I shook my head. There was no way I'd admit I was thinking crazy thoughts about love in the water. I was losing my damn mind.

The crunching of wheels on gravel sounded from outside. Rush frowned as though he hadn't been expecting anyone. We both stood, and my stomach dropped out when I saw the Burke Construction truck pulling to a stop.

Cam was supposed to be at work. He had no good reason for being here.

My heart thudded as I jogged over to him. Rush was right behind me. The second Cam got out of the truck, I saw it in his eyes, in the sorrow there. "What is it? What happened?"

"It's…" He cupped my face. "It's Theo, Beautiful. He's missing."

CHAPTER THIRTY-FOUR

Camden

I'm sorry. Love always, Henry. – Letter from Henry

MY STOMACH WAS in knots. I hated telling Jude this. Hell, I fucking hated that it happened in the first place. Theo meant so much to both of us, and I didn't know what we would do if something happened to him.

"What? Since when? How do you know?"

"I forgot my phone at the condo. I went back to get it, and the police were there with Theo's mom. They wanted to know if we had heard from him. I guess last night he went to his dad's. His mom didn't know. She was at work. I don't know why he didn't tell us, but he came out to his dad. She didn't give me a lot of information, but I'm assuming it didn't go well. Theo left angry and said he was going home. His mom got home late and didn't realize he was gone until this morning."

"Fuck...*fuck!*" Jude shouted. "Did you call Trey?"

"Tyson did. He's at school. He swears he has no idea where he went."

"I'll call everyone," Rush said from behind Jude. "We'll all meet at the condo and then spread out to look for him." I looked up at him, trying to silently thank him. I had to admit, things had felt slightly stilted between Rush and me for a while. I was sure it came from me, from jealousy over how Jude had felt about him. When I gave him a smile, he paused a moment, then nodded and returned it, as if he knew I was saying I was sorry and that I loved Jude, and Rush was telling me it was okay.

I gave my attention back to Jude. Hooking my finger under his chin, I turned his head so he looked at me. "We'll find him. I promise you we'll find him."

"You can't promise me that, but even if we do, then what? There's a reason he ran…or…"

I didn't want to consider the *or* and what it could have meant, so I focused on thinking he ran. I hated that he was right, but first things first. We had to find him, and then we could deal with the rest of it. "We'll figure it out. Let's go."

Jude left his car and climbed into the truck with me. We went back to the condo, where officers were still speaking with his mom. They wanted to talk to Jude too, to know the last time he saw Theo or spoke to him, and if he had any ideas where Theo could have gone.

My hold on Jude's hand tightened when they asked about our friendship with him.

"He just needed someone to talk to," Jude told them, "and I understood what he was going through. Most of the time, we just hung out around here. We've taken him to a few movies, meals, then the holiday party at the LGBTQ center," Jude told them.

"What?" his mom asked with a frown.

Oh fuck. He hadn't told her where we went that night?

"He said he told you where we were going. I talked to you that night before we left," Jude replied. But we never said where we were going, and she had rushed off after a phone call, likely how Theo knew she would.

She stood there for a moment, making my pulse thud harder and my stomach drop further. Then...then she looked at us with tears in her eyes. "I didn't know. He never told me... Why was he afraid to tell me? Doesn't he know I'll always love him?"

"It's not that simple," I said.

She wiped at her eyes and straightened her back. "None of that matters. I just... I want my boy back."

And fuck, that helped. Maybe things could be better

with Theo and his mom after this. Maybe she would spend more time with her son.

When I looked up, the cavalry was arriving—Sawyer and Carter. Jace, Dax, Beau, Ash, Keegan, Owen, Linc, Rush, Tyson, Trey, Mama K, and Ray. All of them there to help us bring Theo home.

We split up into groups to search for him. They'd tried to use the signal to locate his cell phone, but for some reason, it didn't work.

We spent hours looking for him. Jude rarely spoke the whole time. His anger and worry rolled off him in heavy waves, and I didn't know how to fix it, didn't know how to help.

Fuck, Theo had to be okay. What if he wasn't okay?

As the sun dipped behind the horizon and it started getting darker, the worry set deeper into my bones.

"Shit. I have an idea," Jude said out of the blue.

We were in Willow Brook Park when he started to jog. I didn't ask where we were going; it didn't matter. Wherever he led, I would follow.

When we got to the Fever Falls Art Gallery, this little light clicked on inside me. "Good thinking," I said as we went in.

It was a large gallery. I was surprised at the size, having never been there. The walls were all white, with paintings, sculptures, and other art the only splashes of color.

We rounded a corner, and a familiar beanie came into view. Theo had his back to us, his skateboard under his arm, as he stared up at a display.

"Theo!" Jude yelled. The boy started and turned around just as Jude pulled him into his arms. "Jesus Christ, you scared the shit out of me! Don't ever do something like this again. You can come to us. Don't you know you can always come to us?"

Theo looked at me over Jude's shoulder, his brows pinched together in confusion. "What do you mean?" he asked when Jude let him go.

"We have half the town out looking for you! Your mom said your bed hadn't been slept in. Your phone is off. We were worried sick."

He looked down, shame curling his shoulders. "I…I didn't mean to scare you. I didn't think anyone would notice I was gone. My head was all mixed up, and I didn't want to talk about it. I went to this all-night diner and drank coffee and ate pancakes all night."

His words hit me like a punch to the gut. This poor kid didn't think anyone would notice he was gone. That no one would care or paid close enough attention.

"Of course we would," I told him. "Your mom was

worried sick. Your dad came too. Jude and I were out of our minds with worry. Rush called all our friends—Trey and Tyson too. They're all worried about you, and they're all looking for you."

He looked up, tears pooling in his eyes, and Jude hugged him again. "We'll sort out the rest of it later. We're just glad you're okay."

CHAPTER THIRTY-FIVE

Jude

Finally, Awkward Boy didn't feel so awkward anymore...and for the first time, he was comfortable in his skin. ~ Theo's comic

Cam called everyone and let them know we found Theo and were on our way back to the condo.

"Do you want to talk about it?" I asked as we headed home, but he shook his head.

"Can you guys... Will you stay while I talk to my parents?"

"Of course," I replied just as Cam said, "You got it, kid."

We were quiet during the quick drive back. The second we parked, Theo's mom came running out of the building. She pulled him into her arms and started crying. "Oh God. Don't ever do that again. I was so worried about you. I don't know what I would do if something happened to you, do you hear me?"

Theo pulled back and wiped tears from his own face, nodding.

His dad was there too, but he didn't say much. He hugged Theo, but the emotion wasn't there, and it took everything inside me not to tell the motherfucker what a piece of shit he was. Didn't he know he had the best damn kid there was?

There were conversations with the officers, Cam and I never straying far from Theo. An hour or so later, it was the five of us—me, Cam, Theo, and his parents—alone in their condo.

"Thank you. I appreciate your help finding Theodore, but this is a family matter," his dad said, and I could see the panic in Theo's eyes.

"With all due respect," I began just as Theo said, "Dad..."

But it was Annie who made the final decision. "If Theo wants them to stay, they stay. They've been good to him." She began crying again. Maybe she was feeling guilty for not having spent more time with him herself.

We sat down. Theo's leg was bouncing like crazy, nerves making his skin pale. "I, um...I didn't mean to scare everyone. I just...didn't think anyone would notice."

"Of course we'd notice, kid," Cam said.

"Theo?" his mom said, a soft question in her voice, as if she really didn't understand why Theo would feel that way.

"I don't...I don't always feel like you guys care all that much about me. You're both always at work. Dad doesn't care if I go see him or not. I guess sometimes I wondered if it would be easier for you if I wasn't around? Like maybe you didn't want me." Theo wiped his eyes again, and damn, I wanted to let loose on his parents. Wanted to tell them they had a really fucking great kid and I wasn't sure they deserved him.

"That's ridiculous. Of course we want you around," his dad said simply, as if he couldn't be bothered with Theo's feelings. He'd never spoken much about his father, so I hadn't taken him into consideration, and now I knew why he didn't talk about him.

"Why are you always gone, then? Dad has his new wife and son, and Mom would rather be at work than with me."

"Oh, baby," Annie said, and then she shoved off the couch and knelt in front of Theo. "I'm sorry. I'm so damn sorry. You deserved better. Me being gone was never about you. It was about my insecurity and my drive, but never about you, okay? You are the most important person in my life. I love you so much, and I'm going to do better. I promise you I'll do better."

"Even if...even if I'm gay?" Theo asked softly. I held my breath, and looking over, saw Cam's hands were tightened into fists.

"I don't care about that. You're my son. I just want you to be happy," she replied.

"Dad?" Theo asked.

"Like I told you last night, you're too young to make such a life-changing choice," he answered.

"It's not a choice," slipped past my lips. "Would you be saying he's too young to decide he's straight? It's who he is. Theo is a great kid. He's smart and funny. He's an incredible artist. He's passionate and caring. Who cares who he's attracted to? That doesn't change who he is. He's made the past few months in my life much easier. I'm so damn grateful to call him a friend."

Cam reached over and threaded his fingers with mine.

His father's stare locked on us. "I have to say, I wonder if the two of you had any influence on this."

"Dad!" Theo shouted. "They're my friends...like my brothers. I've known for a long time...for like...ever. Can't you see that?"

"That's enough!" Annie said to her ex-husband.

"That. Is. Enough. Don't make him feel bad. They helped him when we didn't. He's our son. It's our job to love and support him no matter what." She turned to us then. "Thank you," Annie said to us, tears in her eyes. "Thank you for being there for him."

"I don't know... I'm not ready to accept this," he answered, and Cam's hand tightened on mine. I thought maybe he was thinking about Henry and why Henry struggled with accepting who he was.

"Then you can leave," Annie told him.

"Theodore. Listen to me—"

"No," Theo cut his father off. "This is who I am, and it's not going to change. I don't want it to change. I've been so scared of who I am...of admitting it and coming out, but I won't do that anymore. I *like* myself, for maybe the first time ever. I'm...I'm all those things that Jude said. I won't be ashamed of being gay anymore." Then...then he looked at Cam and me, and smiled.

My heart banged against my chest as pride swelled within me. I had never been as proud of anyone as I was of Theo.

His father stood and walked out. Rage surged through me. What the hell was wrong with him? How could he give a shit about who his son loved? I knew it happened that way sometimes, but fuck, I really hadn't wanted it to happen to Theo.

"I'm very proud of you," his mom told him. "He'll come around, and if he doesn't, that's on him, not you. Don't ever feel like there's something wrong with you, and I'm so damn sorry you ever had to worry about whether I would accept you or not. I will always love you."

Theo nodded, and they hugged. When he pulled away, he walked over to Cam and me. I stood just as Theo threw his arms around me and cried into my chest. "I'm so damn sorry, kiddo." I couldn't help but feel a little responsible.

"It's not your fault…it's his. His loss," Theo replied.

"Damn right," Cam added, hugging him too.

"I want to thank you both again, for being there for Theo when I wasn't. It really means a lot to me. I'm not proud of how I've acted since the divorce, losing myself in my work, but that changes right now. Theo is the most important thing, and…maybe the four of us can have dinner here together one night? And I'd also be interested in looking for some groups at the center for parents."

"That'd be great. We'd love to," Cam answered. "And we can definitely help you find some organizations. The Fever Falls center has a great PFLAG group that meets there."

We stayed there for another hour or so. We all wanted to make sure Theo was okay, that he knew he was loved and accepted. And before we left, we set plans for dinner with the four of us the next week.

Theo walked us to my condo, and I asked, "Are you sure you're okay?"

"I'm sad, but…yeah. My dad…I figured he would be that way. We've never been close. He has his new wife and his new son, and that's okay. I spent the whole day thinking about what he said when I came out—how I was too young and I could change. I thought about Trey and all those kids at the center. I thought about your friends, and you guys, and it just sort of clicked. I don't want to change. This is me, and I'm a cool-ass guy. If someone else can't see that, it's their problem."

"Damn straight," Camden replied. "I'm proud of ya, kid."

"I'm proud of me too." Theo looked at me…smiled. "Thanks, big brother," he said, blushing.

"Always, little brother."

He hugged us once more and then went back home.

Cam walked toward me, then cupped my face and looked at me. "Are you okay, Beautiful?"

"Yes and no. I really fucking hate his dad. I wanted

to knock him the hell out."

"You and me both."

"But I'm proud of Theo. And this seems to have brought him closer to his mom, and he's…happy. You think he's really happy, right?"

"I do. It won't always be easy, and he'll be hurt because of his dad, but Theo took a big step today. And he's proud of who he is. No matter what happens, he'll have his mom in his corner, and he'll have us."

My whole chest felt like it was expanding as I pulled him close. Goddamn, I loved this man. "What about you? Are you okay?"

"Yeah…I'm okay. I'm sad about Theo's dad, and…it makes me think about Henry. Is that okay to admit?"

"Of course it is. I wondered if it might."

"I hate that he'll never have this…the strength Theo has and the love I feel for you. All because of something as stupid as someone's gender. Why the hell does it matter so much?"

"I don't know," I answered simply. Not everyone got their happily ever after, but I would make damn sure we did.

"I love you." Cam dropped his forehead to mine. "I love you so damn much."

"I love you too. You've made me happier than I ever

thought I would be…but do you know what I hate?" I teased.

He grinned. "What's that? Clothes? Because I hate them too right now. I'm wanting some Naked-Jude time."

Damned if I didn't chuckle. "Yes, clothes, but also…this condo. It's not me." Just like finance hadn't been me and maybe art would be. I was tired of settling. I wouldn't do that anymore.

"What about my house? Is that you?"

"Are you asking me to move in with you?"

"No," Cam said, and I playfully shoved him.

"Asshole."

"Yes…move in with me. We can get a dog!"

I had no idea where that came from, but that was Cam. He would always keep me on my toes.

"Yeah," I replied. "Let's do it." There was no time like the present to be happy. I grabbed his hand and began tugging him toward the bedroom.

"Fuck yes. Naked time! Best boyfriend ever."

"So I really did it? I passed Boyfriend 101?" I asked.

"You fucking aced it," Cam replied, tumbling with me onto the bed, and we got the naked time we both wanted.

EPILOGUE

Camden

Three Months Later

"LADY, COME ON, girl," I called to our chocolate lab puppy, and she came running, ears flopping like crazy. She was going too fast and slid before running into the door.

Jude laughed. "Silly puppy." He bent down and petted her, which made her jump all over him and lick his face.

"She's just like her daddy." I winked at him as we headed out to the truck.

"Yeah, she does take after you," Jude countered.

"I meant you, asshole."

Jude opened the cab door so Lady could jump in, and then we both climbed into the front, with me behind the wheel.

We were on our way to Rush's place. He'd won the Supercross championship the week before, and there was a party to celebrate.

"We're going to be late. I'll text Theo to meet us downstairs," Jude said, and I nodded, starting to drive.

Theo was doing better. His father hadn't come around, but his mom was working hard to mend her mistakes. It was obvious she loved her son and wanted to do whatever she could to support him. She was making more time for him, and Theo had become a regular at the center with Trey. Annie had joined a group for LGBTQIA+ parents there as well.

It felt good to see them both doing so well. Theo was comfortable in his skin in a way he hadn't been before, and I knew part of that was because of the man sitting beside me.

Reaching over, I put a hand on his leg and squeezed. "I love you."

Jude's brows pulled together. "I love you too. What was that for all of a sudden?"

"Nothing. Aren't I allowed to tell my boyfriend I love him?"

"All the time. All day every day," he teased, and I would because I was so damn thankful he was mine.

We pulled up in front of Jude's old condo. Theo was there waiting, beanie still pulled down over his head like always. He jumped into the back of the truck and began giving Lady love. "Hey, guys! Thanks for picking me up. Mom said thanks too. Oh my God, we went out to dinner last night at this really great sushi place. Mom let Trey come too. I think she thinks he's my boyfriend, but he's not…I mean, I'm not saying I don't want him to be. I don't know if I want him to be, but right now we're just friends, is all I'm saying."

I chuckled, because no matter what, he was still the same old Theo and I loved that.

"You have time to figure it out," Jude told him. He really was like a big brother to Theo, even more than I was. Their relationship meant a lot to them.

The drive to Linc and Rush's didn't take long. Theo and Lady tumbled out of the cab almost before I had the truck parked. Methinks he was a bit more excited to see Trey than he realized.

We headed into the house. Everyone was in the backyard, so we went straight for the door. Ray and Kathy were the first people we saw, and they were holding hands.

"Hey, man. What's up?" Rush gave Jude a hug. "Does it still weird you out that our parents are dating?"

"Fuck yes," Jude replied. "But it's cool too."

I tugged Linc closer and ruffled his hair. "What's up, Short Stuff?"

"Ugh. I hate you! Why are you so jelly that I'm prettier than you?"

We all laughed, making our way farther into the yard. Theo had already found Trey, and they were chatting about something or other. Ash and Beau had a game of football going, because—fucking obviously. Jace, Dax, Owen, Keegan, and Tyson were out there with them.

"Come on. Let's go play with them," Jude said, because again, football. Why wouldn't we?

Rush was manning the grill, and Lincoln was chatting with Sawyer and Carter, who were swimming.

"What's up, BB?" I said to my brother as we passed by. He and Carter were doing great as ever. There was nothing like seeing him happy…and it felt pretty fucking great to be just as happy with Jude.

"Hey, did you guys bring swimming trunks?" Sawyer asked.

"Nah…football," I replied.

Carter rolled his eyes. "Your brother is such a dude-bro," he teased.

We played football for a while. When Rush announced the food was done, the game was forgotten so we could all eat.

We were all laughing and chatting. Every once in a

while, I would sit back and just watch everyone. Our group of friends were great.

"How are your classes going?" Dax asked.

"Good," Jude replied. "I'm really loving them." He was planning on staying in school. It made for a bit less time together, but he was happy and doing something he loved, which was what mattered most to me. I had him in my bed every night, right where I wanted him.

"Oh my God, we're great. Do you guys realize how great we are?" Linc asked out of the blue.

"Umm…I mean, we are but you've lost me, Short Stuff," I replied.

"Just all of us…our friends, our community. The way we magically turn men gay or bi."

"Oh God. Not that again," Sawyer grumbled.

"Do I have to go over the evidence again? We turned Jude, Jace, Owen, and Ash," Linc replied.

"I was already bi." Jace chuckled.

"Yeah, but it was my magic dick that made you really admit it," Dax replied.

"Yes, but still bi," Jace said.

"Yeah, gay as hell here too," Ash added. "Sure, I was closeted as hell, but I like to pretend I was waiting for Beau to be ready."

"Aww!" Linc said.

"Always bi here too," Owen chimed in.

"Yep, same here, though it wasn't until Cam that I let myself admit it." Jude grabbed my hand.

"My boyfriend is the best." I smiled. Sawyer made vomiting noises. It was sort of his thing now.

Tyson looked as if he didn't know what to do with us, but then Trey, Theo, Ray, and Kathy approached, and the subject was effectively dropped.

We finished eating and hung out a bit. It was an hour or so later when Rush stood up and cleared his throat. "Can I have everyone's attention for a minute?"

We all quieted and looked his way. Lincoln was sitting in a chair and looked up at him, his forehead wrinkled in confusion.

"As you all know, I won another Supercross championship. It was fucking awesome. The best feeling, and…and I've decided that's it for me. I love the sport, but I want to go out on top. There's so much else I want to do, one of those things is working with Ash and Beau at their sports program."

They both nodded, telling me they knew that part of it.

Rush looked down at Lincoln, and oh fuck, I knew that look. It was the same one Ash had before… Rush lowered down to one knee. Linc's shaking hand covered his mouth. Kathy started to cry.

"Red…I love you so much, baby. You're everything I've ever wanted. You're crazy and high maintenance, but I wouldn't have it any other way. You make me laugh like no one can, and you have the biggest damn heart. I still can't believe you risked it on me, and I promise you, I'll always take care of it. I want to take care of it as your husband if you'll have me."

Rush pulled out a ring, and Lincoln jumped at him, tackling him to the ground before Rush could get it on his finger.

"Yes! Fuck yes! I will *so* marry you!" Then they were hugging and kissing and everyone was cheering.

My eyes found Jude, who was looking at me. "Did you know?" I asked softly.

"Yeah…yeah, I did. I'm happy for them…and I'm so damn in love with you. You're all I'll ever want."

I nodded, but I hadn't needed the words. I didn't doubt what Jude and I were to each other. "Come here, Beautiful." He leaned in and I kissed him, a soft, chaste kiss, and then we were celebrating Lincoln and Rush's news.

They had to find the ring Linc had knocked out of Rush's hand, and then Linc spent the rest of the night with a smile plastered across his face as he showed it off to everyone.

Looking around, it struck me how lucky we all were, how happy. I had a moment of sadness as I thought about Henry and his wife, that they would never really have this, but that was life sometimes. Not everyone got their happily ever after. Maybe things would change for Henry in the future, but we had talked once since we met at the restaurant, and he was adamant he was where he belonged.

It was late when Jude and I headed home. Trey and Tyson were taking Theo back to his place. The truck was quiet except for Lady panting in our ears the whole drive.

We got home and let her out to pee, and then Jude and I took a shower together. Naked time with Jude was still the fucking best. We'd just climbed into bed, the lamp still on, when Jude rolled over and straddled me.

"You want something, Beautiful?" I cupped his cheek as he looked down at me.

"You…always you, Boyfriend."

He leaned down and kissed me, taking possession of my mouth. I cupped his ass and savored the taste of the man who had stolen my heart.

"Fuck me," Jude said, his mouth trailing down my neck. He took me sometimes too, and I loved being with Jude that way, but he'd also become somewhat of a needy little bottom, and there was nothing like being the only man who would ever know him that way.

I rolled us over and knelt between his legs. Jude opened them for me beautifully, the bashfulness long gone now. My dick was aching, and his was so damn hard, the slit leaking all over his stomach.

I pulled the lube from the drawer, the condoms gone months ago after we both had tests run. I slicked my fingers. He arched his back as I pushed two inside him. "So fucking beautiful."

Jude hissed, then rode my fingers as he was so good at doing. When he was panting and begging for me, I wet my cock, put his legs over my shoulders, and pushed inside. We trembled together. He smiled up at me, and there was nothing in the world like Jude's smiles and his hole so tight around me.

I fucked into him slowly, and he gasped. We weren't rushing. His blunt nails dug into my back as I dicked him down in long, deep thrusts. "You like that?" I asked.

"Fuck yes…you know I do."

I leaned forward and kissed him, still taking my time with him. We were sweaty and kissing, when his legs began to shake. "Right there…fuck yes, right there."

He wrapped a hand around his cock and stroked. Watching Jude take his pleasure went straight to my head.

"Fuck, you're so damn hot…so tight. I need you to come."

I took his mouth right as Jude cried out into mine, his whole body going rigid as he came between our bodies. My orgasm rocked through me, my cock jerking as I spilled my load deep inside him. Christ, I loved coming inside him. The first time, I'd lain between his legs afterward just so I could watch my jizz trickle out.

"I can't move." I fell on top of him.

"Then don't."

I kissed his chest. "Best. Boyfriend. Ever."

"So I've been told," he teased. "Should I call you professor now? Since you taught me Boyfriend 101?"

"Have I ever told you what a good idea that was?"

"The best," he replied, hooking his finger beneath my chin so I looked at him. "I'm serious. Jesus, I never knew I could feel this way."

"I think you love me," I joked.

"I know I do."

"Good. Because I love you too."

Then I did as he said, didn't move as he reached up and turned out the light. I slept right there on top of him.

The End

Continue reading for an important message from
Riley & Devon.

Dear Reader,

We wanted to take a minute to thank you so much for spending time with us in Fever Falls! We had a blast bringing this series to you and giving all these sexy guys their happily ever afters. We hope you enjoyed hanging with the crew, dancing the night away at Fever, and getting roped into all sorts of fun shenanigans!

At this time, Boyfriend 101 will be the last book in the series. The original plan was for five books, but then Cam and Jude obviously needed their story told. If any of you are curious about Henry, at this time, there are no plans to tell his story. That can change, of course, but it's not likely. His story is sad, but unfortunately, sometimes those things happen. We're sure you're wondering about a few other characters like Casey, Steve, Trey and Theo, but they have a little growing up to do. Hopefully you'll see them again in their own stories, whether it be standalones, novellas, bonus scenes, or spinoffs. Once they let us know what's going on, you guys will be the first to know! Until then, we have plenty of other projects we're busily working on—together and separately—that we'll be teasing you about in no time.

Thanks again for all the support and giving our guys a chance!

XOXO,
Devon & Riley

About the Author

Riley Hart has always been known as the girl who wears her heart on her sleeve. She won her first writing contest in elementary school, and although she primarily focuses on male/male romance, under her various pen names, she's written a little bit of everything. Regardless of the sub-genre, there's always one common theme and that's…romance! No surprise seeing as she's a hopeless romantic herself. Riley's a lover of character-driven plots, flawed characters, and always tries to write stories and characters people can relate to. She believes everyone deserves to see themselves in the books they read. When she's not writing, you'll find her reading or enjoying time with her awesome family in their home in North Carolina.

Riley Hart is represented by Jane Dystel at Dystel, Goderich & Bourret Literary Management. She's a 2019 Lambda Literary Award Finalist for *Of Sunlight and Stardust*. Under her pen name, her young adult novel, *The History of Us* is an ALA Rainbow Booklist Recommended Read and *Turn the World Upside Down* is a Florida Authors and Publishers President's Book Award Winner.

Find Riley:
Reader's Group: facebook.com/groups/RileysRebels2.0
Facebook: facebook.com/rileyhartwrites
Twitter: @RileyHart5
Goodreads: goodreads.com/author/show/7013384.Riley_Hart